The Sword of Cart

The Sword of Ca.
by
Griff Hosker

The Sword of Cartimandua

Published by Sword Books Ltd. 2013
Copyright © Griff Hosker

The author has asserted their moral right under the Copyright, Designs and Patents Act, 1988, to be identified as the author of this work.

All Rights Reserved. No part of this publication may be reproduced, copied, stored in a retrieval system, or transmitted, in any form or by any means, without the prior written consent of the copyright holder, nor be otherwise circulated in any form of binding or cover other than that in which it is published and without a similar condition being imposed on the subsequent purchaser.

A CIP catalogue record for this title is available from the British Library.

The Sword of Cartimandua

Dedicated to mum who kept on buying me typewriters; thanks for believing in me. Thanks to Eileen, Vicky and David; without you, there would be no book.

Contents

The Sword of Cartimandua i
Prologue 1
Chapter 1 8
Chapter 2 24
Chapter 3 31
Chapter 4 46
Chapter 5 61
Chapter 6 71
Chapter 7 81
Chapter 8 93
Chapter 9 100
Chapter 10 114
Chapter 11 127
Chapter 12 143
Chapter 13 156
Chapter 14 166
Chapter 15 179
Chapter 16 206
Epilogue 230
Author's comment 232
Other books by Griff Hosker 233

The Sword of Cartimandua
Prologue

AD 50 Stanwyck
Claudius might have been Emperor of the largest Empire the world had ever seen but he still hated the rain. This outpost of the Empire was a foul, wet, disease-ridden cesspit. In addition, he had a wicked and persistent cold; he never had a cold in Rome. He sneezed noisily and glowered angrily at the slave by his side. "Well? Why are we still waiting?" His famous stammer disappeared when he addressed servants or was angry and on this wet and dismal morning, he was not at his best.

"I was assured, divine one, that she would be here presently."

He shuddered at the title; like his Uncle Tiberius and his father Germanicus he despised the very notion that a mortal could become a living god. He had hoped that both the horrendous journey across the interminable land of Gaul, the ferocious ocean leading to this end of the world and the barbaric people he had so far met would make the journey worthwhile. The kings and queens who had been presented to him were all barbarians and the not so divine Claudius was glad that his Praetorians were on hand for he did not trust one of them.

Claudius was about to make some barbed comment about divinity when he heard the three blasts on the buccina which heralded the arrival of Queen Cartimandua, leader of the Brigantes. Even Claudius was impressed by the striking young woman who confidently manoeuvred her chariot between the waiting lines of legionaries. He had heard stories of her beauty but he was not prepared for both her presence and power; she seemed to dwarf her surroundings. Her jet-black hair framed an incredibly white face. Her deep-set violet eyes seemed to leap out from her face and her lips, obviously coloured by the crushed body of a scarab beetle, surrounded by remarkably white teeth looked like luscious plums. The Queen was, Claudius realised, everything he had heard and more. He found it hard to countenance that a young woman who looked as though she had only seen a handful of summers as a woman should rule the most powerful tribe in Northern Britannia and had done so, successfully, for over seven years. The way she handled a chariot showed that she was a warrior as

The Sword of Cartimandua

did the skulls adorning the outside of the chariot. He could make out, just behind the chariot, the wretch who was being dragged in chains. Although he had never seen him, the Emperor knew it was Caractacus the leader of the Britons in their fight against Rome. Caractacus was the charismatic leader who had sought refuge with the most powerful ruler in the North of these islands, Cartimandua. Caractactus, he was also the ex-lover of the rapacious young Queen and had been used and then discarded. If there was one thing that Claudius admired it was someone who could scheme, plot and survive as well as he had. She certainly had been a confident young queen who took over the rule of her land, Brigantia when her father was murdered. She ruled the largest tribal lands in Britannia; spanning the country from coast to coast. Claudius realised that she was wise beyond her years; she had seen the power of the Roman war machine and come to an accommodation rather than conflict. Perhaps that was why she ruled this enormous land of wild men and even wilder places. The Emperor of Rome himself would need to be careful about the promises he made.

"Welcome Queen."

"All Hail Claudius." Claudius was impressed that her Latin was flawless, this was an educated woman. "I bring you a gift." She gestured with her arm and her bodyguards brought out Caractacus, the putative King of the Britons, and his face displayed just how much he hated the woman who had betrayed him. The queen to whom he had turned in the hope that, united, they could defeat the monster that was Rome. Instead, she had ensured the safety of Brigantia and her high place in the Emperor's favour. "It is Caractacus. He was your enemy and now he is mine."

Her guards dragged the bound warrior to be symbolically thrown at the feet of the Emperor. Before Claudius could speak, he always gathered his thoughts before uttering anything important, Cartimandua drew from a scabbard in her chariot, the most magnificent sword Claudius had ever seen. Although a cerebral rather than military man Claudius admired beauty and functionality and this magnificent weapon fulfilled both as well as anything he had seen before. Its steel blade was so highly polished it was almost silver, with a line of gold trickling sinuously along its length. It was half as long as the tall

The Sword of Cartimandua

Queen's body and looked as though it needed two hands to hold it, although the warrior queen held it in one. The handle was adorned with a red jewel, the size of a grape and Claudius surmised that it must be a ruby, an incredibly rare ruby as well as blue and green precious stones. The black ebony hilt was engraved with what appeared to be pure gold.

"Would it please the Emperor for me to despatch this rebel and part his sorry head from his body?"

"N-n-no Queen Cartimandua. I wish to take him back to Rome so that the whole Empire can see the power of the Emperor and the Brigante." Her cold callous attitude to execution impressed the Emperor. She had no problem with carrying out the act herself, something the Emperor knew he could not do. He could order a murder or an execution as easily as he ordered supper but he could not soil his hands. Claudius turned to a grizzled centurion who stood at his side. "Gerantium, untie the prisoner and have your men take him away then join the Queen and me inside my tent for we have much business to discuss."

As they entered the pavilion especially erected for the occasion Claudius began to wonder if this island was as wild as he had thought. Although the buildings were primitive and some of the actions of its people somewhat barbaric he could see a sophisticated level of politics which made him think it might become civilised one day. In this young queen, he had seen someone who could have held her own with the senate. She was confident, she was cruel, she was calculating and she was charming. The old Emperor shook his head to free himself from the spell he was falling under. He felt happier now with this island for the northern part would be secure with an ally. He had no doubt that Queen Cartimandua would remain in power and the Emperor determined to support her in that. He was glad that she did not live in Rome for if she did he would fear for his throne.

Aracillium in Cantabria

Himli son of Barcus was concerned about the mare about to foal. The birthing was not going well and he knew that his family needed the new horse for times were hard in Cantabria. Although he had only seen eight summers the boy had the responsibility of the mare as he

The Sword of Cartimandua

was the only one of his mother's children to have survived, a fact which sat heavily on his prematurely aged mother who blamed herself for her lost children. It had made his father into a hard bitter man, a fierce warrior chieftain who had wanted sons to take over the small clan when he passed over to the Otherworld. Himli had much responsibility, not least the fact that he had been named after a famous Carthaginian who had fought hard against the Roman invaders. Those same Romans were now his father's enemies and Himli was desperate to be old enough to fight against them and earn praise from his father, a rare event.

The mare whinnied in pain and her brown eyes looked pleadingly at the boy who knew not how to relieve the pain. His father would know but he was gone, with most of the other men in another raid in the Roman lands to the north. Himli sighed, it was up to him.

"Well, Moon-child, it is up to you and me." He stroked the mare's mane and then looked to see the foal beginning to emerge. "Not long now and you will have your first young. And I hope that the others are easier than this one." His face creased into a frown as he saw that the foal's legs were caught up in the umbilical cord. If he did not do the correct thing then the foal would die. "Easy girl I see what is wrong." He slipped his hands inside the mare, their small size an advantage. More by feel than anything else the young boy eased the umbilical cord over the legs and out of the way. "Come on girl," he shouted encouragingly to the mare that seemed to know that the boy was helping her. With a sudden gush and slip of afterbirth the foal erupted onto the grassy valley side. "There's a good girl." Grabbing a handful of straw Himli began to clean up the foal. His father might be pleased for they now had another horse and the family would be richer. More importantly, Himli had done it by himself. His pleasure and delight were short-lived as he heard the unmistakable sound of a Roman horn. It was a sound which every Cantabrian feared for the horn meant that the Romans were coming and when the Romans left they left only death.

Marcus Aurelius Maximunius, centurion of the second Augusta, held up his hand to halt the century. He could smell the village his scouts had told him was over the rise. He wanted his men fresh for their assault although, in truth, since they had ambushed the Cantabri

The Sword of Cartimandua

war party he was almost certain that they would only find the old, the young and the women but they had to rid the land of this nest of vipers who had preyed on Roman villages and patrols for too long. He also paused to enable the Thracian auxiliaries to get in position on the other side of the village. There would be no quarter given.

The centurion signalled to his men and they took a position in an extended line; this formation was not normally used but he had to ensure that the century surrounded the village and prevent any flight. Nodding to his optio, who signalled the advance, the line moved forward as the buccina sounded. The solid line of soldiers marched relentlessly forward as the villages fled. A few older warriors saw the futility in flight and armed themselves with their short swords, prepared to sell their lives as dearly as possible. Those who fled were suddenly stopped by a wall of mounted men hacking and slashing indiscriminately at young, old and women alike.

Marcus smiled to himself; it had been a good action for there were no casualties and, as far as he could see, no survivors. "Check the huts for anything of value collect the horses and then burn the village." Suddenly there was a whinny from a hidden dell and Marcus ran swiftly followed by a handful of legionaries. As they reached the top of the rise they saw a Cantabrian child with a short dagger guarding a newly born foal. He had such a fierce look on his face that Marcus smiled to himself. "Steady lads, he's just a boy." He held his hand up to stop the javelin that was being aimed by his chosen man. "No Julius, this one did not flee. He deserves to live."

"But the standing orders..."

"I know about the standing orders but the boy has a skill. He might be useful. I'll sell him to the Thracians."

Just then the auxiliary cavalry hove into view, their horses adorned with the skulls of their victims. Himli looked from one set of enemies to the other. He did not understand any of the words he had heard spoken but he had seen the Roman leader stop the javelin which he knew would have ended his short life. His eyes suddenly opened wide as he saw the lifeless, bloody skull that had been his father hanging from the saddle of the Thracian.

"Julius, disarm him and tie him up. You, decurion, how much for the boy? He appears to be good with horses"

The Sword of Cartimandua

The Thracian looked down at the scrawny boy. He would have preferred to have his head but the big centurion was not a man to be crossed. "We have no need of a stable boy."

"I didn't ask that, I asked how much you would pay for him."

The Thracian began to work out how to make money from this. He had taken gold and copper from the dead tribesmen and he could afford the tiny amount the boy would cost him. He would gain the favour of the centurion which was no bad thing. The Pannonians were about to ship out and he had lied for they had no stable boy. He would buy the boy and sell him at double the price to auxiliaries that he would never see again.

The Thracian took out five bronze coins and showed them to the centurion who scowled as he countered. "Five pieces, that wouldn't even pay for an amphora of wine. Twenty."

"Ten."

"Fifteen," The difference having been split they exchanged coins and shook hands, honour even. "Here take him and one more thing. I have no idea what his barbarian name is and I don't want him named after a barbarian so his new name is Marcus Aurelius Maximunius. Right?"

As his men smiled at the conceit of their leader, the Thracian shrugged his shoulders. It mattered not to him what the brat was called for he knew he could sell the slave for a whole denarius. He had watched the boy who, despite his position, had continued to care for the mare and the foal. He was a horseman. "I'll have to take the horse and foal as well."

"That's a denarius." Hiding the smile the Thracian handed over the coin. The foot soldier did not understand the value of horses. He would sell both beasts on to the quartermaster and make two denari profit. Of course, the quartermaster would make more but that was the way of the world.

All that Himli knew, as he was led off, was that he was still with Moon-child and her foal and that was now his family. His hand instinctively went to the halter of the mare and he gripped it as though his life depended upon it. Passing the Roman leader he saw a strangely happy look on the man's face as he ruffled his tangled hair. The Romans were like beasts from another world but as he was taken

The Sword of Cartimandua

to the new world of the Roman army Himli knew that his past was gone, set on fire and slaughtered by his father's enemies. As they were led from the village he saw his mother and grandfather's bloodied corpses lying amidst the rest of the slaughtered village. On the way to the camp, he would see his father's crucified body along with the rest of the warband.

The Sword of Cartimandua

Chapter 1

AD 69 Stanwyck Stronghold
The Queen looked at her face reflected in the water of the silvered bowl in front of her. She could see the hints of grey permeating her jet-black tresses; she could see the crow's feet daily growing from her eyes which, although still bright, drooped a little more each day. She looked down at her body and saw that there was a little more substance around her waist than there had been. Hearing a snuffling behind her she turned to see Vellocatus her lover and she smiled. The young shield-bearer did not seem to mind the ripples of growing flesh or the ribbons of grey, he was satisfied with her. The problem was, the queen thought as she pulled her robe around her, she was not happy with herself. Her body had always been a temple and she had worked out with her warriors using her sword daily and this had kept her muscles toned. It was, indeed, how she had come to take Vellocatus to her bed and divorce her husband Venutius for she had grown attracted to the young man when using him to practice her sword play. The thought of Venutius caused her to frown and she left the comfort of her bedroom.

The Romans had brought some unpleasant things with them, such as their rule, taxes and authority but Cartimandua could not fault their engineering and building. The hall in which she sat was the only one of its type in Britannia; although built of wood, it had been built in the Roman style and was comfortable, clean and, in this damp northern climate, dry. She sat at her table and poured herself a beaker of weak beer and nibbled at the bread left by her slaves. What to do about Venutius? As she ate, she pondered her problem. Since her divorce, which was inevitable even without her affair with the convenient Vellocatus, he had grown increasingly belligerent. If she had not held his close family hostage she was under no illusions; she would now be dead. Her tribe was split and, daily, warriors left the stronghold to join Venutius with the hope of combat and glory against the Romans.

She wondered now about her decision to ally so closely with the Romans. She had seen their might and knew she could not stand

The Sword of Cartimandua

against them but in the past year, she had seen them fall amongst themselves with four Emperors in one year. Hotheads like Venutius had become emboldened by the disarray and lack of focus on Britannia. Now that Vespasian was Emperor, Cartimandua hoped for a reversal of policy. Perhaps now he would send the men and resources needed to tame this wild land. She resolved to stand by her original strategy. She would gamble that the Romans would triumph and she and her people would survive.

Her slave entered to clear away her table. "Ask Gerantium to come."

The tough old centurion must have been hovering close to the door as he entered immediately. His dress was marked by the fact that he alone was permitted to her rooms armed with a sword. It was a sign not only of his status but the relationship he had with the queen. He had been protecting her for almost twenty years and now regarded her more as a daughter than a monarch. He had come to see her capricious actions and sometimes ruthless gestures with the forgiving eye of a doting father. He had also seen the affection which was heaped upon her by the majority of the Brigante. Her people, warriors apart, had seen the tribe prosper under Roman protection. There were now roads, where there had been tracks and there was safety where there had been a danger. Gerantium was rightly proud of what his people had done for the queen and the Brigante but equally, he was proud of what the foresighted young queen had achieved and built.

"Yes, my queen?"

"Send a trusted rider to the governor at Eboracum," she smiled wryly, "as with the Emperors I know not who it will be. I will give a spoken message for I do not want it to fall into the hands of Venutius. I fear that my husband intends to take this home by force and as you know, old friend, we do not have enough warriors to defend it. I need the governor to come to our aid."

There was a silence as both centurion and queen took in the import of what had been said. It would change the relationship between Brigantia and Rome for never before had the queen asked for aid.

"Are you sure, my queen?"

The Sword of Cartimandua

"No I am not, and I would not if I thought we could defend the walls. What are my alternatives? Flee to Eboracum? If I did so I would be abandoning my capital and my people would see that as a weakness. No, I will only do that if disaster strikes and there is no other option."

"I will see to it."

As he turned to leave Cartimandua restrained him and spoke in a quieter voice. "I would also have you do something else for me. Send my sisters and their families to safety, either Derventio or Eboracum. I think your lady should also accompany them."

The old centurion smiled, "Thank you majesty but I know she would not go. She promised to stay with me as long as I lived and I still live." The queen nodded understanding the obvious love and bond between this soldier and his gentle lady. "What of your treasure, should that be sent as well?"

"No, it would only place my sisters in more danger. Bury that in a secret place here and draw a map. I will only need the treasure if all else fails.

Bowing, the centurion withdrew, leaving the queen to ponder her next action. The outer walls of the stronghold were too big to defend and had been strengthened by Venutius. He would know its weak points. In the next few days, she would begin to strengthen the inner ditch and ramparts which were defensible by her smaller forces. She also needed to practice her swordplay for she knew it would be needed sooner rather than later. Drawing her sword from its scabbard she began to swing the beautiful blade back and forth. As soon as she gripped the hilt she smiled as the power entered her body and already she felt not only safer but more at peace. As long as she held the sword there was hope.

Woodland north of Eboracum

Northern Britannia was a wild place at the best of times but in the last year, it had become even more dangerous. The Roman war machine had faltered in the west. Back in Rome, there was intrigue and infighting as the year saw three emperors come and go. Would the fourth last any longer? The Romans in Lindum and those in the newly established base at Eboracum did not know. The vast land belonging

The Sword of Cartimandua

to the Brigante was filled with forests, high hills and bogs. It was not a good place to campaign. The Brigante had been a client and ally of Rome but in the past year, they had shown the restless signs of rebellion and every Roman soldier felt uneasy. Patrols were now made up of larger groups of men as the handfuls they had used had been found hacked and chopped to pieces. It had become increasingly worse over the past five years but this last year, the year of the four Emperors was a crucial one. Every Roman was on edge realising that they were clinging to the edge of the Empire by their fingertips.

Decurion Ulpius Felix rubbed his unshaven face as he peered through the spindly branches of the elder copse. He idly pulled a bunch of elderberries to strip them from the stalk, letting the rich black juice run down his chin. It reminded him of the hill country around his vici in Ad Mures; it was a place he barely remembered having been taken there as a captive when he was still almost a child. Still, he remembered it and he remembered the first taste of elderberries strong and heavy in his young mouth. He remembered the woodland, he remembered the woods and he remembered berries but he could not remember his name before the Roman times. It seemed to him that he had been Ulpius Felix for all of his thirty-five summers. He mentally cursed Aulus Plautius the governor of Pannonia who had decided to bring the Pannonians with him to the edge of the world, Britannia. As the alternative posting was the warmth of Judea he would have preferred that to the capricious climate of this little northern outpost. He would have preferred the evenly monotonous days with warm nights and hot days to the uncertainty of snow in early summer and bright sunshine in midwinter. He would have preferred the rich wines of the middle sea to the weak beer and honey-laced drinks of this northern ice land.

He idly rubbed the angry scar that ran across his white blind eye, the result of an early battle when he was less careful than he was now. It had happened when he had seen but fourteen summers. The stone which had ripped into it could have been deflected by his shield but in those days, he believed himself to be immortal, a warrior hero. He had learned his lesson in the long service to Rome. He could see just as well as any of his men, in fact, some said that he could see behind him but occasionally it burned and tingled, this was one such time. The

The Sword of Cartimandua

pain in the eye was always there; sometimes dull and sometimes so sharp it felt as though his face was splitting in two. At those times his good eye would stream with tears as though he was weeping; those were the dark times, those were the depths of agony far worse than the original wounding. Without reason, the pain could be gone as soon as it came or it could last a whole day. His men had learned to look for the signs for the redder and angrier the good eye appeared the worse was the tough cavalryman's temper. When that pain left it was replaced by the pain of training and working as a Roman auxiliary.

The life of an auxiliary toiling for the mighty Roman Empire was no worse than being a tribesman. The difference was he was fed on a regular basis. The food might be dull but it was plentiful. He also received pay. The caligae in the legions resented the fact that auxiliary cavalrymen were paid at a higher rate and got to ride to battle but Ulpius and his men cared not. He was also worked hard which resulted in a lean, muscular body. His natural ability with horses had soon marked him out as a cavalryman and he was conscripted into the auxiliary cavalry. Fighting mainly Celts, he had spent over twenty years in the service of Rome; another ten and he would qualify for citizenship and a plot of land. Would he live to see it? It was a thought which occasionally flitted across his mind but he had had too many friends who had dreamed of such release only to find the release of death in some corner of the Empire instead. He was the last of that band of warriors who had left their home twenty years earlier. There were others who had survived such as the prefect who had managed to reach the highest rank of any not born in Rome but the majority died early. Roman generals were more careless with their cavalry than with the precious, solid legionaries.

He was brought out of his reminisces when he felt the horse behind him push against the hindquarters of Raven, his own horse. He did not deign to look around; he merely held his hand up in silent rebuke knowing that whichever trooper it was would control his mount. As Decurion of the Second Turma, First Sabinian Wing of Pannonians, his ire would result in a severe and painful punishment. It would probably be young Gaius who had no patience at all. Keen as a young greyhound he was always the first to reach the enemy lines; fortunately for him, he was also handy with the gladius which was

The Sword of Cartimandua

why he had survived so many skirmishes with the Parisi and Brigantes. He was the youngest trooper and as such indulged a little by the other men in the turma. Today he would need all his patience.

Osgar, their Brigante tracker, had discovered the tracks of the war band early that morning. They were a small band mounted on a few of the mountain ponies so favoured by the tribesmen of these hills. Not knowing where they were raiding Ulpius had decided to catch them on their return. Whilst it meant that people would die at least he could recapture slaves, acquire whatever loot they had taken and catch the raiders when they were tired. His men and his horses were too valuable to waste on a few raiders stealing from farmers barely richer than they were. He hoped that some of the Brigante warriors would have gold about them; some of the chiefs lauded their golden torcs as a sign of their bravery as well as the amulets, each one a symbol of success in battle. Ulpius smiled grimly to himself; chain mail would be more effective but he would gladly relieve the corpses of their treasure. He glanced around to look at the auxiliaries following him. Their mounts were far larger than the local horses and fed on grain. They could run all day and carry an armoured warrior. The chain mail of his men, he was pleased to see was oiled and flexible; although it was heavy it was more than effective at deflecting the local arrows. The shields were all slung over their left legs and ready to be used at a moment's notice. The javelins in their sheath behind the leg were less accessible but not so the mighty spatha, the Roman cavalry sword which was far longer than the gladius and gave Ulpius and his men the edge over any foe. He returned his gaze to the horizon, happier that his men were alert and prepared. They would not be caught unawares.

Towards the rear, the troopers rode in a single file with the easy, comfortable banter of men who have worked and fought together for a long time. Drusus and Metellus had to have Lentius and his horse between them because for some reason their horses, Pirate and Chestnut did not like each other and would bite and kick whenever they were in close proximity. This meant that not only did Drusus and Metellus have to carry on conversations with a horse between them they had to suffer Lentius' mount, a black gelding with a small star called Blackie. It seemed to Drusus, who was behind him that the animal suffered from terminal wind added to which he seemed to stop with amazing regularity to relieve himself.

"Lentius if your horse shits one more time I will feed it to you."

"That would be preferable to that slop you passed off as food last night!"

"You can tell that you came from the valleys otherwise you would have truly appreciated the find taste of roast squirrel."

"That's what it was! I had been trying to work out the taste all day."

"Ladies if you don't shut up and keep your eyes peeled you will all be shovelling shit when we get back to the fort!" Marcus' voice effectively silenced the three who knew he would carry out his threat. Drusus reined his horse so that it was not quite so close to Blackie and Metellus spurred his on a little. Marcus smiled to himself; the easy banter was no bad thing it showed that they were confident. He too had found the food unusual but that was because he was the only Cantabrian amongst these Pannonians. It seemed he had been with them for so long that he had almost forgotten his Cantabrian roots. Yet he still remembered the taste of the salted fish his mother had given him as a treat and now he was eating tough roasted squirrel.

Raven told him that they were coming before Osgar's nose sniffed them out. The nodding head appeared to some like an equine message; Ulpius knew that the gelding was just as eager for action and could smell the enemy. Osgar touched Ulpius' foot and pointed north; in truth, the scout was a tiny little runt, far too small to be a warrior but he could run all day and find tracks in the most unlikely places. He had the same animal senses as Raven and Ulpius knew where the Brigante would be, north. Ulpius relied on him more than he liked for the man was of the Brigante and some of those people were now in a state of rebellion; so far he had never let the Roman down but the decurion was always aware that he could change sides at any moment.

"Right boys, today you earn your pay!"

Ulpius could just make out some movement in the leaves. He turned in his saddle and pointed his vine rod to the south. Almost half the turma eased their way deeper into the copse following Marcus, his chosen man. As second in command, he had the responsibility of backing up Ulpius even when he didn't fully know the plan. He had

The Sword of Cartimandua

been with him for five years and most of the time understood his superior's intentions. Today it was easy; he was the shield and Ulpius the sword. Marcus would defend whilst Ulpius attacked. The other half of the turma loosened their swords in their scabbards to ensure they would not stick when they were needed and then adjusted their grip on their javelins.

The raiders were trotting along at an easy lope. The troopers could make out the captives in the middle. They were bound and roped together by the neck. It was obvious that they were not warriors; they looked to be farmers and merchants and by their dress less Brigante and more Roman. Ulpius looked towards the rear of the column. That would be where the fiercest fighters would be, in the place of honour; they would be the target for his twenty men. He lifted his body a little to count them. There were nearly sixty; a large number but on foot and he would have the element of surprise. He looked along the line and saw that his men were ready. He hefted the heavy infantry pilum he carried, an unusual weapon for a cavalryman but Ulpius was incredibly strong and the weapon had given him the edge in many an unequal combat for it was far sturdier than the light javelins they used as missiles.

The end of the enemy column was almost level with him; he could see an older warrior, probably a chieftain at the rear. His face and body had been painted blue but it had worn in parts giving him the mottled look of an adder. His long hair was spiked up with lime and he bore the scars of other combats. Ulpius' greedy eyes lit up when they saw the torc about his neck. It decided him. As he raised his pilum the rest of the turma steadied themselves. As soon as the spear left his hand his men would be upon the raiders like wolves. The spear flew from his hand in a steep arc; even as it was descending he had taken a javelin from his sheath and was kicking forward Raven. His spear took the chieftain in the neck and Ulpius could see from the dark spurting blood that it was a kill. He selected his next opponent. This time he did not throw the javelin until he was almost upon the man. The warrior deflected the javelin as it hurtled towards him but in doing so he revealed his naked torso and the decurion's gladius slashed down opening the man from his neck to his gut. Seeing no more warriors in front of him he reined Raven to a stop and surveyed the

The Sword of Cartimandua

ambush. His men were despatching the enemy so quickly that many were surrendering, for they had not expected any Romans to be operating so far from their fort. He held his sword in the air and his men formed a circle around the few warriors left standing. They all held their javelins at the enemy throats in case of treachery.

Ulpius slid his leg over Raven's shoulder, he did not even bother to look for the trooper who would hold his reins they were a well-practised turma well drilled by the most experienced decurion in the ala. His good eye took in the warriors who remained and he identified the leader. He did not have a torc but from the bracelets about his arms, he had won many fights. His practised eye saw that the man had been wounded in his arm and could not carry on the fight which was why he had surrendered. He walked over to him and, using his sword, knocked the warrior's weapon to the ground.

"So Roman, you cannot kill a one-armed man you must disarm him first!" He spat the words at Ulpius, defiance in his voice and eyes.

"If I wanted you dead your worthless corpse would be spilling its life force on the ground in front of me. I want some information. Where is Venutius?"

"You think I would betray my King? I am Brigante we do not betray our leaders."

Ulpius nodded as though he understood the motive behind the statement. "And what of Cartimandua? Where is she? Is she with the king?" The queen was known to favour Rome and Ulpius had been given instructions to find out where she was. It was rumoured that she had divorced her husband and taken up with a shield-bearer.

"That Roman whore is no concern of mine but she will soon be joining her ancestors."

Ulpius mind took in the threat but his voice feigned ignorance. "I did not know she was sick."

"Sick! You Roman fool. When Venutius takes her, he will burn her body and the Roman house she has built. Had you not taken us I would be watching as the flames licked her diseased body." He spat at Ulpius in a last defiant gesture.

Realising that he would get no more information from him and that the warrior had told him more than he intended Ulpius gave a nod. His men despatched all the Brigante where they stood. In minutes their heads were taken and strung along the saddles, their bloodied, mangled and mutilated bodies left where they fell; despoiled and deserted. The Brigante prisoners watched as their rescuers took everything of value and mounted their horses. As Ulpius was tucking the torc into his saddlebags a portly trader came up to him. "Thank you, lord, you have saved us from slavery."

Ulpius looked at him briefly and signalled for his men to mount. The ex-prisoners stared around in disbelief as the column trotted after Ulpius. "Lord, are you leaving us here?"

"Why? Would you have me escort you back to your farm? For what purpose? We do not escort overweight, whining thieves, we hunt Brigante. Now out of my way before you suffer the same fate." He paused and looked east. "Go that way as fast as your fat little legs will carry you. There is a camp at Derventio. You may make it merchant before the Brigante eat your eyes for their supper and piss in your empty skull." He urged Raven into a trot and they headed westwards.

Marcus fell in beside him. "We could have taken them back to Derventio." Ulpius stared at him in silence. Marcus was one of the few men who could question Ulpius and live. In his mind, Marcus knew there was a sound reason and, equally, knew that Ulpius would only tell him when he wanted to.

The decurion reached under his saddlecloth and removed a piece of dried meat he had been tenderising. As he tore a morsel of the sweat-dampened meat and chewed it he gestured with his head. "Did you not hear what that warrior said? Cartimandua was to be taken; Venutius was on his way to her stronghold to kill her. Think about it Marcus, she was the one who gave us Caractacus. She is the reason we do not need the Second Augusta here. If she is captured by that hothead of a husband we will have the whole of the north of this godforsaken place rebelling against us and remember Eboracum is a half-finished wooden fort. Remember what that bitch Boudicca did eight years ago? I know not how but the tribes know of the trouble in Rome and the many Emperors of this year. They see the chance to evict us. Besides we were ordered to protect her by no less a personage than Marcus Bolanus the Governor himself; it was a standing order that she was a priority. The only reason Venutius has not despatched her yet is that she holds his family hostage. She is a clever woman."

The Sword of Cartimandua

He spat out an inedible portion of meat and glared at Marcus. "Now having spent more spit than I wished on a useless turd with nothing better to do than question his leader's orders I will get back to the task assigned to me. You detail a trooper and tell him to go back to Eboracum and tell the tribune that I am going to Stanwyck to see if I can find out what has happened to the only ally we have in this part of the world! We will need help. I hope the gods favour me and it is Flavius who rides to our aid for if it is that thief Cresens we are dead men."

Marcus smiled ironically to himself as he went to the rear of the column to give one of the younger troopers the task of riding the fifteen miles back to Eboracum. He should have known the old wolf had something on his mind. Knowing his superior as he did, he also realised that the decurion would have worked out how to profit from the rescue of the famous Cartimandua. Since he had first been captured he had seen the power of Roman coins and the way the soldiers of the Empire looked to make a profit out of anything. He had learned much in the few years he had served with Ulpius. He had recognised a wise older warrior and took every opportunity to watch and learn; in many ways, he was the father Marcus had lost all those years before. The chosen man was a superb swordsman, especially with the short sword so loved by his tribe, and could ride a horse better than anyone but he knew his limitations. He wanted to be a leader and he could see in Ulpius Felix the sharpest military mind a warrior could wish for. A man who never took chances but always achieved his objective. He was never careless with his men or his mount which was why he had been selected to lead this patrol for the tribune knew that he would succeed.

Taking his place at the rear of the fast-moving column Marcus constantly scanned the wooded hillsides. He had a keen eye and an even sharper brain. One day he hoped to be a decurion too and be a leader of men. He would have blushed had he heard himself being discussed by Ulpius and the leader of the Ala Flavius Bellatoris. Both warriors viewed Marcus as a future leader, not just of the turma of ala but perhaps a general. The respect shown by Marcus for his leader was returned and both his superiors regarded him as protégé, in Ulpius' case like the younger brother he had left in Batavia, his back

The Sword of Cartimandua

broken by a Gaulish axe. All he needed were the right breaks and a little luck. Fortunately, Marcus was unaware of their thoughts and he could focus on scanning the horizon for enemies who might wish to ambush them. He was a tall man and as his mount was one of the bigger horses he could see further. This was another reason why Ulpius had stationed him in the vanguard. Although the Brigante only had ponies they were light enough to race from the cover of the woods and hack at the auxiliary horses. This was not the perfect place for horses; there were too many streams, gullies and hollows. Happily, for the Romans, they were armoured from their skull cap helmets to the greaves on their legs; even their horses had protection on their heads. He checked the fastenings on Argentium's head and rubbed his ears at the same time. The bond between rider and horse was close and Marcus had seen a steed save his rider on more than one occasion. The care and attention they paid to their horses was often more than the care and attention they gave to themselves. In this part of the world, you needed to know you could get away faster than you arrived.

Young Gaius reined in his horse a little to ride next to Ulpius. Ulpius looked at the young man. He had only joined the ala a few weeks ago but he had shown himself to be bright and brave to the point of being foolhardy. It was not permitted to leave your place in the column and the decurion would have to tell him so but he could see that there was something on the young trooper's mind.

"So young Gaius what is so important that you risk a week of shovelling horse shit just to ride next to an old flatulent one-eyed man who has no patience at all?"

"Why did the decurion leave those prisoners back there? They were helpless."

"They were and so are we. We have destroyed a large war band. It is unlikely that we will meet such a large one in this area. Remember Cartimandua supports Rome. It is her ex-husband Venutius who ferments rebellion. And that is why we are hastening to Stanwyck. We need to warn her that Venutius intends her harm."

"Will the Brigante army not protect her?"

"Since she took up with her shield-bearer she has been shunned by the Brigante nobility. She has few warriors to protect her. Her fortress is not as strong as one of our camps. If they chose they could

The Sword of Cartimandua

easily destroy both her and her men. It is only her status as Queen which protects her and the fact that she threatens her husband's family. It seems Venutius has decided to change that." He held his hand up to silence the next question." And now young Gaius, as you have so much energy for your tongue ride back along the trail and make sure we are not being followed."

Marcus shook his head a grin across his face. He knew why Ulpius had indulged the boy just as he knew why he had indulged him earlier. The turma trusted Ulpius because he always let them know what he was about. This was a dangerous patrol in the heartland of Brigantia. Marcus clucked in annoyance as the young man turned his horse around and galloped hard along the track. Marcus loved horses and hated to see them badly used. The young trooper would soon realise that you saved your horse whenever possible for it was your final escape from the enemy; Roman horses could outrun anything in this desolate northern land. He once again scanned the skyline. They had more than ten miles to go but if Venutius had scouts out they would be seen quickly. Ulpius must have been reading his mind for he stopped the column and Marcus could see him gesture for the first two troopers to scout north and south of their line of march; Osgar was some way ahead weaving from side to side as he sought a sign. The old wolf would not fall into an ambush himself.

An hour later and the whole column looked around as they heard hoof beats pounding up the trail. Marcus realised that it was Gaius who reined in next to Marcus. "Smoke," he gasped, "to the west. I went up a short rise and saw it. About five miles away." Just then the first two riders sent by Ulpius returned and Osgar jogged wearily back to the stationary soldiers. The decurion held up his hand to halt the column and signalled for Marcus to join him. The two Roman leaders dismounted and walked off a few paces where they would not be overheard.

"The scouts report that Cartimandua's refuge appears to be safe still but that there is a host approaching from the south. They are mainly on foot but it looks to be a large number. We will get to Cartimandua before they do but, unless they have horses, we will not escape Venutius."

"Do you think the tribune will have acted?"

The Sword of Cartimandua

Ulpius' one eye narrowed. "I hope our leader," the sarcasm was not lost on his men, "has sent the rest of the ala. A thousand horsemen will be more than enough but I know not. Still, this thirty will have to suffice. If we can be of help then we will do so but I will not risk us for the sake of a glorious death. Come we ride."

Marcus wondered if he would be able to be so calm when leading in such a desperate situation. If he left the Queen to be sacrificed like a helpless goat then the consequences for the auxiliary decurion would be catastrophic. Yet the alternative was to let his men be slaughtered for a heroic gesture.

The town of Cataractonium was unusually crowded; the war band was gathering. Armed and painted warriors milled around eager to see and hear what their war chief had planned. Chieftains proudly displayed their battle scars as younger warriors bragged about deeds as yet unperformed. There was a noise and a hubbub amongst the thousands of warriors which sounded like the roar of the surf on the sea shore. Suddenly there was silence as the door of the hall opened and the crowd breathed in as one.

Venutius was a magnificent looking warrior; his jet black hair hung down his back and his wide torso filled the doorway as he emerged. His arms were covered in amulets, the symbols of successful battles; his body covered by a captured cuirass and ornamented with gold and bronze circlets. His face was devoid of any facial hair and made him stand out from his warriors; it also accentuated his eyes and his nose making him look like a hunting hawk. He was every warrior's idea of a warrior chief and they had all left Cartimandua to join a real warrior before a Queen of dubious morals. None of them approved of her decision to abandon her husband and take up with a young shield-bearer.

He climbed onto a chariot so that the thousands at the rear of the warband could see him. "Warriors! The time has come to show these Romans that they are no longer welcome in our land. The time has come to hurl them back into the sea. The time has come to bathe our weapons in blood." There was a huge cheer at this and Venutius allowed it to continue, revelling in the acclaim. "Our brothers, the Silures, are even now attacking the legions down there." He waved his sword in the direction of the South. "Our Carvetii brothers have joined with our Brigante brothers to make an army which is unstoppable." Again a cheer went up which he stopped with his raised arm. "They think we are cowed because Cartimandua lay on her back like the whore she is. She gave up Caractacus for her own ends and she is a traitor who must now die. We ride to her stronghold and we will show the world who rules when we publicly end her reign in blood. All those who join with us will be spared; all those who oppose us will suffer the same fate." The cheers this time were at fever pitch and it took some time for Venutius to quieten them. "We ride north to destroy the Queen and then the Romans at Eboracum will die. Ride!"

The war host was many thousands strong. There were many horse and many chariots but the majority of the warriors were on foot. Venutius was not worried; he had more than enough mounted men to surround the stronghold and stop anyone from escaping. That he would take the stronghold was certain. He smiled to himself. Did she not realise that it was he who had improved the defences and he knew every tiny part of that huge stronghold? He also knew that she did not have enough men to man the walls. Its strength was as a refuge for the Brigante people, not a few who might hide up behind its mighty ditches. Were it not for his family held hostage he would have taken it in the spring but he was now committed. Hopefully, the queen would surrender without harming his family; if not …The murder of hostages would make his warriors even more passionate in their wars against the enemy.

He looked at his eager warriors, his war bands which gave him a ready reserve that would be eager to emulate the deeds of the mounted Carvetii. His mounted men would easily get by the few guards and take the fortress. There would be little Cartimandua and her bodyguard would be able to do. He had given orders for her to be captured alive for in his mind he was already punishing the false bitch who had betrayed him and taken a lowly shield-bearer as a lover; they would both pay dearly for that mistake. Once she was dead he would rule as the rightful king of the Brigante and with that title came the whole of the north of Britannia. The destruction of the Queen was a symbolic gesture which the whole of Britannia would see for what it was; the

The Sword of Cartimandua

end of Roman occupation and collaboration. It would be the beginning of the revolt.

The Sword of Cartimandua
Chapter 2

Stanwyck

The hill fort of Stanwyck took the young Roman's breath away; it was the largest single structure Marcus had ever seen. Approaching from the south they would see the walls of the Brigante capital stretching away east and west. He estimated it at four or five thousand paces. There was a ditch and a barrier made of palisades, another ditch and then a stone and wooden wall. The gate had two towers with a number of guards and a handful in the open gateway. He could see on a small rise behind an internal ditch the unmistakeable orange roof of a Roman villa. It was the first he had seen on this island. Looking at the tops of the palisades he could now see that there appeared to be few guards walking the walls and only two warriors chatting by the open gate. As Ulpius peered through the trees in the fading light he dismissed the defences as a barrier against the legions but conceded that it might halt tribesmen. It was certainly big. He turned to the men in the turma who surrounded him. "Aulus you and Osgar take the road to the south. When you see the Brigante and Carvetii army, any of them, you get back here as soon as possible. Drusus you take three men and keep watch here. If we have to come out in a hurry I don't want to walk into an ambush. The rest of you go carefully. We don't yet know how the land lies. "He turned to Marcus. "Anything happens to me you get the bitch out and to Eboracum, it doesn't matter how or how many die. Clear?" He glared at Marcus and the rest of the men all of whom nodded. "Let's go."

They trotted forward. They were only yards from the tree line when they heard the challenge from the walls. A dozen warriors, arms filled with bracelets and necks adorned with torcs raced out to the gateway weapons at the ready.

Ulpius' face showed no emotion as he stopped Raven at the barrier of spears. "I am Ulpius Felix, Decurion of the Second Turma, and First Sabinian Wing of Pannonians. I am here with urgent news for your Queen Cartimandua."

There was a silence as the warriors struggled to understand the Roman. The turma were already loosing their weapons in anticipation

The Sword of Cartimandua
of a fight when Ulpius held up his hand. "It is vital that I speak with someone in authority for." He lowered his voice and addressed the oldest of the guards. "Venutius comes."

The words had the desired effect and the most scarred warrior spoke. "Leave your men in the outer ward and come with me."

Ulpius turned to Marcus. "Have the men take the saddles off their horses, feed and water them and find some food. " He turned to the nearest guard. "Have food and drink brought for my men." He marched off with the expectation that his orders, even to a stranger would be obeyed.

Marcus watched him stride off once again in awe of the command of his leader, totally fearless, prepared for anything. "Come on you lot. If Venutius gets here before dark we will have to fight our way out. Make sure the animals can carry us; treat them as you would your lover."

As they dismounted one wag called out, "Atticus already does." The men laughed as the most unpopular man in the turma reddened. Marcus took it as a good sign; if they could joke they would fight and if they fought... Marcus would back this turma against any barbarians.

Ulpius was tall and had to duck beneath the narrow gateway. Behind him, he heard his men leading their mounts through the gateway. The pathway took a sharp right, obviously a defensive strategy to assault an invading enemy from the flank. Behind the outer wall, the land was flat and covered in huts and roundhouses laid out in no particular order or discernible pattern. His military mind took over as he followed the guard weaving between the huts. The fortress had an inner fortress and another steep ditch. To his right, a forceful stream bubbled its way across the whole fort. At least defenders would be well supplied with water. Ulpius noticed how few guards there were and, apart from those he had met at the gate, what was disconcerting was that none of them looked up for a fight. He realised that any defence of the Queen would come from his handful of men. They passed through another gate, ignored by the warriors who lounged there and Ulpius could see the hall before them. Although not on the scale of a Roman building it was, none the less the most substantial structure he had seen so far in this land of round wooden huts. Ulpius

The Sword of Cartimandua
was about to walk directly for it when his guard tugged at his arm. "This way Roman unless you want to meet the queen with wet feet."

Looking ahead Ulpius could now see that the land was boggy and marshy; they were forced to walk a narrow path between the stream and the marsh. He began to understand the workings of the Brigante mind. This would certainly slow up an assault. If an enemy attempted to get across the marsh he would be an easy target. If he took the route past the stream he would be an easy target. The hall was set on a knob of rock which rose higher than all but the earthworks. It looked almost Roman in its design and construction. Away on the right, he could see further concentric circles of ditches marking out the western boundary. As he walked up to the hall he could see, in the distance, the outer defences; by his reckoning, it was three thousand paces from north to south. He could see much evidence of recent building and construction work. A mighty structure but to defend it properly one would need a horde far bigger than the handful he had seen. He turned to his guards, "A fine hall. It looks new."

"Aye Roman your Emperor had it built for the Queen."

"Did he also put the new defensive walls up?"

One of the surlier guards sneered, "No Roman, that was our King Venutius."

Ignoring the implied insult Ulpius stored the key information. If Venutius had constructed the extra defences and if there were still men who remained loyal to the king then it was even more imperative that he escape with the Queen as soon as possible. The defensive qualities were even less if you were assaulted by the man who built the defences.

His guards stopped him at the entrance of the hall. "Wait here, Roman."

As he waited Ulpius turned around to survey the land around the refuge for the hall afforded a fine view across the country. The trees had been cut back for some distance but the only other natural defence was a small stream, easily fordable. He gazed eastwards. That was the direction he would have to take. There was a small outpost at Cataractonium to the south but Eboracum was even closer fifteen or sixteen miles. If his trooper had got there and raised the alarm and, if the tribune had reacted, the ala could be a mere three or four miles

The Sword of Cartimandua

away. It all depended on Venutius and his army approaching from the west.

"Enter decurion." The voice came from a holy man, an old holy man. His hair was not limed as the warriors, it was shorter, cropped but he was a whitebeard and lacked any jewellery. Ulpius detected something about him; he was not a Brigante for he had recognised his rank. "The Queen awaits." His Latin was flawless and as Ulpius followed he noticed the tattoo. The man had been a legionary.

Queen Cartimandua had been a strikingly beautiful warrior queen in her time. She had fought in many battles and held off rival armies very successfully. When she first met the Romans, she realised that they were here to stay and that diplomacy was the best course of action. She dismayed not only other Celts but also her own Brigante people when she treacherously handed over Caractacus to the invaders. She was pragmatic and politic, a rare thing in a Celtic leader. She had further alienated her people when, following her husband divorcing her, she took up with Vellocatus her shield-bearer. This had outraged and shocked her most supportive followers. It was a measure of her character and charisma that she had ruled for a further fourteen years without the support of many of her people. Two things had been in her favour; firstly, the support of the Romans through a series of indifferent governors and, perhaps more importantly, the fact that she held most of her ex-husband's family hostage. The threat of their death kept Venutius and his horde at bay.

So it was that Ulpius first met the mighty Cartimandua. Both her beauty and sexual appetites were legendary. It was said that Caractacus had been a lover before he was despatched. Some of the Ninth Legion from Spain had compared her to the spider called the Black Widow which mated and then consumed her consort. She certainly had a dark look about her but age was creeping up on her. Her raven black hair was now riven with grey. Her eyes, still beautiful were sinking into a sea of lines. Her once taut cheekbones were now puffy and sagged a little. Even though she was a shadow of her former self Ulpius found himself dropping to one knee in awe of this woman who exuded both sex and power, an irresistible combination. As he knelt his good eye took in the powerful warrior behind her. He

The Sword of Cartimandua

was obviously Vellocatus the shield-bearer. Although no longer young he still looked to be a formidable ally and a foe to be avoided.

Ulpius rose and bowed and waited. "So Roman you are here for what purpose?"

"To warn you mighty Queen that Venutius approaches with an army. He intends to destroy you and this citadel."

Whilst the rest of the court displayed various degrees of shock Cartimandua appeared calm. Inside she was deciding what to do. Here in the citadel, she might be safe for a while but she knew that her support was waning. She glanced around her nobles and wondered just how many would stay loyal. Her bluff had been called. All this time Venutius had not attacked for fear of his family. He must have realised that she could never carry out her threat for it would result in her own demise. It was obvious she would have to leave. She looked again at the tall Roman auxiliary before her. Even though her life was in danger she could not help being attracted to this warrior; her sexual drive was still as potent as ever. Perhaps she would see what he was like in bed, but not yet.

"Where are they?"

"My scouts reported them to the south." There was a pause. "They will be here very soon; we barely made it here before them."

"How many men do you have with you?"

"Thirty. Not enough to defend these walls, my lady." He added to avoid the follow up question. He was anxious to leave. "To be blunt your highness I have not seen enough men within these walls to be able to defend them. If I had a legion I might succeed but with my handful. "He paused to let the facts sink in. "We should leave quickly before they are upon us. "

She stood and Ulpius realised she was as tall as he was and, despite being middle-aged moved with an easy athletic grace. She nodded, the decision quickly made. "Go to your men we will be there shortly." She looked at Vellocatus. "Prepare my chariot and take my valuables with you. Have my bodyguards mounted. You, Alerix, despatch the prisoners." Finally, she took the old man by the hand. "Gerantium I leave the defence of Stanwyck to you. I believe they will follow me rather than attack this place but I know you will defend it as you defended me all of my life and for the Emperor before that. I

The Sword of Cartimandua

know that you will protect everything that is precious to me old friend." She paused and her lowered voice told of tenderness and affection beyond that of mistress and servant, it was more of a family member talking to a favourite uncle. "Had I time I would take you and them with me."

"My Queen, ride and I will protect you and your family as long as there is life in this tired old body. I will serve you in death as I did in life."

"If you take refuge in the inner fort you should have enough men to hold them off."

The ex-legionary bowed to the Queen and gave a nod of thanks to Ulpius.

Marcus, even though he was eager to escape before the vengeful Venutius arrived, had been surprised by both the speed of the Queen's decision and her ruthlessness in having unarmed prisoners murdered. She would bear watching. He glanced towards his men who had snatched some food and drink; more importantly, the horses had been fed a little and watered. They had been rubbed down. If they were surprised now they should be able to pull away from the inferior native horses; even so, it was not certain that they could evade the enemy. He turned as he saw first one rider and then another emerge from the woods. From their mounts, he knew they were Roman and from their speed, he knew that Venutius was not far behind. "Saddle up and be quick you idle buggers. They're coming."

Even as he spoke Ulpius erupted from the hall. He nodded in acknowledgement to Marcus letting his chosen man know he had acted well. "I take it you have seen our men." Marcus pointed south to where the riders were racing. "Mount."

The Romans were astride their beasts in a heartbeat. Ulpius led them out of the gateway so that the Queen and her entourage could make a quicker exit. Lentius reined his horse in. "Brigante scouts are just the other side of that wood. They will be with us soon." The unspoken wish was for his commander to lead them to safety.

"How many?"

"About a hundred, on those ponies of theirs but we could make out the main army five miles behind."

The Sword of Cartimandua

Ulpius grunted in answer. "Get your mounts watered. I don't want to lose any more mounts than I have to." He heard a commotion behind and screams from the bowels of the fortress. The prisoners had obviously died. The Queen emerged in her chariot with Vellocatus at the reins. Two warriors ran from a roundhouse wielding long swords they were obviously intent upon murder.

"Murderer. You Roman lover!"

"Traitorous bitch! Whore!"

Before either Ulpius or Vellocatus could react, the Queen pulled a magnificent sword from a scabbard inside the chariot. She swept the weapon effortlessly, slashing one of the warriors across the neck almost severing the head. She then held the sword in both hands and brought it down onto the skull of the other. It split like a ripe fruit showering those around him with blood and brains. Wiping the blood from the weapon she turned to Ulpius. "What are you waiting for Roman? Have you never seen blood before?"

"Marcus, take the lead. Head towards Drusus. Gaius, you come with me we'll take the rear. "The column moved eastwards at a steady trot. The land sloped away and helped the chariot to gain momentum. Ulpius and Gaius waited as the chariot passed by and the twenty bodyguards all riding, Ulpius noted with some disappointment, the little ponies. Already his mind was working out how to sacrifice both bodyguards and ponies to save both himself and the warrior queen. The pace they travelled at was crucial; too fast and their horses would be winded, too slow and they would be caught and the ponies would slow them down. As he looked up at the sky he cursed the northern light. It was high summer and would be lighter for longer. Their only advantage would be they would be riding towards the setting sun which might bring on darkness and the chance to hide.

The Sword of Cartimandua
Chapter 3

North West of Eboracum

As they approached the wood Drusus and his men emerged to greet Ulpius. He signalled them to his side. "I want you to go back into the woods. Wait for the enemy to arrive. When they are within bowshot, kill as many horses and men as you can and then escape through the woods. If they follow you, well, if not you will catch up with us. Clear?"

Drusus looked grimly at his leader. "Do you think we can kill enough to deter them?"

"No. Do not take me for a fool! They will have to slow down. It will appear as though we have tried to ambush them and cause panic. They will reform and attack you. That will slow them down and give you time to escape. Is that clear?" The tone in his voice told Drusus that he had questioned too much.

"Clear decurion."

Ulpius spoke as the four men trotted back into the woods, "And Drusus, be careful. I need you alive, all of you." Turning he rode forward to join Cartimandua looking at the bodyguards as he passed them. Their ponies were coping with the pace but Ulpius knew that in a race they would slow them down. Riding next to the queen he began to speak in Latin, hoping that the guards would not be able to understand them.

"They will catch us your majesty and before we reach Eboracum." She looked at the Roman waiting for him to explain. "The enemy are coming from the south. We are trying to reach safety which lies south-east. We must travel further east to avoid them. They know where we are going and can just cut us off."

"How do they know?"

"Even if they didn't see us when they get near to your citadel they will see our trail and I am sure there are enough of your people who wish you ill to inform on you." He paused as he phrased his next statement. "I fear that the two killers who tried to attack your majesty were not alone and may have been planted by your enemy. I think that your fortress will not last long as there are enemies within."

The Sword of Cartimandua

Vellocatus bridled. "Be careful Roman. The Queen has loyal subjects."

Ulpius laughed sardonically. "Yes I saw her reward two of them for their loyalty."

"Silence! He is right. They will inform on us. So Decurion what is your plan?"

"I have laid a small ambush which should delay them what I need is a second ambush." Again her look made him carry on. "If half of your guards waited until the first of the scouts had passed and then attacked them in the rear it would make them more cautious and they might waste time chasing your guards."

"And they might spend time killing them."

There was a silence then Ulpius said, "That was in my mind majesty. I need to get you safely to Eboracum and the legion. My men and your men are, "he paused, "expendable."

The Queen appraised the one-eyed warrior before her. She was a good judge of men if not of lovers and she liked his honesty. "You are right. When do you want them to make their attack?"

"A little way ahead we drop down a shallow valley to cross a small stream. There is a wood there. If they wait until the last of scouts cross the stream then can attack them and then escape away from us."

The Queen said nothing then called, "Alerix." A huge tattooed man with many trophy amulets on his arms came forward. "When we come to the stream take half my guards and wait in the woods. When the enemy follows wait until the last few are in the water when they will be slower. Attack them and kill as many as you can. Then ride north to Cataractonium."

"We will kill them all majesty."

The anger in her voice was matched by the anger in her eyes. "Why am I surrounded by heroes who cannot wait to die for me? When will I find warriors who want to live for me! If I wanted you dead I would tell you. I want you alive. When you have rested at Cataractonium join me at Eboracum." Her voice softened and she touched his arm. "I still need you and your men this is just a battle it is not the war. We will regain my kingdom from these rebels." He nodded his honour assuaged.

The Sword of Cartimandua

In the woods, Drusus prepared his ambush. He was lucky that he and Metellus were accomplished archers whilst the other two were accurate with javelins. If he fired from the cover of the woods he might be able to get three flights of arrows and one of javelins away before they were attacked. He was under no illusions, the ponies of the enemy would be more surefooted in the woods, and the Romans would only have a few heartbeats to get a lead and escape the woods onto the grassland where they could gallop.

One of the new men asked the unspoken question. "Will we escape?"

"That depends, my friend on two things. One, how well we fight and, probably, more importantly, how does the Allfather view us. I am hopeful that, as I made a sacrifice the day we left on the patrol that we will survive."

"If not," interrupted the blunt Metellus, "our heads and dicks will be paraded by these barbarians on their saddles which in my case means his pony will need longer legs."

The bluff humour made them all smile but they all knew he was speaking the truth. "I hear them."

The four men waited, hidden in the trees at the edge of the wood. As they had correctly assumed the Brigante and Carvetii came on at a pace not expecting a rear guard action when there were so few Romans involved. Drusus and Metellus needed no signal to launch their arrows and they were notching their second flight even when the first was still in the air. Their third left their bows as the first two arrows struck home. The warband veered towards the danger and the last two flights and the javelins flew simultaneously. The effect was immediate for the mounted warriors wore neither armour nor clothing on their upper bodies. A handful of warriors and ponies crashed to the ground disrupting the ones following. Not waiting to see the full effect the four Romans raced off in a line, Drusus leading and the dour Metellus at the rear. As Drusus had feared the enemy ponies were more agile. It was time they made for the open ground where their superior horseflesh would count. Without signalling their intent Drusus took them at right angles to the lighter part of the woods. He could see the edge of the wood four horse lengths away. It looked as though his tactics had worked and they might escape when disaster

The Sword of Cartimandua

struck. The mount in front of Metellus suddenly stumbled and the rider was thrown. Metellus was a superb horseman and he lifted his steed over the recumbent body of the unfortunate trooper. His companion then made the cardinal mistake of stopping to see what had happened to his friend. The Brigante axe embedded itself in his back. Drusus and Metellus had no time to help their comrades and they erupted from the woods like stags. The accident had slowed up the enemy who began to hack at the two unfortunates. Even as they galloped back towards Ulpius, now a long way in the distance, they could hear the harrowing screams from the two Romans who were being eviscerated alive. They lay low over their horses' manes and rode close together to make a low profile and to enable them to talk.

"The first rule of cavalry, be a fucking good rider. The second rule don't fucking fall off."

"Well, Metellus it looks like they paid for that mistake with their lives."

"And the third rule is, don't go back unless you know you can make a difference."

"A few more weeks and Ulpius would have drilled that into them." Drusus looked under his arm as the cries stopped. "Well, here they come. They didn't hold them up for long."

Metellus risked a glance. "I don't know how many there were before but I can only see thirty or forty riders now. Perhaps we can have a bigger ambush next time."

"I think our decurion wants to get the Queen to safety. There is always a risk in an ambush. This is why there are now only two of us!"

The land was full of dips, hollows and mounds with thick copses and it was becoming difficult for Ulpius to see the enemy. "Gaius, ride to the rise. Keep yourself low to the horse and watch for the enemy. When you see them, follow us." Gaius nodded his face eager for adventure. "And Gaius, take no chances. I can ill afford to lose another man. Even someone as useless as you." Gaius grinned as he trotted up the hill. Ulpius urged his horse forward and he joined Marcus at the front of the column.

"Send Lentius forward I want no surprises." Marcus did so and then rejoined Ulpius who had taken some of the dried meat from under his saddlecloth. He looked questioningly at the decurion but realised

The Sword of Cartimandua

he had asked enough foolish questions for one day. Ulpius was just finishing chewing when they heard the distant screams of both men and horses. Everyone in the column looked urgently behind them except Ulpius who took a swig from his water sack. As he wiped his mouth he said, "Drusus!" There was a pause as he put the stopper back in. "I hope the useless weed avoids having his head taken. He still owes me for his scutum." Despite the words, Marcus could hear the affection in his voice for Drusus had been with them both since Batavia.

A few minutes later they heard the sound of hoof beats thundering after them. It was Gaius. He reined in next to Ulpius who had not slowed down. "Half of them followed Drusus and Metellus into the woods the rest are hard on my heels." It was unspoken but they both knew the other two auxilia were dead.

"Right your majesty now we ride and we ride hard! Gallop"

The cavalry horses leapt forward and immediately a gap opened between the Romans and the Celts. Ulpius pulled his vine branch from his saddle and began whipping Cartimandua's ponies who suddenly found extra energy and the bodyguards were the ones left behind.

"We are coming to the stream." Ulpius turned and shouted to the bodyguards. "Here is your ambush!" Alerix nodded and slowed down. The ten guards raised their arms in salute trotting off to take their place in the woods.

As they came up the low rise the chariot's ponies began to struggle and Marcus and Lentius had to help pull them up. By now they could hear the Carvetii following them and as Gaius turned he saw the first of them reach the rise. They would not be able to escape. As they reached the flatter area the remaining bodyguards slowed down. They too saluted their Queen and then formed themselves in a thin line at the top of the rise. Ulpius knew they were sacrificing themselves and he raised his arm to acknowledge their action. Without the ponies to slow them the Roman horses soon put the diminishing daylight between them. He couldn't see the enemy but he saw the back of the bodyguards disappear down towards the stream and hear the class of metal on metal and the whinny of horses. When he heard another cheer he knew that those in the ambush had attacked. Twenty

The Sword of Cartimandua

against fifty. They could not succeed but they might slow them down and cause enough casualties to enable them to escape.

Had he been an eagle he would have been able to look down and see that the Queen's bodyguards were doing better than could have been hoped. The last thing the Carvetii and Brigante scouts were expecting was to be attacked. The shock cost the first warriors their lives. The momentum of the riders and horses threw the rest into confusion and once they were amongst them they began to inflict casualties. They would have been soon despatched for the Carvetii had reformed but their comrades charged into their rear causing not only confusion and mayhem but death to many. Inevitably the twenty died but they took far more of the enemy than Ulpius could have hoped. He knew nothing about this miniature battle for he was racing as fast as he could towards the legionaries at Eboracum. Alerix and his brother were the last to die. Back to back, they slaughtered all who came within reach of their long swords singing their death song. Some of those they killed had been fellow warriors in battles past but they cared not. They were fulfilling their oath to fight and die for their Queen. Their heaven would be to join their brothers.

The war chief of the Carvetii knew that his warriors would sacrifice themselves for the honour of killing the mighty Alerix but he had the Queen to catch. He signalled to his archers; within less than a minute the two warriors were mortally wounded and covered in arrows, even so, they had the strength to raise their swords and shout "Cartimandua" before dying.

After a mile or so of hard riding, Ulpius slowed to a walk. He turned to Lentius. "Wait here. When they come, ride and let me know. Wait until your horse is ready to ride. That will be time enough."

He rode next to the Queen. "There has been no pursuit. Your warriors died well."

"They were oathsworn. It was their duty to die. They will be reunited and live forever." Ulpius nodded. His own people had a similar belief. There was no finer end for a warrior than to die honourably with a blade in his hand.

Ulpius nodded towards the Queen's sword which he could see in her chariot. "I have never seen so fine a blade. It is a noble weapon."

The Sword of Cartimandua
It has been handed down for five generations and came with us from over the water. They say it is an ancient blade with magic and protects its bearer."

"Do you believe that?"

"None of my ancestors died with it in their hand. It was old age or treachery which killed them all. It is always close to my hand."

"Does it have a name as most powerful weapons do?"

"It is called Sax Lacus in our tongue. Sword of the lake."

"I am happy that you have such a weapon." He smiled sardonically. "It will make my job much easier."

She caught his eye as she murmured. "I am happy too Roman." The Queen felt feelings well up in her for this warrior, this man. She glanced at Vellocatus who was a fine and strong youth but she knew that if she ever bedded the Roman it would be a more satisfying experience.

Despite its fine-sounding name, the reality of the sword was somewhat different from the legend. It had been made by the Celts in the land called Gaul before it was conquered by the Romans. It was made by the finest swordsmith who used his own blood in its casting. When the Romans had conquered Gaul one of the last warrior chieftains to leave took the sword with him and went to the land of the Iceni in Britannia. Being a belligerent warrior, he fought and argued with his hosts and decided to travel north with a few retainers to seek a new kingdom. It was in the land of the Brigante in the valley of two lakes when the legend really began. The uncle of Cartimandua's ancestor was hunting with a few warriors when he came across the sword and the unpleasant Celt. They fought hand to hand and the Brigante won. However, his victory was short-lived for the retainers shot arrows in to the Celts until they were all dead. The only one to see where the sword fell was the great, great grandfather of Cartimandua's father. He waited until the following day, waded out and retrieved it from below the surface. It was fortunate for him that other warriors of the Brigante were passing the lake as he emerged with the sword in his hand. Although he had been the outsider to inherit the kingdom the superstitious Brigante felt this was an omen and he was pronounced king. The legend of a sword from the lake calling to him came from his own mind. His great, great, great-granddaughter inherited all of his guile, cunning and adaptability.

Drusus and Metellus had seen the movement of the Queen's bodyguards and, unsure if that was an enemy they had ridden away to the south. Fortunately for them, they were hidden from their pursuers by a line of trees and the curve of the hill so it was that they unwittingly led the Carvetii into the ambush and caused more casualties than if they had not been followed. Hearing the scream of battle they were able to surmise that it had been a Brigante ambush.

"We can rest the horses a little now Metellus. I am not sure we are still following the line of march of Ulpius." His leader had told him to rejoin him but their detour had taken them away from the trail taken by the auxiliaries. Drusus knew that they had to make a choice or die.

Metellus shaded his eyes against the sky. "I think Eboracum is in that direction. He pointed southwest. If we continue in this line we will either see the rest of the turma over there or reach Eboracum. And I don't fancy going back in that direction." He gestured over his shoulder.

"No, you are right there. It is as good a plan as any." Having made a decision the two cavalrymen felt more contented. As troopers, they were normally detached from the main army and both had learned years before that, unlike the legions with their massed ranks and security in numbers, they had to think in the saddle and use their wits. They walked their horses over the flat plain between two low hills giving the winded mounts some time to recover for who knew when they would need to gallop again. They were beginning to believe they would reach Eboracum, as they crested the low hill to the south. The sight which met them made them both clutch at their sacred amulets murmuring for the Allfather to protect his sons. Before them was a whole warband of Carvetii. Drusus estimated that they were about the same number as an ala, five hundred. Metellus who had the sharpest eyes shouted, "That is Venutius!"

They had no choice and they galloped as hard as they could to the north for that was away from their enemy and towards their few friends.

The Sword of Cartimandua

Meanwhile, the light was beginning to dip behind the hills in the distant West when Ulpius heard the hoof beats of Lentius' horse. "No pursuit decurion. They have either gone a different way or given up."

"Excellent." For the first time, Ulpius believed they might make it. The horses could smell the river and were eagerly racing towards it. That meant that they were so close to Eboracum and the safety of the legion that they could have walked there in the time it takes for the sun to set on a spring evening. The last barrier was the river, not as mighty this far north of Eboracum but difficult to cross with a chariot. They were almost at the river when Marcus shouted the alarm; he was riding five hundred paces to the south of the much-diminished band when he saw the movement of mounted men galloping over the rise.

"It is Drusus and Metellus." As soon as they heard the alarm every man took his javelin out and checked the strapping on his oval shield.

Ulpius could see his men riding for all they were worth. The fronts of their horses were covered in sweat and they were almost out on their hooves. Drusus was shouting long before he was close. "It is a trap." He pointed behind him. "The Carvetii."

Venutius roared his pleasure when he saw how pitifully few the Romans were. They would not be able to escape him and he would have the bitch Cartimandua to parade before her subjects a visible sign that he, Venutius, was the rightful king of the Brigante and the Carvetii. The Vellocatus boy would be castrated alive and then left for the crows, ravens and magpies. He drew his sword. "Kill the Romans but I want the Queen and her boy alive!"

Ulpius could now see how clever and devious Venutius had been. The scouts hadn't been chasing; they were the stopper in the bottle, the hound driving the stag on to the spears. The Carvetii leader had known where they would take the Queen and had ridden north east not north-west. His men and horses would be fresher; not that that would be an issue for he outnumbered the Romans by at least ten to one. Behind Drusus, he could see the Carvetii army. There were chariots, horses and foot soldiers. Their enemy intended to cut them off and prevent them from reaching the safety of Eboracum. He made up his mind quickly. The river twisted and turned southward to Eboracum. "Right lads we are heading down there towards the river. The queen can use

The Sword of Cartimandua

the chariot like a boat and float down to Eboracum. We'll buy her time. Let's go." He secretly hoped that the current would take them to the other shore and they would be safe from the arrows and slings of their attackers but at least the river was a safer option.

They rode hard. They were riding towards the enemy but also getting closer to the river. When they reached the banks they dismounted and the auxilia began to strip the chariot of all that was heavy. Ulpius looked over to the approaching barbarians. It would be a close-run thing and he feared that he and his men would have to sacrifice themselves in order to secure the Queen's escape. Decius shouted, "Ready sir."

"Lower it into the river, gently we don't want it breaking up or floating away. "They began to lower the wooden chariot into the water.

"I am not going." The queen's words told the Romans that they would not be able to persuade her. Their ride, the sacrifice of the bodyguards, the deaths of the auxiliaries had all been in vain. They would be slaughtered and without any command, the troopers turned to face the enemy now less than two thousand paces away.

"But your majesty."

"I cannot swim." She smiled an engaging smile that helped to harden their resolve. "Besides decurion as long as I hold the sword I cannot die."

He nodded, he had already assumed he was going to die but he had been prepared to die so that the queen might live. If this tough old queen wanted to join him, sword in hand, then he could understand it. At least they would take a good number of the enemy with them. "Shields!" The men locked their shields into a wall. They were not as solid as legionary shields but they were better than nought. Ulpius gazed at the approaching horde and then his men, their advantage was their shields, their armour and, most importantly, their discipline; typically, they were bare-chested and only a few had any kind of helmet, there were also few shields. That would give the Romans the edge for when they threw their javelins each one would take out an enemy and that would slow up those following on behind. They would still die but they would take many of the Carvetii with them. It was not in his nature to give up hope; as long as he had a weapon and his men

The Sword of Cartimandua
around him Ulpius Felix would always believe he could not only survive but win. "Remember who we are. Remember we fight for each other and remember these bastards only want one prisoner and she has tits!" The men laughed at the irreverence as did the queen who admired the way her rescuer was undaunted by his imminent death. The only one who looked upset was Vellocatus who glared at Ulpius' back.

The enemy warriors were less than five hundred paces away when the Romans heard the unmistakable sound of buccinas. It was the ala! Had they arrived too late? They were unable to see their friends in the gloom but they could see by the way the enemy horse swerved to their right where they were coming from. "Right you useless buggers. Die hard and some of us might live. Those are our brothers coming to help us. Don't let me down! If I die first I'll kick your arses when you get to Elysium."

They laughed at the gallows' humour. "Caltrops. The men in the front row suddenly hurled the many pointed pieces of metal towards the enemy chariots. The ponies were unshod and the caltrops would cause serious damage. The Romans knew their efficacy having encountered them in Batavia- they knew what would happen to this solid line of horses. Their narrow frontage helped and, as the first ponies reared, bucked and tried to turn, the whole of the enemy vanguard was thrown into confusion. Ponies tried to veer away only to hit other chariots or more caltrops. They reared, tossed and threw their riders and chariots into each other. The entire vanguard was stopped and hurled into complete confusion. Taking advantage of the hiatus Ulpius roared, "Javelins!" The first volley flew over the heads of the first rank and totally disrupted the whole attack. As they prepared to launch their second volley some of those who had fallen from the chariots began to hurl axes and spears. "Javelins." The second volley took out some of those who had survived. As they unsheathed their swords Ulpius had a quick look to see their casualties. One of his men had taken a hit to the throat from an axe thrown from a charging tribesman and was bleeding to death. One or two had had cuts but it was Vellocatus and Cartimandua who had taken the most damage. Vellocatus was lying with a spear embedded deep in his stomach-a death-wound. Cartimandua was holding her right arm, a javelin

The Sword of Cartimandua

pinning it to the ground. He had no chance to help her for a huge warrior leapt over the chariots screaming and waving a two-handed broad-axe. He only had time to react. He threw his shield to the left and dived to the right. They faced each other both recognising that they fought an experienced warrior. Ulpius kept his eyes on his opponent's face looking for the movement of his eyes that would tell him how he would fight. He saw his enemies' eyes flick towards his sword and even as the axe sliced down Ulpius thrust the boss of his shield at the weapon. The blade slid off the metal and Ulpius thrust towards the warrior's face. He was too wily to be taken so early and he merely stepped back almost laughing. Ulpius was unconcerned; he had seen how the man reacted. Next time it would end. He swung his sword at the Brigante knowing that he was opening up his left side. His opponent saw the opening and smashed down at the shield. He hit with incredible force and Ulpius turned slightly so that the warrior carried on forward and when his momentum opened up his left side Ulpius stabbed upwards finding a vital organ almost immediately. He had no time for satisfaction as he sensed someone coming from his right. He instinctively struck backhanded and felt the blade sink into soft flesh. He turned and saw that the man fought bare-chested and his blade had cut both the tops of his arms and the top of his chest; not death wounds. He finished the man off by cutting his throat. He looked up and saw Marcus without a shield trying to fight two men with his sword and the broken end of a javelin. Ulpius charged one of the men and almost decapitated him with his sword. Marcus ended the life of his companion with a javelin he picked from a dead body and slid into the unprotected throat of the assailant.

    Drusus and Metellus were fighting as a pair each one watching out for the other. Close by the Brigante scout Osgar was using his sling to mighty effect; to their front was a wedge of Carvetii. The leader fought without any upper body armour save for a golden torc, a blue painted face and a winged helmet. Even as he came towards him Drusus couldn't help musing on this belief from the Brigante that painting your face gave you magical protection. Osgar took aim with his sling only to be stabbed by a spear from his side. Drusus knew immediately that he was in danger and he turned his shield to his left. As he did so the war chief charged forward, his warriors alongside.

The Sword of Cartimandua

Drusus took the thrust of the axe on his sword; he was struck on the head by an axe thrown by one of the warriors. His helmet saved his life but he was knocked down. He would have died there and then but Metellus hacked down on the neck of the warrior striking a vital vein. Before Drusus could thank his companion two warriors sliced and hacked into Metellus unprotected side and his lifeless body fell onto Drusus whose world drifted into blackness.

Marcus and Lentius saw Metellus and Drusus go down and charged into the side of the Carvetii formation. They were enraged and the enemy group was slaughtered as they continued to hack at the lifeless body of the huge auxiliary. With no enemies to their front, Lentius and Marcus dragged Drusus away from his dead comrade. They did not know if he was dead or alive but they could see that Metellus had joined the Allfather.

Venutius was becoming angry that this tiny handful of Roman warriors was thwarting his attempt at ending the Queen's life. The crashed and ruined chariots were a barrier around the beleaguered Romans; his warriors were being picked off before they could get to the enemy. The auxiliaries were using their bows with great accuracy to pick off the warriors as they tried to climb over the barrier. With little or no armour, each arrow took out a warrior who in turn became part of an even bigger barrier. He turned to his bodyguards; he would take his elite and kill these upstarts. "Form on me! Wedge!" Before he could advance he heard the strident sound of a buccina. Romans! He looked in the direction of the river, towards the south and saw a mass of men. It was the garrison of Eboracum.

One of his scouts, bleeding from an arrow wound rode up. "It is the Roman cavalry; they have destroyed Calga and his men. They will be here in a heartbeat we must flee or die."

Cursing his luck Venutius realised he would have to withdraw; he clutched at his sacred charm, given to him by a witch in the hope that its power would help him to survive. Unwittingly the Romans had copied his plan; the Queen and her rescuers were pinning the warband and they were being attacked in the flank. If it was just the cavalry then he might be able to defeat them but if it was the legion…There was still time. He might have lost the battle but this was but the opening of a campaign that would see the end of Cartimandua and the

The Sword of Cartimandua

eviction of the Roman infestation from his lands. "Withdraw!" His standard-bearer waved it in a circular fashion, the signal to retreat. Those warriors who could see it began to withdraw but those facing the two Roman forces kept fighting the bloodlust filling their heads.

There were barely a handful of his auxiliaries left and Ulpius looked up expecting the end. He could see the bodies of his men, some seeping their life into the ground others barely alive but all hope of life leaving their eyes. His horizon was filled with enemies; as the arrows diminished in numbers so more of them made it over the barrier where Ulpius stood like a bronze statue, he hacked and chopped those who stumbled and fell across the sea of bodies and they sank to the ground. He heard a call which brought his fading hopes alive it was the buccina! The enemies before him unexpectedly thinned behind the warrior he despatched with his spatha and he saw, with grim delight, that the enemy warriors to his front were dead or dying and he suddenly saw troopers from his ala were charging and pursuing the rest as they fled the field. The rout was complete as the Romans outnumbered the fleeing tribesmen who would be slaughtered if they faced the fresh Roman troops. He turned quickly to Cartimandua who was lying ashen-faced in a pool of blood. "You fight well decurion. My poor Vellocatus will fight no more." She gently touched the still, silent face of her lover.

Speaking quietly, almost to himself Ulpius said, "Nor will you majesty for I fear for your sword arm. This may hurt my lady but I must stop the blood or you will die." She nodded and, closing her eyes turned her head to the side. Using both arms he pulled the crude javelin from her arm. He tightly wrapped his neckerchief around the arm to stem the bleeding. "You are brave my queen. I have known warriors who would have been screaming like pigs."

"You have saved my life Roman and I will repay the debt. Take my sword until I can hold it again. Guard it as well as you guarded me for I have never seen a warrior like you. You defeated the best of the Carvetii this day. Brigantia owes you a great debt for you have prevented Venutius from killing the rightful queen." With that, her eyes closed and drifted off into unconsciousness. As Ulpius gripped the hilt of the magnificent weapon he felt as though it was alive; it felt like an extension of his arm. As soon as he touched it he knew he

The Sword of Cartimandua
would find it very hard to return it. The balance and feel seemed to make it sing and, as he ran his hands over the Celtic inscription, he felt himself back in the world of warriors from which he had come. It truly was a blade from the old-time and the barbarian in Ulpius thrilled at the thought of using it.

The Sword of Cartimandua
Chapter 4

Eboracum
Vellocatus hung on for a few days. He occasionally recovered consciousness but the legionary surgeon held out no hope for him. The Queen fared better although she too drifted into unconsciousness on more than one occasion. The Greek doctor in the fort was a clever man who knew he had to save the life of the Queen or suffer the consequences of his Roman masters being unhappy. As Ulpius remarked to the tribune and surgeon the enemy were prone to smearing faeces and poison onto their weapons. As soon as he knew that the doctor was able to find the right remedy to cure the angry wound on the Queen's arm.

A day after she arrived in the fort she sent for the tribune Saenius Augustinius. "The soldier who rescued me, what is his rank?"

"He is a decurion, majesty. Why did he do anything to offend you? If so I will have him spread across a wheel."

"Silence! He served both Rome and me well. I would have him promoted." She paused as a look of incredulity crept across the tribune's face. "You can do this, can't you? Or should I send for the governor?"

"No majesty I can do as you wish." The tribune was a politician and he ignored the implied command and changed it to a wish. He didn't see why the ugly barbarian should be promoted but he would make political capital out of it. It would endear the Queen and the barbarian to him. They would be in his debt. "I will see to it immediately."

Making her tone gentler she mollified the tribune a little. "As my ex-husband has stirred up my loyal subjects against me and brought in his Carvetii dogs I would like to invite Rome to make my lands safer."

The Queen's statement suddenly made Saenius see that he had the chance to make political capital out of the situation. The Queen was inviting Rome to take over Brigantia. It would cease to be an allied kingdom and become a vassal kingdom. She had to be protected and Venutius had to be destroyed. He calmed himself to meet with the prefect. He needed to pander to the queen and any sensibilities the

The Sword of Cartimandua

prefect might have would be ignored. Leaving the Queen's quarters he summoned a guard over. "Tell the prefect I wish to speak with him."

By the time Flavius Bellatoris arrived the prefect had maps and reports spread across his table and he had regained his composure. "What do you think of the decurion, Felix, the one who rescued the Queen?"

"He is a good warrior and leader. The men love him."

"Promote him."

Flavius looked nonplussed. "Promote him but to which post? He is already senior decurion the next promotion would be decurio princeps in command of the ala."

The tribune looked flustered; he did not understand the workings of the auxiliary. He preferred the organisation and order of the legion. "Well then just do that."

"With respect sir there are two decurio princeps already in command of the alae."

This was a problem. One could not just dismiss a decurio princeps. "Are they both good?" The pause told Saenius all he needed. "One of them is not. Can we dismiss him? Give him land? A pension?"

"Gaius Cresens has not the required years to qualify for land or a pension, on the other hand, he is not," the rough tribune struggled to find the right words; "perhaps the best man to lead the ala." Flavius himself wished the corpulent cavalryman removed but it galled him that he was being ordered to do so by an outsider; someone recently arrived from Rome without the first idea of what it meant to live, fight and die on the wild frontier.

"Well," said the prefect impatiently, "what can we do with him?"

"As yet we have no quartermaster at the fort. We will need someone who is senior and understands the army to be in command. It would be a better pay grade so I assume he will do it."

"Then do it. Dismiss."

As the prefect left his headquarters, the tribune began to write the report to the Governor; the report that might just make his political career. He was giving the largest tribal area in Britannia to Rome. Perhaps this would be his escape back to Rome!

The Sword of Cartimandua

The turma had suffered. There were ten auxiliaries, including Ulpius who were fit for duty and all of those had scars and minor wounds. Osgar and Metellus had gone to the gods but Marcus, Lentius, Drusus and Gaius had survived. The prefect, Flavius Bellatoris summoned Ulpius to his office the day after the enemy were vanquished. "So, you old goat. You decided for the first time in your miserable life to be a hero." Flavius was an even older grizzled veteran. He made Ulpius at thirty-five look like a young man. He had seen service in Batavia and on the Rhine under Caligula and Claudius. He was known as the toughest cavalryman to fight for Rome but he protected his ala like a father. Ulpius was silent although a slight smile played about his lips. "A good thing that you did. The queen might act like a Pompeian tart and about as popular amongst her people as the Egyptian clap but she is still the queen and had that bastard killed her he would have been king and Mars himself would have struggled to contain the North. He might still be king to many of the Brigante but at least, with the queen behind these walls, we have a figurehead. It was fortunate for you that I was the one who received your message. The tribune likes the protection of these wooden walls. He does not want to venture anywhere where the locals might whip off his balls. " He spread his hand out expansively to the vague south." Bolanus is struggling with the Second Augusta to put down the Silures and the Ninth is still not up to strength. All that trouble in Rome has stretched us a little. We could do with a couple more legions and then the job would be finished. Good job Ulpius." He reached over and gripped Ulpius' forearm in the soldier's grip. "As a reward the tribune," he managed to turn the word into a sneer, "Saenius Augustinius, has asked that I promote you." Ulpius was still silent. "Speak you sneaky bastard."

"I am grateful to the prefect knowing, as I do that it means more pay to be promoted. I am silent because I do not know, as yet, what the promotion is."

Flavius laughed; his laugh came from deep in his belly as though released, like a volcano erupting. "Excellent. Your heroics have not changed your mercenary nature." His eyes narrowed. "I should have known when I heard that you had acquired a torc. I am sure I too will

The Sword of Cartimandua

be profiting from the acquisition. Shall we call it a contribution to the ala funds?"

Ulpius wondered which of his men had let that slip, he would find out and they would suffer. "I have not had time to dispose of it yet."

"Leave that to me. I know a few dealers and I will ensure you get the best price. So you are to command the ala quingenaria. Can you handle five hundred men?"

"I can command them better than the overweight Gaius Cresens. And what is he to do now that I have his command?"

"He is to become quartermaster here. Our Governor has decided to make the fortress more solid and permanent. Our friend will help provision it."

"And my turma?"

"Who do you suggest Marcus? Drusus? Lentius?"

Ulpius thought about it briefly. "Marcus, Marcus Aurelius Maximunius. He's solid as a rock."

"Good. There are some new men coming in over the next week. Fill up your turma and prepare the men for the field. We gave Venutius a bloody nose but he has merely retreated behind his mountains and he waits in the West. We will be campaigning in the spring. Now piss off and have a drink. Thanks to you I have work to do with the lists of dead and wounded." Ulpius turned to leave. "And Ulpius… bring back the torc."

Ulpius went back to his tent happy that he was promoted but seething with anger that he would have to share the golden torc with the prefect. It was not the fact that he would be handing over a share it was the fact that one of his men had betrayed him; one of his men had violated their code. He saw Marcus and called him over. "Find out which of the lads blabbed about the torc."

"What torc?"

"Don't play the innocent with me boy. You know which torc. I know as it wasn't you; if it was you'd be chewing fist. Just find out."

"Atticus."

Ulpius stared at Marcus. Atticus had been with them both for four years and they felt he was a trusted comrade. "That little prick. I'll think up something special for him." He led Marcus away from the

The Sword of Cartimandua

tents towards the horses. "How did the lads do in that last little action? I was a bit busy defending her majesty."

"They did well. Young Gaius saved your life."

"He what?"

"When you were coming to help me out-oh thanks for that I owe you one- there was a big bugger with an axe about to take your head off. The lad had him and then took out two more who were keen on having a decurion's head in their hut."

"Good he might turn out to be alright. And young Marcus some good has come your way, you might make an offering to the Allfather." Marcus looked puzzled. "Pick yourself out a chosen man. You have the turma. I am decurio princeps and I have the ala quingenaria." Marcus beamed his joy and blushed his pleasure. "The bad news is that I will still ride with the first so you don't get rid of me that easily!"

When Vellocatus died, the whole of the camp turned out for the funeral. Although he had only been a shield-bearer he had been the consort of the Queen and the tribune was keen to ingratiate himself with the artful Cartimandua. It was a mark of respect for the Queen rather than the lowly shield-bearer. The Queen herself looked magnificent. Her injured arm was hidden and she wore not only a magnificent jewel-encrusted torc but a small silver crown that accentuated her hair. There were many legionaries and auxilia harbouring lascivious thoughts as they burned her husband's corpse.

After the funeral, the prefect called Ulpius and Marcus to his office. When they arrived, they were surprised to see the Queen reclining on a couch.

"Her majesty has asked us to recover a few of her possessions from her capital," Flavius began, his face expressionless. "There are not only her clothes but her slaves and servants." I thought that as you had been there," he gestured towards Marcus. "You might be the best person to ask. As new commander," he looked directly at Ulpius, "I wondered if you had any suggestions."

Ulpius looked from the Queen to Flavius but could detect no hidden meaning in his words. "The turma is not up to strength I would suggest he takes the third turma their commander Julius Augustina is

The Sword of Cartimandua

still in sick bay with the wound from the battle. We do not know if Venutius went over the mountains or stayed at Stanwyck."

Flavius nodded his judgement in Ulpius' ability having been confirmed. "It goes without saying Decurion that, if the refuge is held, you return here. That would need a legionary intervention." Marcus nodded. The Queen coughed and looked pointedly at Flavius. "There is a box containing," he paused," important items which the Queen requires. They are buried in a secret location. If the old centurion, Gerantium is there he will show them to you. If he is dead then you will have to find them yourself. Here is a map." As Marcus went to take it the prefect went on. "It is important that you share this with no one other than your second in command. Do not open the box which will be locked and return it here. Is that clear?"

"Yes, prefect." He took the map and left.

"Ulpius make sure they have a cart. You will have to see the new quartermaster," he smiled, "that should be an interesting encounter. You took over his command before he had a chance to totally fleece his men."

"I look forward to it." He turned to go.

"I have told the prefect that I am indebted to you. I would like to reward you but we must wait until your men return." A playful, flirtatious smile played upon her lips. "Can you wait that long?"

Ulpius could feel his face colouring. "I er, that is…"

Flavius saved his embarrassment. "He will have to wait, your majesty, he has troopers to train. Dismiss!"

Partly flustered and partly angry Ulpius gestured to the waiting Marcus to follow. Marcus knew his commander well enough to keep his thoughts to himself. The journey to the quartermaster's stores was not a long one but Ulpius had got his temper under control by the time he got there. Gaius Cresens was a huge barrel of a man. It was said that there were no horses strong enough to carry him. He avoided any duty which appeared remotely dangerous but he was a cunning man who had spies and informants everywhere. He gathered information and used it. He was a bullying brute who had risen not through ability or skill but corruption. He had not ridden at the head of his ala for many months. If truth were told Flavius had been looking for an excuse to move him. Cresens did not view it that way. He was a

The Sword of Cartimandua

corrupt, greasy man and he had been cheating his men out of money for years. He had planned to become quartermaster but the decurion's promotion had meant that he had not had the time to extract the last view coins from his ala. He would have to use his new post to do so. Now as he saw Ulpius come in his anger began to boil up.

"Watch your stuff lads, old one eye, the thieving horse shagger is here."

"Cresens your dick isn't big enough to fuck a flea so shut it and show a bit of civility or I will personally show you the business end of my sword!"

As well as being corrupt and a bully the fat quartermaster was also a coward who preferred a knife in the back to a face to face encounter. "No sense of humour that's your trouble."

"Right I need two carts and drivers. We need forty javelins and," he turned to Marcus, "what about shields?"

"About five shields should do us. Oh, and two of the lads need some mail."

"You heard him. While you are back there see if you have some scale armour in my decurion's size."

Gaius Cresens' face became red with rage; his bloated features made him look like an angry toad puffing out his cheeks. "Scale armour but..."

"I know you have some; the prefect told me and this warrior needs it so be quick about it."

The armour was almost thrown at Marcus; had Ulpius known the thoughts racing through the quartermaster's evil mind he might have saved himself and others a great of pain by gutting him there and then. As it was he dismissed him as a blowhard. He was a blowhard but he was also a plotting, calculating vicious thug who would have revenge on the man who had stolen his position and humiliated him. The murderous look which burned into his back as he left would have warned him that not only his life but those he held dear was in grave danger.

The following day Marcus and his men left as dawn broke. The land around the putative fortress had been cleared of shrubs and trees and they were able to make good time as they trotted across the hardened paths which would eventually become roads. They headed

The Sword of Cartimandua

into the still dark west. Ulpius watched from the main gate; it was the first time that anyone other than he had led out the turma and he felt a little sad. Marcus would make a good leader but they were his men. They fought and died as a unit and now they belonged to someone else. He doubted that he would have the same control and bond with the five hundred men he now commanded but that was what happened when you were promoted. It had taken him some time to achieve this position but now that he had he longed a little for the freedom of his turma.

Before he began his reign, some of the lazier men would call it a reign of terror, he had one last piece of turma business to deal with, Atticus. He wandered over to the tents of his men. All the rest were out on patrol but Atticus had claimed he was still injured. Every unit has its weak link and his was Atticus. Drusus and the others fought as though two men with one warrior protecting another whilst Atticus just looked after himself, he was a loner who fought well but for himself. He had forgotten the cardinal rule of the unit; never betray another member of the unit. He had done so. He had told someone else about the golden torc. No matter that Ulpius would have given him, as he would with all the other survivors, some recompense, no matter that he would still make a profit and did not mind sharing it with his superior, he had been betrayed and he was going to have his revenge.

He stood in the tent, towering over the sallow-faced trooper. Atticus knew why Ulpius had come and he began begging, pleading, drool and spittle erupting from his mouth like a volcano. "I am sorry sir. I didn't mean it. I was forced to. Give me another chance."

As he saw how pathetic the creature was he could not bring himself to inflict the physical punishment he had intended. Instead, he bodily picked the runt of the litter up with one hand. "Atticus you are a pathetic little shit. Your mother obviously tried to get rid of you before you were born with wormwood and failed. Just as I failed to make you a soldier. You have let me down. You have let the turma down. You have let the ala down. I don't want you in my ala. I am going to transfer you to the second ala. Let's see if Aurelius Suetonius can do a better job." Seeing the pitiable look of relief on the face of the man he

The Sword of Cartimandua

had just dismissed he added, "And I will be telling your new commander what a slimy, untrustworthy little bastard he is getting."

He went back to his tent where a servant brought him some watered wine, bread cheese and fruit. He munched and drank as he read the reports on his men. There were too many new recruits as some of the time served auxilia had either returned home or settled in Britannia. It was good that they had settled here in the north for it meant that there was a force to supplement the legions and the ala in times of danger. He rubbed his unshaven cheeks as he pondered Venutius and what he might do. Whilst the legions were what you wanted in a big battle they were less than useless at controlling vast areas of desolate countryside and an enemy who attacked and ran. You needed mounted men. As he ran the edge of his knife over his face he began to plan his request to Flavius and the tribune.

The problem with the ala had been Cresens who had used bullying and terror as the means of managing the warriors. They were unfit and resented authority. Their new leader did what he had always done. He led from the front. They drilled and manoeuvred every day allowing Ulpius to see the weakness and post the strengths. At first, the men were resentful of the new regime. The ones who complained soon found that the new leader would brook no mutiny of any sort and his punishments were effective. They also discovered, in the mock battles with wooden swords, that he was the best swordsman in Eboracum. After the more vocal objectors had suffered a few bruises and cracked bones they grudgingly accepted that he knew what he was doing.

Gaius Cresens became even more infuriated as he watched the ala changed from sullen, sulky soldiers to Roman auxiliaries who began to be proud to be a unit. He had hoped that they would have responded to Felix as they had to him and it galled him that they began to look up to him and even admire him.

The ala responded well to the new hand wielding the whip, and whip them he did. They had grown lazy and soft with a commander who just wanted to make money and avoid action. The warriors knew that Ulpius Felix was a warrior through and through; they knew he fought harder than any trooper and they also knew that he had an eye for loot. They suffered the abuse and the blows for they knew that they were softer than they should have been. Marcus and his comrades had

The Sword of Cartimandua

told the tales around the campfires of the enemy they faced and they were under no illusions they had not been Venutius, they had given him a bloody nose. They had fought enough fights to know that an opponent with a bloody nose comes back harder. Next time the enemy would be ready. They would need to practice moving from column to line and back. They need to learn how to skirmish; throw their javelins and perform the circle manoeuvre which kept a constant barrage of missiles striking an enemy. They would need to learn how to fight in the arrow or wedge formation. This was an effective tactic that Ulpius had drilled into him as a child in Pannonia. One warrior was the point of the spear and then two and so on. It was a formation that relied on discipline for the warriors on the right had no one to protect them. In the right circumstances, it would cut through almost any formation. The exception, of course, was the Roman legions themselves as Ulpius' grandfather had discovered when he was defeated by the old Republican legions under Pompey. It took time but soon the ala responded to the signals without thinking.

Every day was filled with training and exercise. Ulpius needed his men drilling so that each unit fought well as a unit but knew how to fight as a whole. The advantage the Romans had over the barbarians was that they could follow orders. The barbarian side of the auxiliary did not last long with Roman training for they had to respond instantly to signals both from their standards and their buccinas. When they were not drilling in their formation Ulpius had them fighting hand to hand with wooden swords for he had seen enough of the Celts of this land to realise that they were formidable fighters. No matter how strategically a battle was planned eventually it came down to a warrior fighting another warrior and Ulpius wanted his men to win.

The queen was tiring of her tented quarters and wished for something more substantial. She had pestered the tribune until he had eventually offered her a stone-built dwelling. There was a smaller river joining the mighty one and it was here, on a small mound that Queen Cartimandua decided she would have her home built. It was not far from the legionary camp and yet private enough for the comings and goings of her confidantes to be assured. The slaves who were building the dwelling were captured Carvetii and rebel Brigante. The Queen made sure that they were worked as hard as was possible.

The Sword of Cartimandua

Her arm was still injured and her inactivity made her short-tempered. Her life was made worse by the fact that she had fled without any of her relatives or servants. She was alone. The servants provided by the Romans were not as trustworthy as those she had had at Stanwyck. Her half-sisters Lenta and Macha had been her handmaidens and she missed their lively banter and infectious laughter. The result of a liaison of their father with a slave girl they were young enough to be the queen's daughters but they were totally loyal and trustworthy. Hated by Venutius who had tried to have them sold as slaves they had been the main support when the queen had decided to divorce the unpredictable warrior.

As she walked along the river, discreetly watched by two legionary guards, she wondered about her future. She had ruled a long time and she had taken many decisions she now regretted. She had taken many lovers but her marriage had been political. She did not regret the affairs only the marriage. She had hoped for a child but the seed of Venutius was not strong enough. She knew it was not her problem as she had had to take the wormwood to rid herself of unwanted babies from lovers before. Poor Vellocatus had fallen into the category of a lover rather than husband; he had been young, energetic but lacked any ideas and thoughts other than those of war.

What would she do now? It would be hard to rebuild her standing in the tribe as long as Venutius ruled for many of the hotheads liked the idea of fighting the Romans. She had no doubt that they would proclaim him king but as long as she held the sword there would be many who would question his right. She was also acutely aware that she had left without her box of treasure and whilst not without access to what she wanted, the Romans were generous, she did not want to rely on their charity. She made her decisions. The Romans could fetch her family and her treasure and then she would persuade them to rid her of Venutius. She had dragged herself from the brink of doom before and she would do so again.

That left the urging of her loins; she had always needed a man, since before Caractacus. She was a woman who was not complete without a man and she did enjoy sex. No that was an understatement, she loved sex; she loved all of it from the play which led up to sex, the act, in whatever shape or form it took, and the comfortable time after

The Sword of Cartimandua

sex. She especially loved waking up to a man in the morning when he was so big she thought he would split her in two. Even thinking about the act made her wet with excitement. Her thoughts did not drift as much as raced back to Ulpius. Although he was not in the first flush of youth, indeed he could be said to edging towards the older side of middle-aged he exuded raw power. He was a warrior in the same sense that Venutius, for all his faults had been a warrior. Perhaps the Roman decurion might fulfil a need at least until it was politically expedient to find a new husband.

The new leader was trudging back from the training grateful for the fact that his new rank gave him a servant to look after raven. He had handpicked the boy who had immediately formed a bond with the old warhorse; Ulpius knew that his mount would be cared for. He was not a man who liked luxuries but right at that moment he would have killed for a bath and to have his oiled body scraped; the temporary camp by the river did not cater for such luxuries. The new stone fortress to be started in the spring would, until then he would have to make do with a sluice down in the river.

He found a quiet spot away from anyone else and stripped off. His arms were tanned as were his legs but his body was a bone white. He ran his hands over some of the knotted scars remembering each one and the battle in which had they had occurred. The bank was steep and he just jumped in, the icy waters shocking the breath out of him. His feet touched muddy bottom and he pushed upwards, the slime oozing between his toes. The water was only up to his neck and he ducked his head back under and began to rub the tufts of hair on his head. If there were any wildlife it would soon be gone. He rubbed his body all over. He was confident that he had neither louse nor flea but he had seen enough troopers who did not look after their bodies, covered in the little bloody bites of those insidious parasites. It was the sign of a weak soldier.

He was about to climb out when he became aware that he was being observed. As he looked up towards his clothes he saw Cartimandua watching him. Unperturbed he waded towards the bank and hauled himself out. He did not attempt to cover his nakedness. He had sought privacy for his bathing and he resented the intrusion. If she wanted to spy on him so be it he would not pander to her by hiding his

The Sword of Cartimandua

body. The Queen appraised him and then slowly passed him his cloak, their fingers touching for a brief second. The vicarious thrill made Ulpius react in a way that was obvious to the Queen who also looked excited by the tiny moment of contact. He was unused to the ways of women and had had little contact with women of any sort. Cartimandua was a powerful woman and a sensual woman both were totally out of the reach of a decurion of cavalry. The first touch he had with such a woman made him forget his annoyance with her presence and made him forget his position and status. He quickly rubbed himself dry and then began to dress, composing himself as he did so. There had been total silence. Neither felt the need for words. It was as though they were thinking the same thought and feeling the same emotion. Her eyes were bright with excitement and anticipation; she could feel the desire for this man burning within her. The bizarre nature of the encounter did not appear to enter into either person's thoughts. The Queen of the Brigante and the barbarian from Pannonia were, for that brief moment just a man and woman who were mutually attracted who both knew that within the next hour would be making love as though it was for the first time.

Even as he had dressed she turned and walked away; the warrior followed, like a puppy dog. It was as though they had spoken and arranged it yet in truth, not a word had been spoken. Had Ulpius thought he would have wondered what was going to happen and where they were going but it was pure lust that drove him to follow. That part of his mind which was sensible told him that this could not end well for he was a lowly barbarian and she was a queen but that thought was driven out by the desire and need to have this woman's body. Her quarters were discreetly hidden behind the tribune's quarters. The legionaries on guard did not move a muscle as the Queen held open the tent flap for him to enter. For just the merest moment he wondered if he ought to have waited for her but in the time it took to think the thought he was inside. As the flap closed behind him he wondered what he was doing here. A barbarian from the wilds of Pannonia was entering the bedchamber of one of the most powerful women in the world. Even as he thought he should not be doing this he found himself willed on by the power of the woman with the most alluring

The Sword of Cartimandua

eyes he had ever seen. The woman who oozed both sex and power, a mesmerizing combination, was seducing him and he was helpless.

He saw that the bed had been prepared with silks and fine linens. The atmosphere was heady with powerful perfumes and scented oils. Had the queen prepared this for him? He felt intoxicated and yet he had not had a drink. Still, not a word had been spoken. It was almost as though they were two animals in rutting season. She took his hand, gently kissing his fingers and running her tongue over the back of his fingers; once again he felt the thrill he had felt earlier and he felt himself growing larger; his reaction was noted by the queen and her mouth opened in the smile of a tiger about to devour its prey. She had to have this man and she cared not that the legionary guards may have seen him come in. All she cared for was this man, this man who would complete her when he entered her damp, moist body.

She slowly began to strip his clothes from him, all the while stroking him gently with long tapered nails which made him even more aroused. As she leaned in to remove the clasp on his armour her lips brushed his cheek and, once again, he became aroused and he became fully erect. As his armour slipped to the ground and he stood both naked and erect he felt her sink slowly down until her lips gently kissed his engorged member. Her mouth opened and he felt her tongue play around the end of his penis. His hands gripped her hair as her mouth moved in and out her teeth exerting the slightest pressure and increasing his thrill. He was not confident that he could hold it in and so he took her head and pulled it up so that he kissed her long and full on the lips. In one motion he lowered to the bed, lifted her dress and entered her.

Later, as she looked at his scarred warrior body she realised that she had never felt such pleasure before with any man. He was totally spent. They lay on the bed, their bodies sweating, their breathing laboured, their thoughts racing and their hearts pulsing. He looked at her, raised himself on one elbow and gently kissed her on both eyes, slowly, one at a time. He felt her pulse quicken and then he kissed her again on the mouth; their tongues twisting, darting and turning as they explored each other. Finally, they lay side by side, his arm curled behind her head, stroking her hair, their eyes locked on each other. She

The Sword of Cartimandua

stroked one finger down the scar that was his eye, leaned over and kissed it.

"Well, decurion I see you perform as well in the bed as you do on the battlefield."

"And Queen Cartimandua, if that is how a queen makes love then I have been making love to the wrong women; I should have found a queen long ago."

"Oh, no Roman there are not many queens with appetites such as mine but Roman we are well matched. You have awoken parts of my body I had never known existed. When you were inside me it felt as though we were one creature, a wonderful, mystical beast with two hearts, two heads but one desire. When your seed spilt it felt like a dam had burst inside me."

They looked at each other with a passion the queen had not felt in a long time and Ulpius never in his life. Suddenly as if by mutual, unspoken agreement, made love again and continued long into the night. At dawn when he finally left to slip back to his barracks they parted with a kiss and the promise that this would happen again for they both felt it was ordained by the Allfather that they should have met and been so well match.

"Would that I had met you twenty years ago Roman."

"I wish that also but we cannot undo the past we can only live the present and pray for the future."

The Sword of Cartimandua
Chapter 5

Stanwyck

Although the return journey was not as fraught with danger, Marcus was taking no chances. This was the first time he had led men alone. Hitherto he had followed the orders of Ulpius. He was doing himself a disservice when he doubted his own ability for the decurio princeps valued and trusted his judgement despite his youth. He had only seen twenty-three summers but he had much experience. He had watched others lead and learned from them. He trained hard for war and was both well-muscled and toned. He was a young man with a bright mind. He did not want to fall into another Carvetii trap. He remembered the last time he had been at the stronghold it had cost him the lives of two of his close friends and he did not have many of those. He sent scouts to the west, south and north. He too believed that Venutius had returned to the safer Carvetii homelands to the north and west but the ruse which had so nearly undone Ulpius was a warning that he was a cunning foe who was able to out-think his opponents. They knew they were nearing Stanwyck when they saw the thin tendrils of smoke rising into the afternoon sky. The western scout returned.

"I could see no sign of life decurion. The buildings are still on fire."

"Did you see any sign of the enemy?"

"There were a couple of horsemen on the low ridge to the west. They did not see me for I approached whilst crawling like a snake. I made sure I checked the places they might hide for I remember when we fled from this place. There were only two and we could despatch them if we needed."

Marcus nodded "Good you have done well," and dismissed the man. Venutius had left men to keep an eye on the stronghold. When they saw the Romans, they would wait to see if this were a scouting expedition or a punitive expedition. The fact that it was only a handful of Romans might make them think it was a patrol; certainly, they would backtrack the trail to see if there were a larger force. It was getting late in the year for a sustained campaign but the tribes of

The Sword of Cartimandua

Britannia had realised that Romans did not always follow rules, as the Druids in Mona had discovered. The other two scouts returned and reported the same as the first one. Their enemies were ahead of them.

The woodland was sparse and spindly and Marcus left the turma in the woods as he scouted the approach to the fortress. It lay on a low mound partly natural and partly man-made. The ditches and ramparts ran away east and west. There was an open plain of four hundred paces all around the walls which meant it could be a killing ground if the walls were manned. He could see no sign of life but then again it could be a trap. He smiled ruefully to himself, he could vacillate all day but there was no Ulpius to make the decisions for him, it was up to him.

He drew his men up close to the walls but out of bowshot. They could just see the impaled heads of some of the inhabitants on the walls including the old centurion Gerantium whose shaven head and greybeard made him stand out, even at this distance. "Drusus, take ten men and circle the settlement to the south. Lentius do the same to the north. When you meet up, enter the refuge from the western gate."

He watched almost half his force disappear. This was his first action in command, were he to get this wrong it could be his last. He turned to the men left under his command. Drusus and Lentius had taken the men they knew from his old turma. Marcus had the rest of the third turma. Not the best way to get to know new men but Marcus was seasoned enough to know that they would follow him and obey orders or risk the wrath of Ulpius.

As he addressed them he looked into their eyes to gauge the mettle of these new comrades. "I've been here before. The entrance is a tricky little place. It twists and turns. If there are any of those bastards left they will be above you. I don't think there will be anybody left but I don't fancy facing your decurion when I return if any of you dozy buggers get a spear up the arse so watch out. Anybody makes a move assume they are an enemy. Let's go."

Marcus took the lead and entered the gate at a gallop. It helped that he had been there before but he was taken aback by the slaughter which had taken place. A quick glance to his left and right revealed severed limbs and headless corpses littered amongst bloody entrails. Women lay spread-eagled where they had been despoiled. The main

The Sword of Cartimandua

hall was burned and the whole turma could smell the cooking flesh of those that had taken refuge in the building. The last battle had taken place just in front of it and the bodies lay two and three deep. No one had been spared. They had seen few children which, in one way, was a relief but on the other meant they had probably been enslaved. He assumed that other adult slaves had been taken but, looking around at the number of bodies, Marcus didn't believe that there were many. This was obviously a warning to the Brigante, support me or this will be the result and a warning to the Romans, all your allies will suffer the same fate. He had a task to complete. He wasn't certain the Queen would have many clothes left but he would have to search and then he and Drusus could seek the hidden box. Having seen the old centurion's head Marcus knew he would have to rely on the map. For some of the younger troopers, it was more than a little upsetting. It was their first view of what the enemy could do. For the older hands, it was significantly worse because of the civilian victims who were slaughtered to make a point. They were well used to what warriors could do to warriors but the Roman army rarely inflicted such cruelty on civilians. It hardened many hearts and Venutius would rue the day he unleashed a Boudiccan savagery upon his own people.

Marcus knew that they would not be able to get back to Eboracum before nightfall and he ordered those troopers near him to make camp. He asked Lucius, the chosen man of the third turma, to secure the gate. As the man turned he looked at the bodies and then at Marcus a look which needed no words for Marcus to understand.

"Yes Lucius Demetrius, we will bury them but for the moment let us make ourselves secure." The man nodded and led off half a dozen men.

By the time Drusus and Lentius arrived there was a little more order. The smoke was dying away from the main hall, the gate was secured and the horses were on a picket line having been fed and watered. Although Marcus was anxious to find the box he knew that his men would not rest until the dead had been laid to rest. He turned to Lucius Demetrius. "Take six men and guard the gate. The rest of you get some shovels we have a grave to dig." They looked at him, an unspoken question on their faces. "Yes I know we should burn them,

The Sword of Cartimandua

make a funeral pyre and in normal circumstances then we would but if we do we'll have the tribesmen here faster than you can say shit!"

They marched outside the walls and found a sheltered spot far enough from the road to be undisturbed. They dug in silence. The ground was hard and Marcus knew that the grave would be shallow; the covering would be light but would at least keep the scavengers away. He wondered if the Queen would come and re-inter the bodies of her followers. "Right lads we aren't going to get it any deeper." The rest of the sentence was unspoken. They all knew they would have to ferry the corpses. One of the troopers found a couple of wagons and they piled on the corpses and limbs. There were trails of blood where the bodies had lain and tendrils of intestines and guts left on the ground. The smell was beginning to become unbearable as they lifted bodies as carefully as they could. In some cases, it was hard to make out the sex of the person such had been the mutilation. The warriors they laid out with whatever weapons they could find nearby. The children they laid with a woman wherever possible. Although they left most of the belongings with the corpses they were soldiers and the odd valuable was surreptitiously pocketed.

They treated the old centurion Gerantium, differently. He had been one of them. They washed his body and put his legionary armour back on his body and returned his head from the walls and secured his helmet. They reverently placed his gladius at his side and coins on his eyes. He was given a solemn soldier's farewell from fellow Romans who hoped that someone would do the same for their bones when they fell, as they knew they would in the service of Rome on some distant shore far from their homeland. Their salute was as much for their other fallen comrades as the grizzled old warrior. The last act was to disguise the burial site but each one of them could have easily found the place.

It was close to dusk as they laid the last sod down. Marcus asked each trooper to get a stone and they made a cairn in the middle of the mound. It was little that they had done but it had at least let the dead lie together. The Romans stood in silence each one with their own thoughts and their own gods in their mind.

The camp was a little easier once the dead had been cleared and the chosen man of the third turma had begun to prepare a cooked and

The Sword of Cartimandua

evening meal. One of the guards had discovered some beer that had not been despoiled and the food and drink made many of them feel better.

When the guards were set Marcus nodded to Drusus who rose and went with him. "Julius Augustus, you are in command until I return. We will check the defences, be vigilant."

The map showed the location of the box with a crude cross. It looked to be in an old hut in the North West corner of the refuge. The buildings were a mixture of typical Brigante, conical huts and the new Roman influences long buildings. The stables, main hall and palace were all oblong whilst many of the older buildings were round. The settlement had been here a long time and showed all the changes of that time. The map showed a hut close to a well and a tower; the layout of the fortress and the different types of dwelling helped the two men to find their way to the right hut. They headed with torches lit through the darkening evening. They had to proceed slowly for they were unsure of the layout and even though it had been searched Marcus was not certain if the entire enemy had left. The map took them past the boggy, marshy area and perilously close to the fast-flowing stream. There was a crude bridge that kept their feet dry and then they climbed the first of the ditches. The scurrying and furtive movements they could hear would be the rats feasting on those burned and cooked body parts not buried for the entire fort was covered in body parts and human entrails. The rats and foxes would have a good winter and there would be many more carrion crows when the year turned. Marcus shuddered, on the morrow, it would be worse when the aerial harbingers of death descended.

The two auxiliaries gripped their swords tighter as they cast a wary eye around them. The tower on the northwest corner was burned and torn down. The hut they were looking for appeared to be intact. The door was thrown down and they both drew their swords. Inside it was a scene of destruction and devastation. Tables and crude chairs were smashed and cast aside; there were broken shards of pot littering the floor. The hut also appeared to be of a higher status than the others for none of the others had had any furniture. This was definitely the right location. The light from the torches revealed the floor where the map indicated the box would be buried. Both Romans were dismayed

The Sword of Cartimandua

when they saw that there had been something there but it had been removed. They could see footmarks on the floor and signs of human scrabbling close to the hole. Someone had dug it up, someone who knew what they were looking for. From the size of the hole, Marcus estimated it would have been as long as his arm and about half as deep. It would have been heavy. From the drag marks, it had been dragged and then lifted. They had failed in their mission. They searched the outside as thoroughly as the inside but it was obvious from the map that someone had been there before them.

Drusus looked at his friend as they went back to the rest of their fellows. He admired Marcus and looked up to him probably more than he did to Ulpius. Drusus wanted to be just like Marcus and it dismayed him to see the decurion so obviously crestfallen. What angered Drusus was the fact that it was not their fault; they had been sent too late but it could follow Marcus and stop him from becoming the leader Drusus knew he could be. A failure was a failure; Ulpius had succeeded because he had had the luck. Marcus had not had the luck. The fates could be cruel.

Night had fallen by the time they arrived back at the charred and blackened remains of the Roman-built hall. There were a few guards who stood warily as they approached. "How goes the watch, trooper?"

"All quiet decurion."

"I will take the first watch, you sleep Drusus. I will wake you." His second in command needed no urging to grab whatever sleep he could. You learned to rest when you could, eat when you could and steal when you could for who knew when death would strike in this wild land so far from home. Marcus needed to think about the report he would have to make to Ulpius. His first task as a decurion and he had failed. It did not matter that he couldn't have prevented the box from being taken nor could he prevent the queen's belongings from being desecrated; his task was to succeed. He supped a beaker of weak beer and chewed on a piece of hard stale bread, the joys of a soldier's life. He would have to work even harder on his next mission if there were to be the next mission. The prefect could take away his promotion just as easily as he had given it to him. The thought burned in Marcus' mind for he felt worse about letting Ulpius Felix down. Just then the trooper who had challenged him approached.

The Sword of Cartimandua

"Decurion."

"Yes, what is it?"

"I saw a movement out there," he gestured towards the east. "I thought it was my eyes but I saw it again."

"An animal?"

"I don't think so, it looked too big and the movements were wrong. I think it was someone, not something."

Marcus did not know the man who was from the third turma but he had given an honest report. Marcus shook the shoulders of the four men asleep around the fire. "Get your weapons." He went over to Drusus who was already waking and strapping on his sword. "Wake the men and have them stand to. Tell Lucius Demetrius he is in command until I return." Taking the four men and the guard he trotted towards the eastern gate. He looked at the two troopers guarding the gate. They were not from his turma and he did not know them. "Have you seen anything?" From their guilty looks, he suspected they had been gambling rather than watching. He would deal with them later. "Right well keep your eyes peeled now while we investigate the movements you should have spotted." The guards let them out and then slotted home the bar on the gate. He gestured to the observant guard and whispered, "Where?"

The man pointed at the grave they had just made. It was halfway between the woods and the walls. He could detect some movement but he could not tell if it were an animal for the moon had not come out and the shadows blended into the woods. Marcus pointed to two of the guards and gestured that they should go south and to the other two, he gestured to the north. They were a small half circle with swords drawn and they approached the grave gingerly. The movements stopped and the shadows looked like the shadow of the grave. Had it been an animal and gone? This could be a trap or they could have spotted the scouts seen earlier by Lentius. Either way, he was taking no chances. They paused when they were all about twenty paces from the grave. He was about to raise his arm to signal to charge when suddenly three small bodies stood up.

"Do not harm us, Roman. We are unarmed."

The three had swords at their throats in seconds. Marcus peered down and saw that they were women. He would take no chances until

The Sword of Cartimandua

he knew who they were. He remembered the stories of the savagery of Boudicca and the Iceni; women in these lands were warriors just as the men were. He had seen the queen fighting and knew that they had skill. He scanned the edge of the woods and could discern no movement. If this had been a trap to lure them from the safety of the fort then there would have been a sudden rush of warriors to attack them.

"Move!" The auxiliaries hurried the three women towards the walls and Marcus watched their backs. Every Roman was awake when they arrived at the walls. Julius Augustus had lit torches at the gates to guide them in. Marcus nodded his approval at the chosen man as he led the women into a hut close to the gateway. Dismissing all the troopers except for Drusus and Lentius left as guards the decurion held a light to the women. They were Brigante; two were younger women, they looked as though they had seen twenty summers or so whilst the third was as old a woman as he could remember seeing. What attracted his attention and caused a gasp of surprise was the box carried by the taller of the women.

"Who are you?"

The taller one looked directly, without fear into the eyes of Marcus. "I am Macha handmaiden to the Queen. This is my sister Lenta and this is Aurelia Gerantia, widow of the Roman Flavinius Gerantium."

"I am sorry for your loss lady. We buried your husband with honours."

The old woman merely nodded and Macha added. "We saw. It was good that you treated our dead with respect."

"Why did you not come out sooner? Why wait until dark?"

"The woods are filled with scouts. We thought they may have attacked you and then we would have been in a worse position. The speaker gestured at the older woman. Aurelia Gerantia wanted to pay respects to her husband. If it were possible we would have remained hidden but they would have searched the wood once you began to leave. I assume you will be leaving on the morrow?"

Marcus could see that she had wisdom beyond her years as well as a cunning and supple mind. "Are they still there?"

The Sword of Cartimandua

"Yes. It took us many hours to work our way close to the grave. We were resting, intending to make the last few yards in daylight."

"You need not fear. The scouts will pose no threat to us. You will be safe for you are correct we will be leaving in the morning."

Lenta spoke for the first time. There was anger in her voice. "It is a shame that you did not protect our people when you could. Many would have lived. Perhaps you feared to face them then!"

Marcus looked closely at the angry young woman who coloured up with eyes wide and fierce. He could see that there was more to her than met the eye; she was more than a handmaiden. She was not afraid to speak up to a Roman officer who towered over her.

"Peace sister. My sister is overwrought. Her husband and child died in the attack." She looked at her sister. "Remember sister the warriors were too few to defend us and their duty was to protect our Queen." She turned to Marcus. "The Queen lives?"

"Aye, she asked us to return here to save what we could and," he looked pointedly at the box, "to return a precious item which was buried."

"Aurelia's husband led us here even as you were leaving. He dug it up and gave it into our safekeeping. We were on our way out by a secret passage when some of Venutius' supporters attacked the guards. That is when Lenta's husband died and her child taken. We too would have died had not Aurelia's husband fought off our attackers." She put her arm around the shoulders of the old woman who was now crying silently. "He bought us the time to flee with his life. Even though mortally wounded he killed the last of the traitors. Perhaps had he lived they might not have taken Stanwyck. Who knows?"

"You have done well, you have all done well. Keep the Queen's box and guard it." He turned to Drusus. "You and Gaius are to guard these ladies and the box at all times. It is important that they are returned safely to Eboracum. Now get some food and drink and then rest. We leave at dawn."

Macha looked at this seeming boy but one who had such command of his men. She could see that he was a leader but more than that he was a man and she felt herself curiously attracted to a man for the first time in her short life. She touched his arm. "Thank you. I

The Sword of Cartimandua

can tell that you are a good man. Forgive my sister's outburst. She will look kindly on you when she is over her grief."

Marcus turned at the softness in her voice and her touch. Her eyes seemed to suggest an even more personal message but perhaps he was imagining it.

"Lady you need not explain. We are doing our duty and tell your sister that if we could have prevented the death of her family we would gladly have given our lives to do so." He paused, the delicate question almost catching in his throat, "The child?"

"That is why she is so angry. She blames herself and feels that she should have protected the girl but there was nothing she could have done. Had she attempted she would have been captured raped and then killed. It would not have saved her daughter."

Marcus noticed that Macha had not referred to the child by name. He understood that for by not naming the child it gave a detachment that it was someone else. Soldiers often did that. "Will she be sold do you think?"

"That is the small hope and consolation that we both share. What we fear is that Venutius and his animals will use and then kill her. If she is a slave then when Venutius is gone and the Queen has control again we may find her. Until then Lenta will be not the happy, laughing Lenta I know. She will mourn and yet not mourn for the child who is neither alive nor dead."

The Sword of Cartimandua
Chapter 6

Eboracum
Gaius Cresens was looking over his books. He had already lost money and it was down to one man, Ulpius Felix. He had planned to sell the scale armour to a local chieftain who had managed to acquire some gold. The quartermaster suspected it had been illicitly acquired but he didn't care. He would have made a small fortune. As it was he was out of pocket and for the shields and javelins as well. He would not only have to pay back the one-eyed horseman he would need to remove him permanently for he would thwart all his schemes which relied on his cunning backed up by his thugs. His associates were all ex-legionaries none of whom had covered themselves in glory. They all had one thing in common; greed and Gaius Cresens used that. He would have to arrange for an accident. The accident would have to wait until his armour returned and then the decurion could join his leader in Elysium. He then applied himself to working out how to make money from his new post. It would not be quite as easy as there were Imperial clerks whose sole task was to scrutinise the dealings of people like Cresens in the far-flung corners of the Empire. It would be more difficult but, potentially, more profitable.

The cavalryman was blissfully unaware of his fate as he slipped from between the Queen's sheets. She half murmured a kitten-like noise which almost drew him back into the bed and more lovemaking. Her sleep-controlled hand wandered over to the warm space his body had occupied. Much as the tough old warrior wanted that he knew his duty came first and he had to drill his men. As he dressed his thoughts wandered from the bedroom to the battlefield and he wondered how Marcus had fared. The task had seemed simple enough but he had been in these islands long enough to know that simply did not always work out.

Even as Ulpius was thinking about him Marcus was in action. They had found some items of clothing for the Queen and a few items such as brushes and brooches forgotten in the aftermath of the massacre. The problem would be how to get them and the ladies safely

The Sword of Cartimandua

back. There were no horses to be had. He ruefully took the decision to harness four of his horses to the wagons and use them to transport the women back to Eboracum. It would not only slow them down but also make them more vulnerable to attack. They were safe from Venutius as long as they were mounted; now they would be yoked. His one advantage was that he knew where he could be ambushed and he would avoid those places. He wondered, not for the first time, why they had not sent the whole of the ala quinquigeria. It would have made more sense and would have allowed them to find out just where Venutius was. As it was they were blind and Macha's comments about the woods being filled with the enemy filled him with disquiet. He could only do one job at a time and his job now was to get the women and the box back safely.

As his men trotted away from the refuge Marcus gave the signal and his men began firing the fort. It was little enough but it would, at least, prevent Venutius from re-occupying once he had left. He was certain that the tribune would return and there would be a proper Roman fortress soon, one which would not be so easily taken.

Marcus allowed the third turma the honour of leading the small column back. The more experienced second turma provide the rear guard and flank guards. They remembered well enough the places to look out for. Marcus himself rode next to Macha and Lenta. He was more than a little curious about the box they guarded but he could not bring himself to ask. Instead, he asked about them and their relationship to Cartimandua.

"It is an honour that we serve her majesty. She is not only the Queen she is also the high priestess and the mother of our people. This is why Venutius cannot kill her for she would be reborn or else the land would die and he could not risk that."

"What does Venutius know of our people?" interjected Lenta, her face still filled with anger and hatred. "He is of the wild Carvetii. They live amongst rocks and know nothing of growing and rearing just hunting and killing."

"They are a wild people, "agreed Macha. "I sometimes think this is the reason our Queen married the wild man to protect the lands to the west as the sea guards our lands to the east."

"And what of the south and the north?"

The Sword of Cartimandua

"We never feared the south, until you Romans came and our Queen was wise enough to live with you. As for the north, no one can tame the Pictii but they only hunt cattle and slaves. Stanwyck always withstood their pathetic attempts to capture it. It has been many years since they tried. But they make life difficult for our people who live near the big rivers to the north. Even Venutius feared them and he has made Stanwyck the fortress you saw. Perhaps you Romans can, at last, tame them."

Marcus had not had such pleasant conversation in a long time and he was disappointed when Gaius came racing up with news that a patrol from the ala was coming to meet them. They were home far too quickly for Marcus for soon he would not be able to speak so freely with the Brigante beauty who had ensnared him. He smiled ruefully when he saw that the patrol was being led by Ulpius. The big warrior obviously wanted to get all the information before they arrived at Eboracum. Marcus shook his head, he had much to learn about being a leader but at least he had a good teacher.

The quartermaster looked nervously about him as he left the safety of the temporary fort. He was treading in a dangerous area. The civilian encampment was made up of some legitimate merchants and providers of services but there were a far greater number of villains, thieves and chancers. As soon as the Romans arrived in numbers then there would be many people some honest, some dishonest who would want a share of the money they brought. From bread makers to whores, from beer sellers to bodyguards they were all drawn to the honey pot that was a Roman fort. He had some contacts but he also knew that this throat could be slit for the price of a pair of sandals. He had taken no one with him. He was vulnerable, as he made his secretive way past crude dwellings and groups of locals who, to the quartermaster, looked like murderers and thieves. This assignation had to be secret otherwise he would have made the journey in daylight. . The message he had received was a verbal one from a local who sometimes acquired women for the corpulent Cresens. He would have ignored the request were it not for the silver piece which had been passed over and the frightened look on the man's face. Whoever wanted to speak with him was powerful enough to scare a whoremaster. He was not making as much from his new position as

The Sword of Cartimandua

quartermaster and he was a greedy man. Even though it was a risk Gaius Cresens had found that sometimes great risk brought great reward.

The path he took left the main inhabited area and dropped through a small copse to a stream. By the stream were two wicker huts. He approached them gingerly, cautiously for he was known to be a man who had riches. He would see no apparent sign of life, suppose this was a trap? Just when he was about to turn and leave he felt a sharp blade prick him behind the ear and the rancid smell of grease and unwashed body; it was a warrior.

"Where are you going fat one? I thought you had a meeting."

Without warning, he was propelled unceremoniously into the darkened interior of the hut. The entrance was so low that he found himself on the dirt floor. A dying fire gave the outline of shapes but he could not make out the faces of any of the men who squatted around its embers. He did see, however, the mail they wore and the blades that lay at their feet. There were warriors and he was alone, a Roman amongst rebellious tribesmen. The wrong word could end his lucrative career here and now.

He tried to raise his head but was sharply forced to the ground by a blade in the back of his neck. The figure in front of him, hooded and dark raised his sword in the direction of the Roman. "I hear you are a man with the love of gold?" Gaius nodded, unable to speak. A small leather bag was thrown from behind him and landed at his feet. "Here is gold. Examine it." His greedy, podgy fingers opened the pouch and poured the contents into his hand. "Is that the sort of thing you had in mind?"

"Yes... lord. It is just the sort of thing. How would I er, earn this?"

"Call this a down payment for loyalty. It is yours to keep. What it buys is your services for me and, "he added threateningly, "your silence. I will request information. I will do so frequently. When you provide it I will supply more. Is that acceptable?"

Aware that the wrong response would see his throat cut the ex-cavalryman was cautious in his reply. The blade was not pushed so hard into his neck and glancing up at the hooded figure he became aware that the man was enormous. His shoulders seemed to fill the

The Sword of Cartimandua

hut and, worse still, he could see many amulets on his arms; a sign amongst these Britons that he had killed many. He swallowed hard; he was getting into dangerous territory. It could result in great fortune or crucifixion but if he betrayed these animals it would be much worse. "What sort of information?"

"Nothing difficult. Nothing that you cannot handle. Numbers."

"Numbers?" There was surprise in his voice.

"Numbers of troops here, Lindum. Military information."

"That is dangerous, I could…"

"You could die here and now fat man. You could die when we drive the Romans into the sea. You could die if we informed the Romans of your treachery. You could die if we told your comrades how you mixed lead with their flour. You could die if we told of your pleasure in young children. There are many ways for such as you to die. The question is when and where? This way you live, no matter what happens and you make gold. For when we win we will spare you. It is a clear choice Roman, obey us now or die! Which is it to be?"

Put that way there was little choice. "I will live and become rich."

"Good. I thought you would see sense. When you leave here, go into the next hut you will meet my contact there. She is the only one who you will ever see and she is the one who will pay you. You will come here once a week and she will ask you a question."

"Will it not look suspicious if I come here regularly?"

"She is known to be a witch and a soldier's woman. I am sure your comrades will believe that you still have desires." Gaius nodded. Knowing his luck she would be a toothless old harridan. "Now go."

Gaius was ejected from the hut and thrust into the next one. From the noises, he heard as he left he knew that the men were leaving. His desire was to see who they were, the jewels on the man's arms and his bracelets suggested an important man but his desire for life outweighed it. He did not want to die and he was under no illusions for even though he was close to the fort his throat could be cut and his body disposed of in the time it took to sigh.

The new hut had a brighter fire and he was able to see the face of the woman. He was surprised. She was younger than he had thought probably in her twenties; his loins began to react immediately as his mind began to relish a weekly meeting with such a woman. He unconsciously licked his lips with a spittle covered tongue.

The woman had noticed his arousal and ended his thoughts in an instant. Drawing a lethally sharp dagger she put its point at his genitals. "You are here for information. The story about me as your lover will be just that, a story. If you try to touch me I will geld you." The look in her eyes and her tone of voice left him under no illusions she would do as she said. He sat back all thoughts of lust dissipated by the appearance of the knife. "Come when the other soldiers find women, which will look natural. The first information we require is the full strength of the ala and the legion here. Is that clear?" He nodded. "Now go."

He was about to leave and then a thought struck him. "Are you a witch?"

"Why do you want to know?"

"If you are a witch then you have potions do you not? You can make spells. Tell the future."

She laughed. "If you want a potion to keep your cock hard then you will be wasting your money."

"No I want," he paused and leaned closer, "a poison. To kill a man."

"Ah, then I can help you but it will cost and, "she looked pointedly at his pouch, "I know you have money, much money."

"I do and for this?" He tossed a heavy silver coin at her.

"For this, I can give you poison. I will give it to you when I have the information."

As he walked carefully back to camp he realised that this could work out well for him. This had turned out better than he had hoped for he now had a regular income, protection if the legions left and someone who could provide him with poison. It had been a good day.

Fainch watched his back with some disgust as he left. She and her sisters worshipped Mother Earth. She had spent many years, as a child, in the lands of Mona where she studied with the Druids. She had been there when the Romans had first desecrated the holy places and slaughtered the Druids. As she had hidden she had seen the ruthless Romans slaughtering the priests, killing those that she thought of as family. She swore an oath then on the holy shrines that she would have

The Sword of Cartimandua
revenge and drive these Romans from her land. It had taken all her willpower not to slit the throat of the Roman she had just spoken with. Since she had arrived back from Mona she had become more patient. She had seen that these Romans built solidly whether a building or an army or a country and she would need to bide her time and choose the most opportune moment. She would use Cresens and then he too would die. As she chanted a spell she began to grind up the mushrooms, herbs and roots she would need for her next potion. This potion was for herself; it was a potion that allowed her to leave her body and communicate with her sisters and Mother Earth. It allowed her to fly, without leaving her dwelling. She would create an alliance that would defeat these Romans who had disembowelled and crucified the only man she had ever loved; Vosius son of Lugotrix a king killed himself by the Romans. They had killed the only chance she would have of happiness; she would ensure that they had none. Her revenge was begun.

    Ulpius walked to headquarters blissfully unaware that murder, his murder was being plotted. He was blissfully happy because his lovemaking with Cartimandua was getting better and better. He did not know if it was their ages, it certainly wasn't his experience or lack of it, whatever it was they had sexual chemistry which left both of them satisfied, replete and totally at ease with each other. He worked hard with his men each day but he so looked forward to the long nights of lovemaking; rather than sapping his energy it seemed to give him energy.
    Having met Marcus and the Queen's handmaidens he was heading to make his report. He had gleaned all the necessary information on the last few miles of the journey. Marcus had filled him in completely. Both were curious about the contents of the box but Ulpius had hidden a secret smile for he knew the Queen would tell him all. Marcus could now have a bath and some food, he had deserved it. The guards outside headquarters snapped to attention as he strode past them.
    Flavius looked up from the reports he was reading and gestured for Ulpius to sit. "They made it then?"
    "As I said he would."

The Sword of Cartimandua

"And the er...box?"

"Safely delivered to the queen with two handmaidens." He paused. "Gerantium, the centurion didn't make it but the lad brought his widow back with them."

"We'll find something for her. You never met him did you?"

"Just the once when we rescued the Queen."

"He was an absolute hero; fought in Germany, Batavia and here in Britannia. The divine Claudius took a real shine to him. Thought he was some sort of lucky omen. There was him and that elephant he brought with him. Good job he didn't leave the elephant. It was him as arranged for him to look after the Queen. Sort of bodyguard. Obviously did his job well as most of the rulers in this land have short lives and violent ends. How did he die?"

"According to the lad, in battle, took a dozen or so with him. They gave him a decent burial."

Flavius nodded. As a Roman soldier, especially an auxiliary, decent burial was something you hoped for but didn't expect. "And Venutius?"

"Still hanging around. We ran into a few of them and Marcus said there were more in the woods and hills. They trailed him all the way back. Not enough for us to waste our time chasing them but just enough to let us know that he hasn't gone. The handmaidens told Marcus that there were hundreds spread all over the place. I think they are getting rid of the Queen's supporters so we have a little time but not much."

Flavius rubbed his chin and poured them both a goblet of wine. He gestured for his friend to drink. "What do you think he is up to?"

"The lads burned the wooden parts of the stronghold so he can't refortify that, at least not without us noticing. Besides, it was only built to hold back barbarians. Apart from the northern side where there is a double rampart and double ditch, there is nothing to stop legionaries. Even that wouldn't hold them up for long. It is mainly earth and wood. Greek fire, bolt throwers, even stones would easily crack that nut. There is nowhere south of the big river that is fortified which leaves over the hills in Carvetii, his stronghold of Brocavum which, the Brigante tell me, is smaller but much harder to attack than Stanwyck. He must know we'll come after him but he will hope that it is in the spring when his men have had time to rearm themselves and gather more men."

Flavius pulled a map over. "You are right about his stronghold Look. Here is his capital, Brocavum. Nasty little place. It's on a steep hill with a moat and ditch going around most of it. And the little bugger has made it of stone. I visited there a couple of years ago with Paulinus, a courtesy. It was when Venutius was only a lad and his dad was still king. It would take at least a legion to capture that. And the road to get there is no picnic. Right over the tops of the mountains. A cold, desolate and windswept place. He thinks he is safe until spring. If I had my way we would be after him now before he gets too comfortable before he can get his army together but we will have to wait for the Governor to come and light a fire up the tribune's arse. I am worried that he will get other tribes to join him. Somehow, they got wind of the trouble in Rome. I suppose no new legions gave him an idea about the situation."

"It's shame that Caesius Alasica isn't here. He knew how to fight in this land. "

"Aye, he was handy in a fight, it is a shame we only have a couple of legions over here. They should have finished the job the first time. Trouble was the Iceni. Everything was going well, they pulled the legions out and then some dozy prick decides to have his way with the Iceni women. Fucking stupid. Just shows you are safer with your dick inside your armour." Having revisited the past, the cavalryman got back to business. "Right you keep on at your men, keep them sharp, keep them ready to move at a moment's notice and I'll see if I can get you a long patrol to round up these Carvetii and rebel Brigante." A broad smile filled his face, "That is if you aren't totally shagged out you old goat!"

Saenius Augustinius did not use his clerk for this most important letter. He could trust no one with this information. The intrigue in Rome which had seen a succession of Emperors meant that every province in the far-flung Empire was at risk. Those on the extremes were in an even more parlous state. Added to that Britannia was an island and could only be supplied by sea and the sea they had to cross was capricious at best. The tribune needed to secure his position. He

The Sword of Cartimandua

was gambling that it would be Vespasian who would still be Emperor and there would be a steady hand at the helm. He was also counting on the fact that Vespasian had served in Britannia during the invasion and knew what the problems were likely to be. He would inform the Emperor that it was he, Saenius Augustinius, who had ordered the Queen's rescue. The promotion of Ulpius Felix should have ensured his cooperation. He added that the fortress of Eboracum would serve as a sound base from which to invade the far north. Once the Emperor realised that Saenius had done so much it would not take much for him to recall Bolanus and, perhaps, give the governorship to him. Perhaps Britannia might prove to be a route to even greater power he just had to make sure he held on to Cartimandua and stopped Venutius from rising in the spring.

The Sword of Cartimandua
Chapter 7

Eboracum
The pleasure at the return of his acolyte was diminished for Ulpius by the fact that the Queen now had an entourage and he could not be as close to her as hitherto. He would have to forego the pleasure of waking up in her arms and making love before the dawn broke. He smiled to himself; there was no doubt that the queen would be missing it too. The few times they were in contact there was an audience. He had enjoyed the nights spent in her arms and the joy of awakening to her each morning. That was now ended and he had to get his pleasure where he could in small ways. He took a young boy's pleasure in accidentally brushing her fingers and she reciprocated every action. He was sure that people must see their looks and almost smell the animal attraction they had for each other but everyone appeared to be oblivious or, perhaps, too tactful to comment.

It was on one such occasion that the love-struck cavalryman had a body blow to his nightly visits. He was summoned to headquarters. Not only was Flavius there but also Queen Cartimandua and, most unusually, the tribune, Saenius Augustinius. The tribune was a small unimportant looking individual. He had the frightened look of a child found with his fingers in the sweetmeats. He had been given the post by his uncle in Rome, an uncle who wanted an incompetent out of the way in the wilds of Britannia. If the truth were to be known he had hoped that he would have been killed before now and from that he would have made much political capital. Tribunes had paper power but most were only in post for a year or two and then they would return to Rome and feast out on stories of the frontier. Although he was cowardly he had cunning and guile that matched his uncle. He knew that he could gain much credit for the rescue of Cartimandua. He had visions of returning to Rome with her on his arm, not as a bride but as evidence of his courage. He would emulate Claudius who returned with Caractacus in chains.

He shifted uncomfortably upon his couch when Ulpius entered with the leader of the other ala quinquigeria, Aurelius Suetonius; he found these auxiliary cavalrymen too uncouth and wild. They were not

The Sword of Cartimandua

Romans and he could smell them before he saw them. He thought they all had the air of barbarians and they were, after all, only one generation removed from barbarians. They might wear Roman armour but their hair was still long in the style of their peoples, they wore amulets and still insisted on carrying the decapitated heads of their enemies; barbarians still. He was quite happy to waste their useless lives; it was the legionaries who would protect him behind their solid phalanx of shields. It was the legions who would defeat these tribes not barbarians from some eastern backwater.

He looked at the tall decurion princeps and found much to dislike about him even excusing the disgusting mess that had been one of his eyes which he, apparently, had lost it in the service of Rome; could the man not wear a patch? He also disliked the insolent look he normally gave to the tribune on the rare occasions when he actually had to speak to him and now he noticed looks exchanged between the Queen and this cavalryman. He had heard rumours, not only about Cartimandua's sexual appetite but also her liaison with a Roman. Heaven forefend that it should be this barbarian. All in all, he decided that he needed to be rid of this ugly barbarian who might have too much influence over the Brigante queen. Even though the days were shortening and the harvests were being gathered he would have him away from the fortress. He was a constant reminder that the Queen had not been rescued by him, the tribune, but a wild barbarian. Once he was rid of him the story could change and move him into a more prominent light.

"You have done well decurion princeps and you have been rewarded. I have another task for you. Take your men and sweep away the last of these rebels."

Ulpius looked incredulously at the tribune. "With five hundred men? Venutius will have at least ten times more!"

"Not afraid are we?" He sneered. "Is this the mighty warrior who snatched the beautiful Queen Cartimandua from under the nose of her husband?"

The Queen's face coloured a vivid red. "Enough! I know of the courage of this man and I dislike your implication tribune. Be careful you are still a guest in my land. Think before you speak little man." The threat was a powerful one for the Queen held the affection of many of the Brigante. Venutius just had the hotheads. If she chose to

The Sword of Cartimandua

make the north rise then all the gains made in the last few years would be wasted. Augustinius visibly quailed before her onslaught. She was as wild a woman as any barbarian.

She turned to Ulpius her voice softened, almost gentle. "The tribune did not explain himself well. There are reported to be a number of bands still wandering on this side of the mountains. We wish you to destroy them before the onset of winter so that we..."

"That is all you need to know," interrupted the tribune.

Flavius decided that the meeting had gone on long enough. "Take enough supplies for fourteen days. You need not go further than Calcaria in the south, Cataractonium in the north and Virosidum to the west. That should scour the land around Stanwyck and anything further away is too far to harm us with winter approaching." He paused as he wondered about giving Ulpius a task that ought to have been carried out in the summer. "If you deem it safe and the patrol is successful investigate the great river to the north for we may need to cross that in the spring if we take the war to the Carvetii." All of them avoided mentioning the fact that many Brigante were still rebelling not only against Rome but the queen. All of them were diplomatic enough to realise it would only antagonise the queen. Even Ulpius had learned not to be the plain-speaking warrior he had always been. The enemy was always Venutius and his Carvetii, not the Brigante.

"If you find any of my loyal people please bring them back to me. I am feeling lonely. You may come across some of my bodyguards."

"I am afraid not, my Queen. When my men returned with your handmaidens they reported finding the slain bodies of all your guard at the river crossing where they laid their ambush. None of them made it to Cataractonium. He said they died well."

"Good for I do not want the oathsworn to have died in vain. Be careful warrior I have still to reward you for saving my life." The look was subtle but Ulpius saw it and felt a warm glow. Flavius also noticed it; he would need to have a word with his friend when he returned from this patrol for he knew the antipathy felt by the tribune for his friend. It would not do to have him risk the enmity of such a powerful and well-connected patrician. Flavius had only survived as long as he had by holding his tongue and flattering the younger Roman

The Sword of Cartimandua

popinjays. He did not intend to end his days on a cross in this empty land far from his homeland. His friend would need to curb his tongue.

As Ulpius left he spoke to the ala clerk. "Get all my decurions at my tent now." His mind was already formulating a plan even as he walked. He would play the Carvetii at their own game; he too would use cunning and guile. His advantage was he had Roman discipline and weaponry.

He counted only fifteen men. "Ask Lucius Demetrius to join us as his decurion is still in the hospital." He decided he would have to get a better clerk one who was able to think for himself. "This will be the first time you have fought under my banner." Even though he was Roman he knew that the men in front of him still remembered their barbarian, tribal past. "My rules are quite simple. Obey me instantly. I do not like unnecessary questions. If you are still confused ask the new decurion of the second turma I am sure he can enlighten you." They all smiled at Marcus' obvious embarrassment. "Look after your horses and your men. That is it, those are my rules." He nodded at Lucius who had just entered. "We are going out for a patrol. We will be heading southeast towards the Parisi just to make sure they haven't got any ideas from Venutius. We will need enough supplies for twenty nights. We ride in an hour." As they left he noticed Flavius standing by the tent entrance.

"Are you making up your own orders now decurion princeps?"

"No prefect. I will be obeying your orders and, once we are a good way from the fort I will issue new orders."

"I am curious. Do you not trust your men?"

"I trust my men, not their tongues. There are too many people around here we do not know yet. I don't believe in taking any chances."

Flavius nodded. He had chosen well. His friend was a good leader and would go far and, more importantly, would not risk Rome's soldiers unnecessarily.

The five hundred warriors made a magnificent sight as they left the security of the fort. Their horsehair pennants danced in the autumn breeze and the early morning light reflected from the gleaming mail. At their head sat Ulpius now with his own red horsehair standard carried by the beaming Gaius delighted that he had been chosen.

The Sword of Cartimandua

Ulpius allowed himself a rare smile. He had been touched by the youth's devotion and having had his life saved he felt honour bound to reward him. It was little enough he had done for the life of a standard-bearer was considerably shorter than that of an ordinary auxiliary.

They were five miles from the camp heading towards Petuaria when the decurion princeps called a halt. He summoned his decurions whilst the troopers ensured that their saddles were tight and their equipment secure.

"Now that we are safe from prying ears and mouths too full of their own importance I can reveal where we are actually going." He drew in the soil a crude map and pointed as he did so. "Lucius Emprenius will take turmae nine, ten eleven and twelve towards Calcaria, then to Verbeia and meet with me at Virosidum. Fulvius Agrippa, you have the harder ride. You will head for Stanwyck with turma thirteen, fourteen, fifteen and sixteen and thence Cataractonium and you too will meet me at Virosidum. You have seven days. Be careful near to the fort and approach cautiously for Venutius may have fortified it again. I will take the rest of the ala directly to Virosidum." His officers looked at him and Ulpius realised he could not be as close-mouthed as when he had been a mere decurion. He needed his officers to know his mind, he needed to trust them. If he fell in battle they would need to carry out his orders. He was learning the lessons of command. Marcus noticed the change in his leader and saw too that he would also need to change with his new responsibility. "I am stealing a trick from Venutius. You are to drive any groups of Brigante towards me. I will be going slower than you. It is important that no one escapes south or north. You need to keep in touch with me. The senior decurion will assign a rider to give me a daily report; where you are and what you have encountered."

"What if we meet with a larger group? Larger than we can handle?"

"We are cavalry. We can move faster than anything they have. The only danger is when we are in their woods. Avoid them if you can. Any more questions?"

"If we do meet a larger force what then?"

"Shadow and send for me. We will be never more than a hard gallop apart. The land we will be travelling is supposed to be peaceful

The Sword of Cartimandua

and any warriors you meet will be the enemy. I will be the anvil to your hammers. Conserve your men and horses. Seven days is ample time to get to our meeting place. We will not be able to replenish any supplies and, more importantly, we have the best horses. If you lose your horses you become a foot soldier and you will lose your head. Speaking of which, we are trying to leave a message. When your troopers take heads make them into a pile, a marker to show all rebels the folly of rebelling against Rome."

"I thought they were rebelling against the Queen?"

Ulpius fixed the young decurion of the tenth turma. "That is one and the same thing. The Queen is an ally of Rome what is hers is Rome's. Now get back to your men and ride."

Cresens couldn't wait to get to his contact. He had information that would rid him of Ulpius and would further cement his position with the barbarians. He ran his tongue over his fat lips as he anticipated meeting with the witch. She excited him; the women he could afford were skeletons by comparison with the alluring and seductive witch. Her power and sexuality excited him and he felt himself becoming larger as he thought of her. Her threats did not worry him. He had taken many women against their will in the past and when the time was right he would have her and she would be in no position to fight back, but for now, he would be compliant; the lure of gold was strong.

There was a faint plume of smoke coming from the hut and he tentatively tapped on the wood. "Come in Roman."

His first thoughts were, 'how did she know it was him' and the second was 'was she alone'?

"You smell like a girl Roman. I knew it was you when you were a hundred paces from my home."

He was so taken aback that he could barely speak; had she read his thoughts? She truly was a witch! "I have news. Five hundred of the auxiliary are heading south to the big river. They will be gone for twenty nights." He paused, expecting a reaction. "Are you not pleased?"

"I merely pass on the messages it is our master who will show pleasure," her mouth opened in an evil smile which did not bode well,

The Sword of Cartimandua

"or displeasure." She passed over a piece of gold. It was not a Roman coin but he had not expected it to be. It was gold and he quickly pocketed it. "Now go."

As he left he wondered how she would deliver the message. Hearing a flutter of wings over his head he realised that she would be using pigeons. He was beginning to understand that these barbarians were not quite as primitive as he had first thought and he would need to watch his step he would need to be wary and choose the best time to betray them and preserve his corpulent neck. These were not the poor he regularly swindled or abused; these were cunning and crafty.

Venutius was close to the Brigante fortress of Stanwyck when he received the message from his rider. The Romans were securing their base before tackling him they were heading south and east to pacify that area. Good that suited him for he had not had time to order his people to gather food for the winter. He had been so confident of defeating Cartimandua that he had thought he would have been able to take what he wanted from her. If the cavalry had been in the north they could have prevented his men from foraging. He turned to Brennus, his leading war chief. "Send out your men in small parties; I want every morsel of food, every weapon, every animal collected and taken to Brocavum. The Romans must find nothing that will help them. When the earth warms we will take the war to them. We will be rested with full bellies while they will be tired and hungry. I want every Roman killed and every sympathiser slaughtered."

"How will I know they are sympathetic to the queen?"

"Give them the chance to join us. If they do not, they die. Do not be gentle Brennus." As Brennus rode away to give his orders Venutius smiled to himself. The first part of his plan, the death of Cartimandua, had not gone well but he was well placed now to destroy these Romans. The messages from the south were good. The Romans were not having an easy time in Mona and the wild mountains. The invaders were like fleas, annoying but few enough in numbers so that they could be picked off before they became an infestation. This was the time to strike before they could bring more legions in the summer before they could reinforce their garrisons. Now was the time, his time!

The Sword of Cartimandua

The warband headed north-west through the darkening skies and threatening clouds. Wrapping his cloak even closer around him the king felt, not for the first time that Mother Earth was on their side. Fainch and her sisters could summon the power of Mother Earth to their aid. Winter would soon be upon them when the food would disappear and the cold of these islands would become a weapon against the enemies who came from a much warmer climate. Venutius smiled to himself; this land belonged to him and his people and the land itself would fight to rid them of this relentless enemy.

Less than a half a day's ride away the very Romans who Venutius was cursing were huddled in their cloaks as their mounts plodded through the sharp shower which had emerged with incredible ferocity from the thick black clouds massing on the skyline. Marcus nudged his mount closer to his leader. "Just like being at home eh?"

Ulpius smiled a grim smile. "Aye, we all thought that joining the Romans meant warm Mediterranean postings, wine, women and song. It seems we have traded one cold and damp corner of the outer world for another one."

Marcus turned in his saddle to look back down the line of troopers and to make sure none were lagging behind. Satisfied he scanned the horizon. "Do you think we will catch any?"

Ulpius rubbed his chin thoughtfully and nodded. "I would expect to. They will think that we are tucked behind our palisade licking our wounds. They think because we bathe we are soft; much as we thought when they came to Ad Mure. They do not like fighting at this time of year and they will think we are of the same mind. Remember they do not have an Empire to supply them. They have to gather in the food and make their clothes and weapons. They cannot do that whilst they are fighting. This is why we will win Marcus. We have a behemoth at our back. You travelled as I did across the Empire and across the seas to get here. Think of the cities and peoples we saw. Think of the fields filled with crops and animals. Britannia may have treasures under the ground but they cannot be eaten."

"That means they may all have retreated back to their homelands."

The Sword of Cartimandua

Ulpius shook his head. "There will not be many but they will be out here. There are outlaws and bandits who will take advantage of the chaos that we have made. There will be survivors who are mounted and there will be others, scavengers, looking for easy pickings. Remember Marcus there are ordinary people of this land who go about their lives and they will now be gathering in as much food as they can to survive the winter. They do not have the luxury of galleys from Rome bringing grain and wine as we do." He paused as his good eye picked out movement in the distance. His hand came up instinctively to halt the column and they, in turn, loosened their weapons and became more alert. Everyone relaxed slightly when they realised it was their two scouts who had been more than five miles ahead.

The two men reined in and saluted. "Just ahead decurion princeps, there are raiders. They are driving animals north to the river. They are twenty in number."

Ulpius nodded. Twenty was manageable and the animals would augment their rations. He turned to his troop. "We are going to capture some of the brigands who killed our comrades. If we can I would like at least one prisoner but take no chances. These are like snakes." He addressed Marcus. "Take twenty men and the scouts sweep round the north. If any escape us you will take them." Marcus marked off his men and they rode at a fast gallop. Ulpius signalled for his men to spread into line formation; dangerous against formed infantry but perfect against a handful of bandits.

They saw the smoke from the fire over the hill and Ulpius knew that they were close. He drew his sword and his men mirrored his actions. They came over the rise silently, like wraiths. The grey overcast sky helped to mask their outlines and the Carvetii were too busy killing the last of the villagers. They had been so confident that they had posted no sentries; it would cost them dear. The smoke helped to hide the Romans until they were within javelin range. The Romans charged silently to appear suddenly from the smoke. The raiders were despatching their last few victims and the first they knew was when swords sliced through the air taking heads and limbs in a frenzy of destruction. The action was over in a few heartbeats; the surprise had been so complete that the fallen had barely had time to realise their plight. They were too busy slaughtering unarmed

The Sword of Cartimandua

villagers and had made the cardinal sin of not leaving a sentry to watch. The action was so sudden and swift that unfortunately none had survived and the decurion princeps had no prisoners to question. While that disappointed Ulpius he was also pleased that his men had survived intact and in his heart, he knew that it was difficult to get information from these tribesmen. He was not even sure that these were part of a grander plan. He suspected that it was a few men trying to profit from the chaos of the war.

They had just finished stripping the bodies when Marcus arrived. "We saw the smoke. Looks like we are too late for the fun."

"Aye but we eat well tonight. We will camp here and move off in the morning. "

Marcus took in the bodies and the lack of wounds on the Romans. "If this continues we will end the war before it has begun."

"This is not the war. This is Venutius preparing for the war. I fear that the tribune's plan will not work. The fox has fled and we will just have a few scraps of men to pick at." While some men began slaughtering one of the animals others began making a small pile of Carvetii skulls. The Pannonian intentions were being made clear.

Leaving a handful of men to drive the remaining animals back to Eboracum, Ulpius took the rest of his men towards the meeting point. He hoped that the rest of the ala had been as successful as he with no casualties and many Carvetii heads. They rode warily until they recognised the other Roman riders who appeared on their left and right flanks. Within a day he had the whole of his ala. As they reported to him he realised that the majority of the Carvetii had to have fled west for they had only encountered pockets of resistance and they, as with his raiders, had been scavengers rather than warriors. He was about to order their return to the comfort of the fort when their Brigante scout reported signs of a large body of men heading west. Ulpius quickly made up his mind. "Fulvius Agrippa, take all but the first. Second and third turmae back to Eboracum I will see where this trail leads."

The moors seemed much emptier to Marcus as the rest of the ala took the path south. Gaius turned to him. "Would it not be better to take the whole of the ala with us?"

"I think the decurion is thinking of his whole command. Some of the mounts were looking a little weary as were the men. We have little opportunity to replace either. I am beginning to see that command is never as easy as it looks," he grinned and punched the younger man on the arm, "when you are a tadpole."

Gaius laughed, "Aye but one day I will be a frog and then you will hear me bellow."

It was later that day when they arrived at the first great river they had seen since Eboracum. It was a dangerous place for beyond the river there were no Romans. Ulpius went forward with the Brigante scout and they dismounted in a small wood just on a bluff above the river. Bellying up they could see the river below with a bridge. It appeared to be unguarded. The bridge itself was a crude wooden affair and Ulpius doubted that it would take much punishment. If the legions ever came they would need to build a new one. He sent the scout down to make sure there were no enemies in hiding and he watched as the man scurried down the bank peering from the tree line as he checked for signs. It was with some relief that Ulpius saw him sprint across the bridge for that meant there were no Carvetii. After a few minutes on the other side, he made the all-clear signal and Ulpius stood to summon the rest of his men.

Once they were safely across the bridge Ulpius summoned his decurions. "Marcus I want you to guard this crossing with your turma. The rest of us will continue to follow. I need to be sure that when we return we can cross. Protect this crossing."

Although Marcus was disappointed he knew that he had a greater responsibility as he was to make sure all of them would return. "I shall do so decurion princeps."

Ulpius smiled, "I know you will. We should return within two days. My scout tells me that Brocavum is but two days march hence. I suspect that is where they will be going."

The scout was right and, on the evening of the following day Ulpius could see, some distance away, the stronghold of Brocavum. Leaving the turma under the command of Lucius Demetrius he took Gaius and the scout with him to see close up what the problems of assaulting Brocavum might be. It was almost nightfall when they arrived. They had the advantage that they rode from the east and the stronghold was silhouetted against the setting sun. They tethered their mounts in a copse and ran from bush to bush until they were within arrow shot of the walls. They were so close they could smell the cooking, feel the heat from the fires and hear the noise of feasting. There were guards on the palisades but they appeared unconcerned with events outside the fortress. The gate of the fortress was barred and there was a ditch around it. They were safe. The three of them slid like snakes to the edge of the mound which surrounded it. As they peered over Ulpius could see that there was not only water in the ditch but also sharpened spikes. It would be a death trap. They made their way back to their horses.

Later, as they walked back to the safety of a small clearing where they would camp Gaius finally asked the questions which had been racing around his head. "Is that kind of place easy to attack?"

Ulpius looked down at his eager young face. "Attacking any kind of fort is never easy but our legionary brothers are adept at it. That one, my young friend is particularly difficult for the ground nearby is rocky and uneven that makes it hard to get the siege engines into place. The legionaries work better if they have a flatter area in which to manoeuvre."

"That ditch looked nasty."

"Nasty? I can think of stronger words to describe it. There may be traps hidden below the water, the banks are so steep and deadly that you could lose a cohort just crossing the ditch. I think that if we are to defeat Venutius we will either have to starve him out or defeat him in open battle."

The Sword of Cartimandua
Chapter 8

Eboracum

Cresens was incandescent with rage when the turma returned to camp. He had hoped that Venutius would have finished him off but he returned without a wound and, it appeared, without having lost a man. What was even worse he was bringing in supplies and arms taken from those Carvetii who had perished during the patrol. He hastened off to see the witch; he would have to put his more direct murderous plan into action.

Eboracum was now a little more civilised. The marching camp had been fortified into something more permanent and dwellings were erupting all around the periphery. The Queen, of course, had a house which whilst not a palace was more fitting. The foundations and lower part were made of stone found in a quarry not far away. The upper part was wattle and daub. Inside there was a fire and separate rooms for the queen and her handmaidens. The door was guarded by two legionaries. The tribune was anxious that the only ally they had should not be murdered. Although her food was prepared in the legionaries' kitchen it was prepared by the tribune's cook, a man with epicurean tastes much as his master.

Despite all this Cartimandua was not happy. She was surrounded by Romans. Her people were kept outside the fortress and her conversations were limited to her handmaidens. She had always enjoyed power and this vacuum did not suit her. She was not making the decisions; she relied on others to do that. If the Romans chose to discard her she would be nothing, at the mercy of her own people and the evil Venutius. She was under no illusions, she would not last long. In her heart, she knew that the real reason for the disquiet, the sadness, the ache was there was no man to share her bed. Ulpius had been on patrol for a moon and she longed for his touch. She had important news to impart and she needed him. Lenta and Macha had learned to walk quietly around her for any minor inconvenience that could result in a tirade. Just as the queen they were overjoyed when they heard the signal of the returning patrol.

The Sword of Cartimandua

Cartimandua began to prepare herself for her warrior. She ordered Lenta to bring to her the most expensive and alluring perfume she possessed. Macha began to apply the eye paint she had seen on the Egyptian slave girls. When she was as ready as she could be she waited. When would he come? As a queen she could not go to him she had to wait, her loins aching for the moment her man would appear. She chewed her lip nervously. She wondered how he would take the news. When she had discovered it she felt a riot of emotions shock, happiness, incredulity, fear. She had thought when she missed her bleeding that her time was changing and she could no longer bear children. When she began to vomit in the mornings and when she felt the strange sensation in her belly she knew that she was to have a child. She also knew that this one she would keep for in Ulpius Felix she had a man who could be a father. She had a man she would love to grow old with. She just didn't know how he would take to becoming a father. Neither of them had discussed it; it had not even been a fleeting thought for they both had assumed she was too old and they had enjoyed the act far too much to think of the consequences.

The other problem would be with her people. How would they take to her cohabitation with a Roman, an enemy? Although she cared little for their thoughts their opinion might make them shift to support Venutius and then all her work would have been for nothing. She had six months before the child would be born. It would be simplest if she kept out of the public view. That would also give her more time to plan a strategy to include Ulpius in her life. She smiled to herself; at least motherhood was not softening her political and strategic mind.

Ulpius was too busy with his report. He knew Marcus and Drusus would ensure the animals and the men were looked after but the reality was he would have to account to the tribune for the delay in returning. Flavinius and Augustinius kept him cooling his heels for what seemed an age. Ulpius ached from the hard riding and the hard fighting. All he wanted was a bath, food and some wine. Eventually, he was summoned. It was the tribune who addressed him. "You seem to have taken rather longer than we planned for this foray." He paused and glared aggressively at Ulpius. "And I see neither prisoners nor slaves."

The Sword of Cartimandua

"I would have brought both had the enemy not been so careless with their lives. They fought like demons. Those that were not killed in the fighting died of their wounds."

"Well, get on with your report."

"As ordered we swept towards the hills to the west and Carvetii stronghold. We found groups of warriors collecting animals and food, laying the land bare. There were many groups. We followed them as far as the great river in the north. The other turmae had joined in the sweep and there were many hundreds. Most died in the battle, some were swept away down the river and a few escaped north."

"And why did you not follow them?"

The horses were tired and the river fast flowing. Most of the enemy who tried it died. I did not think the tribune would want me to waste his cavalry in such a reckless adventure."

The tribune's voice took on an even more threatening tone. "Have a care decurion princeps. Do not be impertinent with me! Do not presume to read my thoughts! Do you think I care how many of you savages die!

The prefect coughed, "Where are the nearest Carvetii warriors?"

"We followed them to the highest passes and they went west. I tracked a large band of warriors who went back to their stronghold at Brocavum. It is many days travel on a horse. I believe he has gone there to winter and prepare for a war in the next year."

There was silence as the tribune peered at the rudimentary map. "You believe! And who are you? The mighty Germanicus?"

The prefect spoke again. "Did you see many of the Queen's people, the Brigante?"

"We saw signs but only of women and the old. We saw no warriors. The ones we spoke to said they feared Venutius would return and punish them for their queen."

The prefect and the tribune pondered this. Ulpius continued, "I have seen his stronghold it is better built than Stanwyck. "

The prefect sighed," You are right taking a hill fort is not the work for cavalry."

The tribune snorted. "It seems that there is little work which is suitable for these auxiliaries. "He managed to imbue the word 'auxiliary' with an invective normally reserved for a curse. "But

The Sword of Cartimandua

maybe you are right that is work for a legion. Perhaps when the new military governor arrives."

"He is due then?"

"I believe he is travelling even as we speak."

Ulpius stood, feeling foolish as the two men spoke as though he was not even there. I want your cavalry out all winter on patrols. I do not want to be surprised by a winter attack."

"But tribune the horses will suffer. There is little enough feed for them as it is. Would it not be better to rest them for the campaigns next year?"

"Prefect I have made my decision. Carry out your orders!" With that, the tribune left.

The two cavalrymen looked at each other. "He is a fool"

"Yes, Ulpius but he is the commander and he makes the decisions. Perhaps when the military governor comes we may be better off but I do not know the man." He looked closely at the decurion princeps. "How hard do they fight?"

"They are wild. They appear to have no regard for their own safety. They hurl themselves at man and horse. One wound will not slow them down. My men learned early that you go for the killing blow for they will not stop until either you or they are dead. If Venutius has an army of them it may be harder than we think."

"Wine?"

"Aye, I need that." He took a long draught. "There is something else. My Brigante scouts speak of people from the north, allies of Venutius who are even more ferocious. They fight naked and paint their bodies blue." The prefect laughed. "I do not jest and I believe my scouts."

"I do not laugh at you for I have heard the same. The queen told me of these people. Until her marriage to Venutius, the Brigante people were plagued by raids. No, I smile at the thought of a man fighting naked. Why is it that the fools think that a bit of blue paint will stop an arrow? I prefer mail and good discipline."

"That is one good thing. They wear little armour but their weapons are good. At least they have few archers otherwise we would suffer."

The Sword of Cartimandua

"Is there any other news I can pass on to Governor Bolanus when he arrives?"

"There are no roads. There is little food and no shelter. It will be a hard campaign. There is little grass for the horses. The hill forts are only made of wood and earth but they will need legions to take them."

"Rest. I will send the other troopers out on patrol. Ready your men and watch yourself. I fear the tribune does not like you."

"I have shat bigger turds than him."

"Maybe but those turds couldn't have you crucified; he can, without even blinking. I have met his type before. He was born into power and he thinks that we are little more than slaves. Remember how Romans treat slaves. Think on that."

The sun was setting when Ulpius finally got around to thinking about the queen. He had been away some time. Perhaps she had someone else to pleasure her. Perhaps he had dreamed the whole experience. Perhaps he had imagined it to have greater import than she. He did not know what to do. He decided to walk past her dwelling it was on the way to the kitchen area.

As he strode through the camp acknowledging the shouts, waves and salutations from comrades he did not notice the fat quartermaster studying him through half-lidded eyes. The ex-soldier was on his way to see the spy with the information he had gleaned from the tribune's clerk a man whose indiscretions were known by Cresens and who was the fount of most of his information. He would get money for his information and then he would get the poison that would rid him of Ulpius and regain him his power.

Ulpius for all his confidence with his men was less confident with women- the camp followers and whores were not a problem but the queen was a different proposition. The two guards saluted as he went by the door to her domus. He was about to head for the canteen when he felt a tug on his sleeve. He turned quickly and saw that it was Macha. She spoke quietly and softly so that the grizzled warrior had to bend down to listen.

"My lady would speak with you. Follow me."

Ulpius was perplexed as he turned towards the doorway. What was the queen thinking? The guards would surely see him enter and then the whole camp would know. Just as he arrived at the door Lenta

The Sword of Cartimandua
came to see them. "The Queen would have words with your leader about the state of her kingdom. She is not pleased that you did not report to her immediately upon your return!" The girl played her part remarkably well and her scolding tone made the hint of a smile appear on the faces of the two guards who took great pleasure in the apparent discomfort of a decurion princeps.

"I am sorry, lady, but I had to speak with the tribune. My time is now hers for as long as she needs me."

With that, he entered. Cartimandua did not speak a word she just threw her arms around him and kissed him oblivious to the startled looks from Lenta and Macha who quickly scurried into their own room. After an embrace that seemed to last forever, she murmured into his ear, "You are so cruel; you knew I was waiting for you."

"I was trying to be, what is the word? Discreet."

Cartimandua threw her head back and gave such a hearty and loud laugh that the guards turned in surprise at the noise emanating from the domus. "I was never known for my discretion my love but come," she led him by the hand to her bed and lay him on it. All the time she was speaking to him she was undressing and kissing him. "I have news, Great news. Well, it is to me. We are to have a child."

Ulpius looked up in shock. "A child but how?"

"The how is easy. When we lay together a child was created but in truth, I thought my childbearing days behind me. The gods had other plans."

"When will it..."

"In five moons or perhaps six."

They kissed and he began undressing her. He was already engorged and the queen hungrily took his whole length in her mouth. Using his great strength he rolled her on her back and was about to enter her when he stopped.

"The child?"

The queen thrust herself onto him. "The child will be fine it is the mother who needs this."

Their lovemaking went on well into the early hours of the morning. The guards were changed. Lenta and Macha went to collect some food and still, they coupled, seemingly insatiable. When Ulpius could no longer raise himself they lay in each other's arms.

The Sword of Cartimandua

"What will your people think?"

"My people do not think much at all and they certainly don't think of me. If they did think they would believe that it was Venutius' or Vellocatus'."

"And are you happy about that?" His one eye searched her face for deception or lies but could see only truth and love.

"I am happy that we will have a child and more I believe it will be a son and one day he will rule this whole land. He will be the union of Brigante and Rome."

Ulpius smiled at her. "I am Roman as a soldier but I am Pannonian by birth. I think our son will be the better for that for he will have my warrior skill and your mind and," he bent down to kiss her eyelids, "your beauty." The rest of the night saw them continue their lovemaking until they fell asleep, exhausted in each other's arms.

Lenta and Macha had been asleep long before the two lovers but they had heard all the lovemaking.

"When will you take a man sister?"

Macha looked at her younger sister. "When the right man comes along. It does not always happen quickly, look at our sister. She has seen almost forty summers and now she has found the right man."

"The right man? How can you be sure?"

"Look at her eyes, listen to the words when she talks of him, look how they are together and look at the man. He may be scarred but it is on the outside. Venutius was scarred on the inside. Ulpius Felix is a good man. He is like the noblest of we Brigante. He will protect her."

"You have not answered me. When will you take a man? Has not the right one come along?" There was a mischievous lilt to her voice and she suppressed a grin when Macha coloured bright red.

"You are foolish. I do not know what you mean."

Realising that she had made her point she turned over to sleep leaving her sister aching for Marcus between her legs making her feel like a woman.

The Sword of Cartimandua
Chapter 9

When Venutius heard the reports from Brennus he seethed with anger. The warriors he had lost were a grave blow but the lack of supplies from the lands to the east of the hills was an even more disastrous loss. He had hoped to weaken his enemies but they had weakened him. None of his roving bands had returned with any provender and those who had arrived had all suffered wounds at the hands of the Roman cavalry. Venutius wondered if his subordinate had sent the right men. He knew that some of his warriors were little more than robbers; they served a purpose but he would have preferred to use warriors who had the aim of driving the Romans into the sea rather than raping women and butchering cattle. The Romans had surprised him; he had thought them soft and unwilling to campaign in the harsh land of Brigantia. He had learned a valuable lesson. The reports from his spy were even more alarming for the spirits of the Romans were high and the fortress was already a formidable structure. The jetties and docks at the river mean that supplies were coming into the heart of the fortress making his enemies stronger and stronger. Soon they might be too strong for him. He resolved to contact the Novontae, Selgovae and Votadini. With those tribes supporting him even the mighty Roman army might be beaten.

Leaving his chiefs, he went into his hut where he kept those sacred objects given to him by Fainch. Perhaps he had not made enough sacrifices, enough promises to the Earth Mother. Before he met with his allies he would make another sacrifice. He had seen a small child prisoner brought from Stanwyck, it was rumoured she was related to the Queen. She would make a worthy sacrifice and the Earth Mother would drink her blood and look kindly on his endeavours.

The Roman army was represented by someone who at this moment was not happy with life in Britannia. Marcus Bolanus hated everything about this forsaken corner of the Empire. If it were not for the gold rumoured to be hidden under the wild mountains to the west there would be no reason to be here. He peered out of his carriage at the windswept uplands without a tree in sight. He cursed to himself.

The Sword of Cartimandua

They would have arrived far sooner had it not been for the floods which forced him and his forces up into the higher, colder more desolate land. The early winter rains had turned the wide plains into an enormous lake. As his carriage crashed and jolted he wondered if this land would ever have real roads and civilisation. He had plotted and schemed his way through various minor posts, he had destroyed many lives and literally taken some. He came from a noble patrician family who had fallen on hard times when they chose the wrong leader. He was determined never to have hard times himself. He was now as rich as any man in Rome but he dreamed of more money. He had secured this post so that he could acquire some of the fabled gold and copper this land held but first he had to destroy these barbarians and destroy them he would. He was already plotting his next move, out towards Parthia with its fabulous lapis lazuli and the lucrative spices. Then he would be the richest man in the world.

Once again, he studied the reports he held in his hand. At least Cartimandua was safe. The revolt by Venutius and the uprising had been the reason his predecessor, Marcus Trebellius Maximus had returned to Rome in disgrace. He had been too mild-mannered and had not been ruthless enough. Marcus Vettius Bolanus would put down this rebellion and return to the luxury that was Rome by the next summer. At least he had a secure base now that he had built the legionary fortress at Lindum and he could call on a legion at a moment's notice. He began to work out how he could claim the credit for the rescue of Cartimandua. Perhaps he would see a way when he reached the end of the world that was Eboracum. He shivered back into his robes and tried to sleep his way there.

His clerk coughed discreetly waking the military governor from his disturbed rest. "We are here master."

Bolanus peered out and although he had not anticipated much he was depressed by the sight which greeted him. The Roman camp was as the others spread throughout the Empire; perhaps a little sturdier than most temporary camps with towers and solid looking gates. That reassured him. He would not be over-run by the savages of these parts. It was the rest that make him think about returning as soon as possible to Lindum. There was a straggle of huts close to the river with, what looked to him, like half-naked savages. There appeared to

The Sword of Cartimandua

be no stone to be seen and little evidence of either gold or jewels. He hoped he had not been misinformed about the riches of this land if so someone would pay dearly for their error. He glared at his clerk who shivered in fear.

"Well do you expect me to walk into the camp? Move!"

The guards at the gate recognised the retinue of the Military Governor and the word was quickly sent to the tribune and prefect. As he rushed towards the tribune Saenius Augustinius was more than a little nervous. He had had the support and the ear of his predecessor; would he enjoy the same privileges and perks? He licked his lips nervously. Had his letter to Vespasian arrived? He dreaded the possibility that it had been intercepted by one of the Governor's spies for he had been less than complimentary about his superior.

Marcus Bolanus looked at the two men with distaste when he climbed down from his carriage. One was a barbarian, an auxiliary whilst the other was a small man nervously licking his lips, obviously the tribune. Although a Roman he looked more like a shopkeeper than a Roman officer. He did not deign to introduce himself; he assumed they would know who he was. "Well? Your report."

Mentally the tribune sighed. From the governor's comments, he did not know of the letter to Vespasian. He was still safe. "Saenius Augustinius at your command. Perhaps we could go to my, er your quarters and be more comfortable."

The governor peered round. "A ditch would be more comfortable than this. Lead on."

"And so I affected the rescue of the Queen's half-sisters and the treasure."

"I am pleased to hear that the tribune risks his life in the barbaric north for the Emperor." Marcus looked keenly at the tribune whose account of the rescues sounded as though he was another Horatio at the bridge, a true Roman hero. His spies had told him a different story.

"You misunderstand. I didn't actually go myself, I sent cavalry. Just as I did when the Queen herself was rescued."

Bolanus waved his hand dismissively, the information was not news it confirmed that his spies told him the truth. "The box? What was in it? Was it an artefact, a religious object? Come on man out with it!"

The Sword of Cartimandua

The tribune looked suitably embarrassed; despite numerous requests, the Queen had consistently refused to discuss it. "I don't know, the Queen has it and she, well, she won't discuss it."

Rather than the anger, the tribune expected the governor showed quizzical interest. He was secretly pleased for he suspected it was a treasure and he wanted no one else to know of it. He felt sure he would be able to persuade the barbarian to hand it over. After all, the other wild queen, Boudicca had been a savage who was slaughtered like an animal; her only tactic had been a full-frontal attack and her people had all died as a result. No, this queen would be as wax in his hand, he would mould her to his own ends.

"Have your cooks prepare some decent food and invite the queen to dinner. I will apprise her of the Emperor's plans.

The feast was richer than the tribune had enjoyed for some time but to Marcus Bolanus it was like eating hard rations. The cooks had received a delivery of spices and rich ingredients with the Governor's caravan. They had been proud of the repast they had presented. The Governor and tribune looked at the dishes with differing views as they awaited the arrival of the queen. She was late but Bolanus put that down to the woman in her. He nibbled on some olives which had been in the jar too long as he waited for her. The wine was drinkable but only because he had brought it with him. His hand stopped halfway to his mouth when she entered. Even the tribune was surprised. All hint of grey was gone from her and her face had a pink healthy glow. The dress she wore was a vibrant red colour which matched her lips painted with cochineal. The Governor could not believe that this was the same queen who had met with Claudius. He had expected a toothless hag instead he found it hard to estimate her age. Her arms were laden with golden bracelets and on her fingers, she wore rings with precious stones. But it was the torc around her neck which excited them both. It was the largest single piece of gold either man had ever seen and it gleamed in the light like the sun. The gold made his mind race with the thought of owning that gold and the treasure, perhaps it was even more fabulous than that with which she adorned herself.

The Sword of Cartimandua

"Governor, welcome to my land; my people and I welcome the representative of our ally Emperor... Just who is the Emperor these days? Is it still Vitellus?"

Inwardly Bolanus fumed. The cunning bitch had taken the initiative away from him. She welcomed him to her land as though they were allies rather than the clients they were. He was also angry about the Emperor jibe as the whole Roman world knew they were on their fourth emperor in one year.

"It is the divine Vespasian who is now the ruler of this Roman Empire." Feeling that he had scored points now by calling the Brigante land the Roman Empire he magnanimously waved his arm for the queen and her sisters to sit. "Please ladies sit."

The Queen had dealt with people like Bolanus all her life. She knew the men who used power as a weapon and who resented women. He was crushable but first, she had to ascertain her position. She was politically astute enough to realise that she had no power base any longer; her people would only support her if she returned at the head of an army and that army had to be the Roman army. She would be pleasant to this weasel until she had what she wanted. "I am pleased that Rome is in such safe hands. Does the Emperor plan on visiting us at any time soon? If so I will need time to plan a celebration and, of course, make sure that the rebels who have driven me here are destroyed."

"I fear that his divinity is busy in the Eastern lands but be assured your highness that he will visit just as soon as possible. Now please, eat, drink and enjoy the food, poor though it is."

They nibbled at the food and the Queen's sisters watched, carefully, the reactions of Bolanus to the Queen's questions; they would have to report to Cartimandua later.

"It is a shame, governor, that it is so poor. Perhaps if there were a port here at Eboracum we could acquire the food that would please the Emperor."

The governor stopped eating and wiped a hand across his greasy mouth. The woman had a good idea for a port here that would secure the Roman presence and enable a rapid supply chain. "I am sure we could come to some arrangement."

The Sword of Cartimandua

"Of course, we would need to have a fortress here to ensure that the rebels do not ravage this place," she paused meaningfully, "again."

"Again, I am sure we could come to some arrangement." He looked carefully at this woman who was showing all the guile of an Eastern potentate.

"That, of course, means that there would have to be a legion here. Are they not all accounted for?"

Marcus Bolanus stopped mid-chew. For someone so far away from civilisation she was remarkably well informed. He thought quickly. The only legion he had available was the Ninth Hispana that was busy building Lindum fortress; the others were busy in the west putting down the last of their rebellions. If he was to use another legion it would need to come from Rome. Perhaps he could turn the Queen's request to his advantage and gain another legion; with another legion, he could conquer all of this forsaken land and then his return to Rome would be truly a triumph. "That is true but we can begin the building with the troops already here." He looked shrewdly at her. "Have you any more requests?"

Cartimandua paused, delicately wiped her mouth and then looked directly at the governor. "Well once you have made Eboracum secure with adequate accommodation for a queen I am sure you will give thought to defeating the rebels and returned my lands to me."

"Your lands your majesty? Are they not part of the Roman Empire?"

There was a silence and Bolanus wondered if he had gone too far. Suddenly the Queen stood and in one movement pulled her sword from its scabbard. The blade was pointed at the centre of the table but her eyes bored into the Roman's." I am Queen Cartimandua of the Brigante and this is Sax Lacus the sword of my ancestors. As long as a member of my family wields this mighty weapon then we rule the land of the Brigante and all the people know this." She slowly returned the blade to its jewelled scabbard. "If the Emperor wishes to help us to conquer my rebellious enemies then the sword of the Brigante will serve the Roman Empire as a, I believe they are called, client kingdom. Certainly, that was the arrangement I came to with Emperor Claudius."

The Sword of Cartimandua

The governor was white for the sword had been so close to his face that he was under no illusions that, had she wished, she could have taken his head. Next time he would have guards in the room, and the bitch searched. The comment about Claudius caused him some worry. He had been sent to Britannia without speaking to the new Emperor, perhaps there were arrangements in place he knew naught about. Even now the Emperor was in Judea making sure that the new d place there would do as he was bid. Perhaps this was true in Britannia; He chewed to help him regain his composure although, in truth, he could taste nothing. He wondered how she knew about client kings. If she truly knew about them she would know that, as in Judea and Egypt, they soon became Roman. "Of course, your majesty that is what I meant."

"Excellent and now I fear we have imposed too much upon you and you have had a long journey. We thank you and bid you goodnight."

The three walked silently to their quarters and when Macha looked as though she were going to speak the queen held her hand to silence her. Once in the room, Lenta closed and barred the door and they retreated into Cartimandua's chamber.

"Well?" said the Queen.

"He went along with you," began Macha.

"But he went along for his own reasons," added Lenta. "I would not trust him. He will betray you."

"Once he has defeated Venutius he will try to rid himself of you."

"I know." The Queen looked hard at the two young women. "And it is you he would replace me with."

"But we would not do that."

Cartimandua's face softened. "I know for you have had the chance before but you have to know that he would try and you must be careful and I must ensure that you have some protection. Perhaps marriage to a noble or powerful Roman."

Macha looked aghast. "I will choose my own man!"

"Of course, but I will choose your husband."

"I have had one husband whom I loved I do not want another."

"You will have another if I say so. Remember I have always looked after you and I will continue to do so. Have as many lovers as

The Sword of Cartimandua

you like." She smiled to herself thinking of Ulpius. "But, as I did with Venutius, you sometimes have to marry for power."

Lenta murmured half under her breath, "And looked what happened there."

There was a sharp intake of breath from Macha who wondered if her sister had gone too far. "True sister it was a mistake. Instead of keeping the wolf from the door, I brought him into the fold. Let us see if we can find a hound who can be trained and controlled instead of a wolf eh"

Although Bolanus resented the Queen and her attitude he realised that it made sense for him to improve the defences of Eboracum. He set the legionaries to work building stone towers at the corners of the wooden camp. He used slave labour to begin the construction of the port which was adjacent to the camp. Meanwhile, he sent a messenger to Lindum to request another legion. In his report to Vespasian, he exaggerated the treasures Britannia had to offer. He enthused about the potential treasures to the north, treasures which would become Imperial with another legion. He also made quite clear that Queen Cartimandua would accede to all his demands. The governor had no doubt that the Emperor would look favourably on his demands. Finally, he sent for two more cohorts of the Ninth Hispana just to ensure his own safety.

The winter hardened from the gentler time of early winter; there appeared, to the Romans, to be little difference between the two. The main difference was the lack of leaves on the trees a phenomenon unknown to many of the legionaries. The weather could change from a glorious sunny day to one where the skies turned black and then emptied themselves upon the land and all in an hour. The mighty river running through Eboracum could rise higher than a house overnight and just as quickly disappear. The more superstitious Romans attributed this to the evil and witchcraft which abounded, they believed. Any land that would follow a woman, and a wild woman such as Cartimandua, was a land which would be as capricious as a woman.

Ulpius had little time to enjoy with the mother of his unborn child as the tribune kept the decurion princeps and his troopers on patrol as much as possible. The times they had together were precious. As she

The Sword of Cartimandua

was trying to hide her pregnancy she kept indoors as much as possible which made life much easier for Ulpius. There were now more Brigante warriors drifting into Eboracum. Once Cartimandua had vetted them for loyalty she executed those not to be trusted and enrolled the rest into a bodyguard. She was still as ruthless as ever and seemed to have the ability to almost sniff out those who were not loyal subjects who wished to serve her. So it was that Ulpius found it easier to access the queen getting past guards whose loyalty was to the queen and not Rome.

When not on patrol they lay in each other's arms, talking like young lovers long into the night. The queen was fascinated by his scars and questioned him at length about the origin of each one. The Roman, for his part, was curious about the life of a warrior queen. His own tribe had held women in esteem but had not made one their leader. Cartimandua explained about the sword and its symbolism. When Ulpius held the sword, he could understand the power of the weapon. His own people viewed all swords as magical but the sword of the lake appeared to him to be the ultimate magic weapon.

"Promise me that, when I die," she held her hand over his protesting mouth, "when I die for I am old to be a mother and childbirth is hard even for younger women; you will make sure that my son has this sword. Guard it with your life for as long as this sword is wielded by one of my family then Brigantia will live. Swear!"

"I so swear but you will outlive me. One of these patrols will see me gutted. I cannot avoid every arrow and sword for I have outlived all of my people who joined the Romans. The gods alone know why I live."

"Live you must for if you died, all meaning would go from my life. We will soon have a child and he will need us both."

They embraced and silent tears coursed down the queen's face. The unborn child was changing her and making her less of a warrior. Shaking herself she looked at Ulpius. "Swear too that you will protect my sisters and family for there will be many who would cause them harm or use them as Venutius tried to use me."

"I swear but I have little power. The tribune wishes me gone."

The Sword of Cartimandua

"We will deal with the tribune. Perhaps if he were sent away from Eboracum for a while…"

"I cannot see the weasel wishing to leave the safety of these walls."

"Nor can I but something may arise." The Queen's razor-sharp mind was already plotting; unlike the military mind of Ulpius, she had a political mind which had enabled her to survive for so many years with so many enemies. The governor might think he understood politics but he had not come up against a formidable opponent such as Cartimandua.

Gaius Cresens surreptitiously peered over his shoulder as made his way towards the woods and the dwelling of Fainch the witch. He had long ago ceased from sexual advances and had begun to fear the dark-eyed vixen who appeared to know far too much for someone who appeared never to leave her hut. He had yet to acquire the poison he had requested and he suspected that she was holding it back for some reason. He had good information this time and he hoped she would give him what he desired.

"I have some news."

"If you are here to tell me that soldiers are coming from the south then you can leave for I know it already."

Cresens inwardly cursed. He had hoped that the information was a secret. "No, it is greater news than that."

"So, you are not going to tell me that the governor intends to attack Venutius before the festival of Eostre?"

Gods! The woman had other spies. "No, it is news which cost me dear to acquire." He paused significantly.

"On with it Roman. Don't stand there licking your greasy chops."

"I know you know that there are legionaries coming from Lindum but you do not know that Bolanus has sent for another legion from Rome." Her silence told him that this was news indeed. "Is not that information worth gold and, perhaps, the little favour I asked?"

"Here is some gold but the rest and the, er favour, will have to wait until I have the information confirmed."

So she did have other informants. Cresens determined to keep his ears open. "Thank you for this. I will return next week."

The Sword of Cartimandua

"As a small favour, I would not send for any supplies for the next week. They may not arrive."

The quartermaster looked in surprise. There would be an attack on the supply routes. The soldier in him wondered why and the thief in him was already plotting how to profit from that news.

Saenius Augustinius gnawed nervously on a fingernail. The new governor was not making his life easier. The fool appeared to go along with the Brigante bitch in all she said and did. Even now her quarters were being improved and her guards increasing by the day. He was rarely consulted on anything remotely important. He could see his military career-ending ignominiously and he would have to slink back to Rome a failure. This was, as his father had told him, his best chance for glory; the primitive warriors of Britannia were no match for the Roman legions and he had pictured himself returning with the laurel leaves of a victor. What was even worse was the lack of respect he had from the barbarian cavalry. The prefect Flavinius Bellatoris paid lip service to him and the only respect he had was to his office and not to him. He seethed and blamed that one-eyed barbarian Ulpius; he had chosen to disregard him and he had the backing of the Queen. He had thought that by promoting him he would ensure his loyalty and he would do as he wanted. The decurion princeps had not done so. The Queen also seemed to regard him as something unpleasant into which she had stepped. Would that they were both dead! He had tried to engineer Ulpius' demise by constant patrols but he seemed to thrive on the action. His only pleasure came from the fact that he was keeping him from the whore's bed and that gave him pleasure.

He finished writing his weekly report and stood to peer into the camp. It was a desolate place now that the leaves had left the trees and the cold was biting into his bones. He pondered wrapping his bearskin around his shoulders but he knew it would be colder later on. Across the camp he noticed the quartermaster watching him. The tribune knew of some of the illicit deals the man-made but he chose to ignore them as he benefited sometimes. Perhaps he could use this obvious criminal to his own ends. He signalled him over.

The Sword of Cartimandua

Cresens wondered why the tribune needed him. He had been of service to the patrician on a number of occasions, normally involving women and twice with boys. Perhaps the tribune needed servicing.

"Come in quartermaster. Sit." He leaned forward, put his hands together and peered at the ex-soldier over the tips of his fingers. His eyes were sharp and watched for any reaction from the corpulent Cresens. "How is your new position working out then, "he paused trying to remember the fat old cavalryman's name, " Gaius? How are you enjoying being a quartermaster?"

"It is an honour sir although if truth be told I would still prefer to command the ala."

Saenius smiled at the thought of this fat man sitting astride a horse but he hid the smile behind his hands. "Ah yes, it is a shame that we no longer have a Roman as decurion princeps but still Ulpius Felix is a brave warrior is he not?"

"He has brave men with him but I find it interesting that others die and others are wounded and yet the man who leads them always comes back without a scratch."

The tribune now knew what he had suspected, there was no love lost between the two men and he could use that to his advantage. "Perhaps you may have something there."

Emboldened by this apparent support Cresens continued. "There are rumours about the decurion princeps and the Queen."

"Are there? Well, I think there are rumours about many things in this camp but, "he paused significantly and lowered his hands, "if you should hear anything of a more solid nature I am sure you would tell me first would you not?"

Gaius' face lit up, he had an ally, "Of course, of course. I will keep you informed of anything which would be of interest to yourself and Rome." He paused. "Has the tribune noticed that the Queen is becoming larger?"

"Well good food."

"One of her servants hinted that she is, well she is with child!"

"Don't be absurd. She is too old." Even as he said it the tribune wondered if that were true. It would explain much. It would also give him more power as knowledge was power.

The Sword of Cartimandua

"Good. Well thank you for your time and he added significantly for the information. You will not lose by my friendship." With a wave, the quartermaster was dismissed but he left not feeling rejected but accepted. His star was on the rise and he was already calculating how to profit from this new liaison.

So the longer nights and shorter days drifted into a similar pattern. The queen grew larger, the patrols increasingly fraught as fodder and food diminished and the buildings grew apace. It was in the depths of winter when the nights were the longest and the weather the coldest that the change came. Even the tribune had to accept that the patrols were no longer relevant and besides the first ships had arrived at Eboracum with fresh supplies of wine, olives and delicacies such as the Romans had not seen for months. The governor called a three-day holiday with just the guards on the camp walls and the slaves working.

Cresens took the opportunity to visit with Fainch. Although she would have known about the lull in activity he thought he might be able to get something for his information. According to his slaves, this was the local festival of Yule; perhaps she would be more forthcoming with her favours. He had only been in her hut for moments when that hope was dashed. "Have you brought information fat one or are you here to lose your manhood?"

"I bring news that there is a holiday for three days and no patrols."

"Is that all? I too knew that." In truth, she did not know how many days nor did she know that the patrols had ceased but she did not want to give away too much.

"And there is a boat arrived from Ostia. It brings many luxuries from home."

Surprisingly that information seemed to interest the witch. "There will be feasting?

"There will be much for the Romans will celebrate Saturnalia."

"Do you still wish for the poison to rid yourself of Ulpius?"

His face lit up with malice and mischief. "Yes, give me, give!"

She tantalisingly held out a phial. You may have it provided," she dropped her voice; "the Queen and the Governor also die!"

The Sword of Cartimandua

The quartermaster's face went ashen. To kill the decurion princeps was one thing but to risk the governor was quite another. "You are mad! I would be discovered!"

"Think you cowardly lump! Have they not brought rich delicacies from Rome? Have they not brought spices and sweetmeats which will mask flavours? It will be easy. The queen and the governor will have the choicest of foods all you need is someone to put the potion in their food. "The one-eyed barbarian you hate, he could also die, "she shrugged, "I am sure it could be hidden in his wine."

He chewed his lip nervously. The witch was right, this was the perfect opportunity. If he timed it right he could be safe from blame; as quartermaster, he had access to all the foods as they arrived. He knew which ones would be chosen by the governor. His only problem was ensuring that his ally, the tribune did not eat the same food. "Give. I will do as you bid." He would not use the wine for he was not sure that they would all drink it. He needed to find another means.

"When they are dead there will be more gold for you."

This was proving to be an excellent meeting. Ulpius would be gone and he would be richer, perhaps rich enough to return to Rome.

Chapter 10

The Queen's quarters Eboracum

Lenta smiled when Macha volunteered to pass a message from the Queen to Ulpius; it was not the first time that she had done so. Lenta was pleased for her sister, she knew that she and the soldier Marcus had an understanding and as a woman who had known a man Lenta wanted her sister to enjoy the same joy. Macha, for her part, felt Lenta's eyes on her back but she felt no shame but secret delight that she would pass by the Roman she believed she loved. She would never know until he held her, until he caressed her, until he kissed her and, yes, until he took her. She also felt the eyes of all the soldiers in the camp appraising her and imagining themselves with her. Her position as the queen's sister ensured that no one would dare make a comment or a gesture but she knew they were watching her. She hoped that Marcus would be near to Ulpius so that she could snatch a few moments with him.

Her heart lifted when she saw him in conversation with Drusus outside the decurion princeps' quarters. She coloured a little when she saw the grin on Drusus' face and the reddening face of the man she loved.

"Lady," Marcus and Drusus both bowed their heads.

"I have a message for the decurion princeps." It was as though he had been awaiting the message for Ulpius strode out.

"Yes, my lady? What is the message?"

"The Queen wishes to discuss the training of her bodyguards."

Ulpius wiped the grins off the faces of his subordinates with a glare of his eye. "Marcus check sick roll." Hearing the laugh from Drusus he added, "Drusus, make sure the horses have had their quarters cleaned." As he strode off to his lover's chambers Ulpius couldn't help grinning at the discomfort of all three young people. It was good that Macha and Marcus had found each other. He could not believe that he had found love so late in life. He did not care if people knew but he preferred to keep it a secret for the dignity of the queen.

Left alone Marcus and Macha were at a momentary loss until Macha said, "Could I help you with the roll?"

The Sword of Cartimandua

"That would be, yes thank you, kind lady."

In truth checking the sick roll was a quick job, as Ulpius had known and it was finished far too quickly for the two would be lovers. Macha felt obliged to fill the silence as Marcus had shown in previous meetings that he was tongue-tied in the presence of women. "Are you looking forward to Yule?"

"Yule? I am sorry we do not celebrate at this season. We just hunker down until the days lengthen."

"As we do but we make sure that we feast. We light a fire that burns until the days lengthen and we eat all the foods we have saved from the harvest. That is why we were so happy when your ships began to arrive for now we have the spices we need to make the food taste so good. We cut green leaves and put them in our homes and we guard our homes against evil with the magic white berries. Then we drink the brews from the harvest, sing songs and tell stories."

Marcus laughed. "We have a similar festival, we call it Saturnalia but we drink more than we eat. Yule sounds like a better way to celebrate. I look forward to my first Yule. Does everyone celebrate together?"

Macha's face darkened a little. "When we had our own home and hall yes, all our people came together but here our quarters are so small that we could only host ten or twelve people." Her eyes twinkled when she added, "Perhaps my sister will invite Ulpius and some of his senior officers." When Marcus coloured and grinned like a child Macha laughed out loud. "Your face my love can be read like the stars."

"Your love, you mean..."

Macha was torn; half of her was upset that she had told him first that she loved him and the other was joyous that it was in the open. Before she could say anything, Marcus had thrown his arms around her and kissed her passionately on the lips. Any outrage at the impertinence was soon replaced by a magical thrill that coursed through her body. When they came apart they stood staring deep into each other's eyes. "I think you have your answer and I have mine but," she cautioned, "as with my sister we must keep it secret. At least for now." She leaned forward and gave him a quick peck. "And now my love I should go. I do not want to but I must."

The Sword of Cartimandua

In the Queen's quarters, the warrior who would soon be a father was gently stroking the queen's hair as she lay with her head in his lap. "How is the child?"

"As restless as a young colt. He will be a warrior. It will not be long now my love."

"What will your people say when he is born?"

"What they will say is long live the prince what they think will be a little different but I am queen. Whatever I do is right by my people. You can see from the warriors joining us now that they tire of Venutius and the Carvetii. Soon we will be able to join with your Roman army and defeat him."

"That will be easier said than done my love. I saw his stronghold at Brocavum. It will take at least a legion to storm that and the land before it is inhospitable and barren of food and shelter. With only two alae we would struggle to protect our lines."

"Did you visit the land further west?" Ulpius shook his head. "It is very fertile it is a land of water, hills and woods. The grass there would provide rich fodder for your horses. There are many lakes and it is close to the western sea. If you had a fort there you could supply it from the sea which is but a day's ride from there. We do not have ships amongst the Brigante but I know that you Romans can use the sea as a road."

Ulpius laughed a deep laugh. "You truly are a warrior and a general. Other women talk of children and clothes but you, my love, can talk of war and talk wisely of war. I will mention this to the prefect. When the days become longer I will take my ala.

Marcus Bolanus was holding a meeting with the tribune. Much as he disliked the tribune he knew that he would have to work with him until he had appointed tribunes of his own. The last thing he wanted was a debacle like the Scapula campaign against the Silures which had resulted in the only defeat of a legion in these lands. He would have to tread carefully until the Emperor despatched another legion to help the ninth subdue the north.

"Well tribune, are your troops ready for the invasion of the north?"

"The horses of the Pannonians are not as strong as I would like and our replacements have not arrived but, other than that yes we are ready. But as we both know we cannot subdue the strongholds without the legions."

"True and that is why I have summoned another legion. We must use your cavalry to pin down the barbarians and prevent them from gathering strength."

The tribune had already discussed this with the prefect of cavalry and they both knew that the major problem was a secure base. They needed a fortress close to where they would be operating to enable them to strike quickly and control a large area. The Carvetii had no cavalry of their own and their horses were pathetic ponies. As the legionaries said 'pathetic ponies for the pathetic Britons'. "Perhaps we need to establish a base from which they can strike? Somewhere to the west? The legions subduing the Silures would protect their rear and they are close to the coast."

The governor looked at the tribune in a different light. He was not the fool he took him to be. "Perhaps we could begin in the next few weeks. The barbarians will still be asleep and we could steal a march on them. Have you troops ready?"

The tribune grinned a wolfish grin; at last a chance to rid himself of the troublesome Ulpius. Ulpius Felix and his ala have already had great success, rescuing the queen and ridding the lands of the Brigante and the Carvetii." It stuck in his craw to admit this but he wanted to be rid of the troublesome barbarian who could not have a charmed life for long.

"It would be dangerous."

"Yes but we would be risking just five hundred men and, I assume, there is another ala coming with the legion?"

"Yes, I heard today that the Samians are coming which will give us two thousand auxiliaries. We can let him have a couple of centuries of legionaries and with the dismounted troops, he should have enough men to defend a fort and still harry the enemy. Make it so."

Flavinius stared at the tribune. The fool had just signed the death warrant of seven hundred men. To send a Roman force in the depths of winter was folly indeed. To send them through enemy territory bordered on the suicidal. Of course, his objections had been overruled for the popinjay had the backing of the military governor. He had not had time to get to know the new man but what he had seen he had

The Sword of Cartimandua

disliked. He yearned for a decent governor like Caesius Alasica but commanders such as he, were viewed with suspicion for who knew when they might decide to become Emperor. Successful generals who were loved by their men were watched, monitored and investigated. Vespasian had done well to rise to become Emperor and Flavius hoped that his old commander would survive into a second year for he gave hope to the soldiers. He sighed as he wondered how he would convince his old friend, Ulpius, that he had a chance, which, of course, he had not.

He watched Ulpius striding through the camp. The man had a presence; had he still been in Pannonia he would have been a chief for he had the warrior's instinct for survival and a keen strategic mind. If anyone had a chance on this foolish foray it was Ulpius.

"Come in decurion princeps. The Governor has a task for you. You are to take your ala and a vexillation of the Valeria Victrix and build a fort in Carvetii land to the west." The prefect expected a reaction but Ulpius merely nodded. The decurion had long since given up expecting all orders to make sense and in truth, he had been expecting some sort of mission. Too many Romans came to the army to make political careers, their ladders were not the scaling ladders of sieges but the bodies of the dead soldiers they trampled upon. The poor caligae were the ones whose bones littered Parthian deserts and German forests. He also saw in the tribune and military governor two men who appeared to want him to disappear. Since their arrival, he had spent more time out of the fortress rather than in it. The second ala enjoyed mocking Ulpius and the men from the first ala as they enjoyed the benefits and comforts of barrack's life.

"The twentieth are good soldiers. They did well against the Iceni. How many in the vexillation?"

"Just two centuries. They are to help build the fort and then provide the guards." Again, there was no reaction from the auxiliary which again surprised the prefect.

"At least they are not the Ninth. Remember they spent thirty years in our homeland and they are the laziest bastards I ever met."

"And the most untrustworthy. Back in forty-three they almost mutinied. I wish they had, a good decimation might have made them more reliable."

The Sword of Cartimandua

Ulpius nodded. "Do I choose where to build the fort?"

"Yes," his curiosity was aroused for Ulpius' face became more animated. "Have you something in mind?"

"If I am to pin down the Carvetii I need to be close to their lands do I not?" His commander nodded. "Yet, if I am in their lands, I would have no allies and risk raids by small bands so I was thinking of something a little further south in Brigante land. Venutius is stronger in the north. The west has few people, narrow valleys and would be perfect for a fort. The Queen has told me of a site which should be perfect. If we are to travel over the short days I would prefer to be able to travel as far to the south as I could to avoid contact with Venutius. If the Queen loaned me a few of her bodyguard we could ensure that the locals were on our side and we could still harry the enemy."

"That sounds like a good plan. This place the Queen told you of can you find it?"

"She said it is easily defended, close to the coast, good water and with a day's ride of Venutius' stronghold."

"You old fox. Don't tell me you know how to get to such a place?" He nodded. "Not such a death ride as I expected. You will need to leave within the week."

"One thing, Flavinius, "he dropped his voice to a conspiratorial level so that the clerk could not eavesdrop. "I want no one to know our precise destination. Just somewhere in the Carvetii lands will suffice. The raids on the supply columns convince me that there are spies in the camp. I will do as I did before and tell my men once we leave the comfort, safety and ears of this fort."

"Yes, I agree. I too am convinced that someone is passing information. Too many couriers are being lost. I will look into it while you are away. Things will be quiet here and not only for you. He looked knowingly at his old friend. He could see that he wished to say more. "And?"

"We are old comrades and, I hope, old friends."

"Yes. I hope this is not a request to borrow money?" He joked.

"As old friends, we trust each other and we can confide in each other."

Flavinius was intrigued. "I am interested where this is going."

The Sword of Cartimandua

Taking a deep breath, the decurion princeps launched into it. "The queen is with child, my child. I know that you would protect her but her condition means that she will need even more. You will watch over her. While I am away she will need your eyes, both of them to make sure she is safe. If I have some of her more trusted warriors she will be more vulnerable."

"You are a fool. She is the queen! If the governor were to find out."

"If the governor were to find out then we would have to deal with that but you are the only one who knows. I am trusting you."

"I will watch over the queen my brother but I can do nothing for you if you are discovered."

"I know but in the unborn child, I have a future. I will be leaving something in this world when I depart instead of a few belongings to be shared out by my comrades. I will leave a little of Ulpius Felix; something of me will live on."

The prefect nodded in agreement. To have a child was to have a future. "Be careful then and tell no one else." They grasped each other's forearms in the soldier's salute. "When you return we will celebrate with a libation to Mithras."

"I will hold you to that. My next problem is to persuade the Queen that she is to stay here without me."

"Well, old friend I cannot help you there. You are on your own."

The queen had mixed emotions when she heard of his departure. She was fearful that she would be alone when giving birth but the warrior in her was excited at the prospect of a battle that might return her lands to her. "I will give you ten of my young bodyguards they will take you to a good place to build your fort. It will be hard my love. The hills through which you travel will soon be filling with snow; if you do not start soon you may not get there."

"I know. We have a week to prepare."

"And I have a week left to love."

Rome

In Rome Vespasian threw down the report in disgust. Marcus Bolanus was obviously an incompetent fool and he needed replacing. He was ineffective allowing too much disruption in that part of the Empire. Right now the Emperor needed the gold mines of Britannia

The Sword of Cartimandua

producing gold to finance his war in the east. He needed the tin and copper to make even better weapons. He needed Britannia to be peaceful. The fact that the Queen of the Brigante had almost died was too much. Client kings were the mortar of the Empire. They held its fragile structure together and allowed its soldiers to defeat the barbarians at the gates. He called over his scribe. "Send for Marcus Caesius Alasica and Quintus Cerialis."

As the man disappeared Vespasian wondered why he had not thought of his young friend Caesius Alasica. He was a superb warrior and, more importantly, had been the first to come out in support of his claim to be Emperor. Quintus was a solid man who would make a good governor. He would brook no revolt and would handle the province with efficiency. Although it would take them some time to reach the outpost of the Empire by the time the spring arrived Britannia would be in safe hands again and this time the whole of the island would be conquered. A secure northern border would allow him to set his sights on the Parthians, the nemesis of Rome. First Judea would be subdued and then Parthia. He would recapture and return the eagles of Crassus to rest in Rome.

Eboracum

Standing at the main gate Gaius Cresens was shocked to see Fainch, the witch, walking towards the camp. She was shuffling and had a ragged cloak about her head and shoulders making it difficult for anyone to see her but he recognised her immediately. He noted with some disquiet that she appeared to be heading towards him. He looked nervously around. No one, apart from the bored guards at the gate, appeared to be watching him and there was no one else within earshot but even so it was a dangerous thing to do. As she approached him she looked up at him and gestured for him to follow her. She led him away from the settlement through a grove of elder and blackthorn to the bank of the river. The spot she took him to was overgrown and could not be seen either from the river or the camp. When there she squatted down and pulled him down next to her. "For anyone watching you are taking me so while I talk make noises as though you are."

"What?"

"Pretend you are fucking me by making noises, you useless fat man! I have a message." He grasped the idea and began to moan as she spoke. Whilst speaking she put in an occasional moan and moved the branches close by. "We know that the Romans are to move a force towards Venutius in the next seven days. You must find out precisely where he is going."

"I have tried but no one is speaking."

"Try harder. As a reward, I have more gold." She showed him a bag containing more gold than he had seen before.

"That is a good reward." He looked suspiciously at her. "Just for information."

"You are becoming wiser, just talking to me, we wish for the queen to die now and if the cavalry leader dies too then that will delay the Roman plans."

The quartermaster thought about it. He had already decided to do it. This gold would mean he could leave in the spring and return to Rome. "I will do it."

"Good now squeal as though we are finished." He did so. As he walked through the gates he saw that the guards were leering at him. Obviously, the deception had worked and now he could begin to plan the death of Ulpius and try to work out how to acquire this information.

Fainch also left to continue her work. It was midnight when she met her inner circle of killers. They had killed most of the messengers sent from the fort. If it were not for the ships tied up at the jetties no news would arrive. This time she told her band that they had to find out where the Romans were going. She did not trust her spy and if she could augment her information she would.

Drusus and Marcus were drinking heavily in the soldier's canteen. They were talking as quietly as drunken men talk. Most of the soldiers around them were ignoring them drinking as heavily as they could, knowing that in the next few days, many of them would be heading towards privation, danger and, probably, death. There was an exception. In the corner, hooded, but close enough to hear them sat Gaius Cresens who had made it is his business to follow the men of Ulpius' ala when they were drinking. He had not risked asking questions but he knew the cavalrymen, he had been their decurion princeps and knew that the decurions would know where they were headed. So far it had been fruitless but he still had three days to go.

Drusus looked around furtively. "This place we are seeking. Morbium?"

"That is what Ulpius told me."

"Where is it? I have not heard of it."

"It is to the north. We found it on a patrol a few weeks ago. It is a place where we can ford the North river. There is a hill overlooking the ford and it could be fortified. Ulpius and the Brigante think it would be a good place to defend. We could assault the Carvetii and yet be within a two-day ride of Cataractonium."

"Well, at least the decurion princeps is not thinking too much of glory. He has us a bolt hole."

"Ulpius is a wise warrior and he will not throw our lives away lightly. Come we have yet to check the picket lines." The two soldiers left staggering and lurching a little as they did so. Cresens did not move. He had the information he needed although he did not know where Morbium was. He hoped the witch would for to ask further questions would invite too much suspicion. Besides the new wine just arrived from Rome was going down remarkably well.

Later when Marcus reported to Ulpius on his patrol of the picket lines he was walking in a less drunken manner. "Well?"

"I think I have missed my calling I should have been in the theatron as an actor."

"You said the words I told you?"

"Word for word."

"Did anyone leave just after you, or follow you?"

"No we waited but no one emerged. The wine was too good."

"Were there any strangers in there?"

"No. There were a few fellows we did not recognise but all wore soldier's garments."

"Hopefully one of the many spies will have been in there. You have done well."

"Well enough for you to tell me where we are going?"

Ulpius smiled. "The Queen tells me that at Yuletide they give a surprise to friends and family. This will be my surprise present to you," he paused, "I will tell you and the men when we are on the road."

Cresens had delivered his information to Fainch who had looked more than a little pleased. His next task was to work out how to poison the Queen and Ulpius. He had decided that the festival of Yule would be the best opportunity for that was when they would eat and drink to excess. His problem was he did not yet know what they would be eating. He knew what Roman tastes were but not Brigante. As he sat in his quarters chewing on the last of the figs stolen from the Governor's supplies he had an inspirational idea he would ask his slaves. He shouted for Annowre, the woman who cleaned for him and serviced him when he could get nothing better.
"Tell me of this Yule festival. What do you savages eat?"
"Any of the chickens or geese which will not live through the winter."
"What special foods?"
"There is a pudding made of the last of the summer fruits, the old meat which we can no longer eat, some spices when we can get them, and they are soaked in the wine made from the elder tree."
"And does everyone eat?"
"It is considered a dishonour not to eat," the Briton was shocked at the lack of etiquette from the Roman. Everyone knew that to eat the pudding brought good fortune for the following year. Why would people not wish to have good fortune?
He dismissed her with a wave. Here was his chance the alcohol and the spices would mask the taste. It was one dish they would all eat. He cared not if Lenta and Macha also died. He just wanted Ulpius to die and he was being paid to kill Cartimandua. He would have to try to keep the tribune away from the food but if he died then he died. Cresens would not risk all to save an alliance that so far had brought him little.
He strode over to the kitchen area with the newly arrived spices from Rome. The cook was pleased to see him, as he knew he would be. Cresens for his part was fulsome in his praise for the cook.
"Thank you, Gaius. If it were not for these magic ingredients I would struggle to make the swill they call food here edible."

The Sword of Cartimandua
"Just so Julius, just so. And what are we making here?"
"This is the pudding the Brigante like to eat. The queen has asked me to make a special one for her and she has given me this." He held up a bottle of the spirit distilled from the elder wine, a rare libation reserved for special occasions. "Here," he looked around guiltily, "try some."

Cresens felt his throat burn with a warm sensation. The taste continued after he had swallowed. "A rare drink indeed. Will you put it all in there?"

The cook leered at the quartermaster. "I feel sure I will have a little left for us to share."

"Is the pudding finished then?"

"Almost. I have tasted it and it is now ready for the liquid."

"You do not taste after the wine has been added?"

"There is no point it would only taste of the drink." There was an almighty crash behind him and the cook turned to beat the slave who had dropped the dishes. Cresens took his opportunity. He poured the phial of poison over the pudding. By the time the cook had turned around the liquid had soaked into the other ingredients.

As he left Cresens almost did a dance of joy; the queen and Ulpius would die in the next three days and when next boats arrived in the spring he would return to Rome a very rich man. He needed now to ingratiate himself with the tribune and governor to make his return to Rome even easier.

Ulpius and his lover were oblivious to their impending danger; as was their normal practice they lay in each other's arms forgetful of their responsibilities of people and troopers and only mindful of each other. They indulged in the trivialities which had been absent from their lives for so long. They talked of names for the child, their plans for his future and how they would live together. Both were aware of the impracticalities but the queen was certain they could be overcome.

"If needs be I will buy you out of Rome's service but I am sure, as with Flavius Gerantium, the Emperor will allow you to serve me." She gave a flirtatious giggle. "Not necessarily as he did but serve me you shall."

The Sword of Cartimandua

He raised himself on one elbow. "What of Marcus and your sister? Will they enjoy life as we have?"

"I am sure something will be arranged. What is the point of being a queen if you can't make things happen? We might be a client ally of Rome but, until Rome has conquered all of these lands she will need all the allies she can get. I realised that long ago. I saw how Togadunum and Caractactus were destroyed, wafted aside by your legions. If they could not stand, the most powerful tribe then we had no chance. Boudicca proved that when she tried to take them on. Some people may resent what I have done but my people still prosper, my people still have their homes and customs and they still have their own ruler."

"And still a beautiful ruler."

She reached up and pulled him towards her. "If that is your way of saying you are ready again well so am I."

The Sword of Cartimandua
Chapter 11

Eboracum
Considering it was supposed to be the depths of winter, the feast of Yule arrived on a bright sunny day. To the Brigante, it was a good day, although the Romans found it far too cold for their taste. The governor had decreed that only essential guards need be on duty whilst the rest could enjoy the feast. He was annoyed that the queen had declined his invitation to join him for the feast and rumour had it that she was to dine with some barbarian cavalrymen. His decision to send them off was a wise one. He picked at his olives and looked around at the senior officers gather around him. He yearned to be in Rome, to be surrounded by beauty and baths not this primitive, cold and unappealing hole. He wondered if he should have insisted that she attend but then thought better of it. He could have his special pleasures with his special friends in private.

Gaius Cresens was pleased that the tribune was not invited but distraught that the governor was also not to be invited. Fainch would not be happy and Cresens knew that she had information from inside the fort other than his own. He determined to leave sooner rather than later.

That view was not shared by the two auxiliaries for Marcus and Ulpius were being waited on by the queen's slaves and eating food far richer than they were used to. In deference to her Roman guests, the Queen had arranged for some Roman delicacies such as roast dormouse, the sauce liquamen and pickled eel. In truth, they had never eaten such food but they devoured it in honour to the queen. The wine was honeyed and less watered down. By the time they had finished the prima mensa, they were almost full.

"Before we have, as you Romans would say, the secunda mensa, our Brigante pudding I have a gift." She signalled to a slave who disappeared into her chambers. "It is the custom at this time of year to give gifts to those we regard as special. As you, Ulpius Felix has served us so well." Lenta and Macha giggled until silenced by a stern look from their elder sister. "And as you are shortly to help me to recover my lands I would like you to have until our son is born,"

The Sword of Cartimandua

Ulpius noted that no-one seemed surprised at this news including Marcus, he would have to have words with his decurion," my sword. The sword of the Brigante, the sword of Cartimandua." The servant presented the sword reverently to the queen who first kissed it and then presented it, hilt first to Ulpius who stood opened mouthed.

"I cannot take this, my Queen. It is the sword of your people."

"It is the sword of my family first and you are now part of our family. You will guard it better than I ready to give to our son and you will use it to help me regain my lands, the lands of my people."

"I take it my Queen and I swear that I will not dishonour this holy weapon and I will use it for you, your people and your land." He grasped the hilt and slid the weapon from its scabbard. In the candlelight, it appeared to glow with a life of its own. It was as though its maker had put part of his life in the weapon. Without even testing it he could see how sharp it was. Marcus came over to admire it.

"While the men admire my sword, we will do honour to our pudding."

The slaves brought out the steaming, gleaming bejewelled dish. The slaves put portions on the platters. Macha and Lenta topped up the warrior's drinks and so it was that the queen was the one to eat the poisoned dessert. "My love, hurry and eat yours for it is so delicious that I will devour this and finish yours."

"I forgot that you are eating for two. Fear not I will match you mouthful for mouthful." Sliding the sword back into its scabbard he sat and picked up his bowl. He was just about to take his first mouthful when he was stopped by the sight of Cartimandua reaching up to her throat and retching. Macha and Lenta ran to their mistress whose face had taken on a most unhealthy blue colour. Her eyes rolled back in her head as she continued gagging and vomiting.

"I..." the Queen looked at Ulpius and tried to say some last words but the rest of the sentence died along with the light in her eyes and the life in her body. Ulpius held her in his arms and looked plaintively at the two Brigante. Death on a battlefield was something he was accustomed to but he could not even begin to fathom what had just happened. He had had the most perfect night of his life and he was as

The Sword of Cartimandua
happy as a warrior could be and then the Allfather had taken half his life away on a whim.

Macha put her ear to the Queen's chest and shook her head. "She is dead."

"But how?" questioned Ulpius who could barely speak.

Lenta looked at the body and the dish lying on the floor. "I have seen this kind of death before. It is from poison, a quick-acting poison. She can only have taken it moments ago."

"But we all ate the same food, drank the same drink how?" Marcus could not believe what he was witnessing. The evening had gone from celebration to disaster in a heartbeat.

"It must have been the pudding!" Lenta looked at the dessert as though it would bite her.

"But how…"

Ulpius changed from a man in shock to a warrior enraged; it was not the Allfather but someone, some person who wished the Queen dead. The idea suddenly rushed into his sharp mind, the poison had been meant for them all. "Never mind that we must tell the governor. There is a murderer loose in the camp. This food was prepared in the camp kitchens others could be poisoned. This could be the plot of Venutius." The warrior in Ulpius took over. He would mourn later. He would grieve later. He would get his revenge, later. He called to her bodyguards who were stood outside the door. "Guard the Queen, let no one touch the body and let no-one in." They looked at each other, at the Queen's body and finally at the Queen's sword in his hand and nodded assent.

Ulpius and Marcus moved swiftly through the camp to the quarters of Marcus Bolanus. He was busy feasting with the tribune and other senior officers. Bolanus saw him at the door and murmured something to the prefect who rose to speak to Ulpius.

"The governor is not happy about having his meal disturbed."

Ulpius look directly at his leader. "The Queen has been murdered. Poisoned!"

"Poisoned but…are you certain?"

"We all ate the same food except for the dessert. The Queen began to eat it and she died." Ulpius stared at his leader who seemed

The Sword of Cartimandua
unable to function. "The food was prepared in the kitchens here. Your food may also be poisoned. There is an assassin loose."

Finally comprehending, Flavinius raced back to speak to Bolanus. If the situation were not so tragic and serious Ulpius might have laughed for the first thing the governor did was to spit out his food. He signalled the decurion princeps. "Come. Speak. Are you certain the queen is dead?"

"She is dead. I have seen enough corpses in my time to know when one is dead. We must secure the camp, governor, there is an assassin in the camp."

"Do not presume to tell me what to do decurion princeps. I am aware of my duties." He turned to the prefect. "Have the gates locked no-one in or out." The prefect left taking Marcus with him. "How was she poisoned?"

Once again Ulpius went through the events in the queen's quarters. "The pudding was not prepared by the queen; she gave the recipe to the cook."

Bolanus nodded, enlightenment illuminating his face. "You," he pointed to a centurion fetch the cook and his assistants now, here." The man scurried out calling to his men who were nearby. Outside they could hear men shouting orders and the noise of arms and movement. "What of the Queen?"

"Her sisters and her guards are watching over her."

Bolanus looked down at the sword in the decurion princeps' hand. "Is that not the Queen's sword?"

"Aye, she gave it to me just before she died and I will use it to kill the man who ordered this."

"That is for me to decide."

Ulpius looked coldly at the man who seemed to take delight in petty victories. Regardless of what the governor said he would end Venutius' life. He knew who had ordered this murder. The ones with blood on their hands would die but he would have his revenge. At this moment he could not mourn. The fact that his heart had been ripped from his body, his future shattered like a glass bauble and all meaning in his life gone did not stop him from hardening his resolve and putting aside all thoughts of tears and the rending of clothes. There would be a time for mourning, for thinking of his lost love and lost,

The Sword of Cartimandua
unborn child, but that time would come when her killers were dead, by his hand and by the very sword which she had bequeathed him, the sword of Cartimandua.

Even before he heard that he had failed to kill his enemy Cresens was already fleeing the port of Eboracum. He was outside the camp when he heard the commotion from within. He smiled with malicious joy; his enemy would already be dead but before he celebrated too much he would make himself scarce. They would seek out the cook and whilst the cook had not seen him put the poison in the pudding he might remember his visit. He had decided that he would leave. Eboracum was too dangerous a place to be between the witch and the governor his life might soon be risked. He would take a trip to Petuaria and check up on the uniforms which should have arrived there. That would give him a good seven days away from the questions and he would also be in a good position for flight. He went to his quarters and the first thing he did was to get his saddlebags containing his ill-gotten gains. He did not intend to be parted from the wealth he had garnered. He had converted most of the gold and silver into precious gems which were smaller and easier to transport. He struggled to fasten the leather cuirass about him but he did not trust anyone. He would kill any of whom he thought might get in his way. He was ruthless and he would take no chances. He covered the leather with a tunic. He also took his bearskin; it would be a long cold ride. As much as he wanted to take guards with him he had to be invisible. He had to travel the dark roads where only thieves and robbers ventured. He could not relax until he had left the island behind and then he would become the rich man he had always wanted to be. No-one saw the portly quartermaster leave, no-one that is, save Fainch who smiled to herself as she had known what he would do. She would find him when she needed to.

The trader he boarded was heading south to Regulbium. From there he could disappear into the cesspit that was Londinium. The captain of the trader suspected that Cresens was fleeing and had charged an appropriately large fee. He smiled to himself; when he returned he would earn another reward for informing on the fat quartermaster.

The Sword of Cartimandua

The guards herded the terrified cooks and kitchen assistants into the governor's quarters. Bolanus had already ordered the brazier and irons to be made ready for the torturers who were readying their implements. The terrified cook fell to his knees before the governor. He had not the first idea of why they had been summoned. Perhaps the food had not been to the new governor's liking? Whatever the reason the cook felt helpless.

"Was it you prepared the queen's pudding for her feast?"

"It was sir. She gave me the recipe and I made it. I made two for I wanted to try it myself first and taste it."

"Would it surprise you to know then that the queen was poisoned by your pudding?"

"But I ate the other one and my cooks did as well." He waved a vague arm towards his cooks who cursed him for including them in his guilt.

"So if you did not put the poison in the pudding then which of these did?"

The assembled throng quailed as his gaze fell upon them. There was a cacophony of noise as they all screamed their innocence. "Take these men away and question them all one by one. I will ask the questions here."

The guards led out the terrified men while the white-faced cook stared in horror at the irons. "But I am innocent."

"I will be the judge of that." He turned to Ulpius. "Go guard the queen's body and ask her sisters about the Brigante arrangements for death."

Ulpius was glad to leave for the face of the cook had told him he was innocent. He would be tortured and, hopefully, the name of the real killer would emerge but it mattered not to Ulpius who knew the man he would have to kill, Venutius.

Although the cooks were tortured none of them could add any further information. The chief cook, Julius, had suffered more than his helpers and he had already lost an eye and an ear when he finally remembered something. "The only other visitor when we were preparing the food was the quartermaster, Gaius Cresens but he was in for a short time."

The Sword of Cartimandua

"Why did you suddenly remember him?"

"He asked me what I was making and he gave me some spirit to put in the dish."

"Did you put that spirit in your own as well?"

"Yes, I think so."

Bolanus held his hand up and the punishment ceased; this was a new name and the man clearly had no further information. "Send for the quartermaster. Take this one away while we decide if he is telling the truth."

As he sat in his chair sipping some warmed wine and water he debated upon his course of action. It would not look good for him in Rome if it was discovered that the queen had been killed in his camp. The majority of the legionaries in the camp only knew that there had been an attempt on the life of the queen. He could dispose of the cooks easily, his senior officers owed their loyalty to him, and his problem lay with the bodyguards, her sisters and the auxiliaries. When he did divine his strategy he did not know if it was the wine or his natural brilliance which gave him the solution. The queen's sisters said that she had to be buried near one of the secret holy places in the hills to the west. He would kill all the birds with one stone. The auxiliaries would escort the Brigante to the holy place and then continue to create a new base in the west. Either the winter or the Carvetii would destroy them and the queen's death would appear to be an accident of war. The auxiliaries' foray would distract Venutius who would not want five hundred Romans harassing his supply lines. The remainder of the Roman army would be able to advance on his stronghold and defeat him. It was a winning plan and he smiled to himself at his own genius. The tribune did not know that the plan had been his all along. He needed every witness of the debacle away. If he could have engineered it then Flavius would have gone with them. When the dust had settled and the vexillation massacred the death of the Queen would be forgotten, the treasure would be his and Brigantia would be Roman without a native ruler. Saenius Augustinius could then be blamed for the disaster that would ensue when the vexillation and the last of the Brigante royal family died at the hands of Venutius. The plan had a beauty about it that appealed to the convoluted mind of

The Sword of Cartimandua

Marcus Bolanus. The order to march away was signed by Saenius Augustinius; the governor's hands were clean.

The next day he summoned Ulpius who frowned as he looked up at the crucified bodies of the cooks and kitchen staff. He shook his head. They had been largely innocent but it was the roman way to make the punishment as severe as possible to encourage all to obey. He saluted as he entered the headquarters.

"Ah, decurion. I understand that you are to escort the queen's sisters to her burial."

"Yes sir."

"Good well I am going to give you some further orders, "he gestured to the prefect who sat, unhappily in a chair at the side of Bolanus. "You are to take your ala and a cohort of legionaries to the west of Brigante land. I want you to secure a base from which you can harry the enemy. Later in the year, when we have reinforcements we will begin our invasion and we will use your new fort as our base. Understood?"

"Yes sir but we can't go yet."

The face of Marcus Bolanus began to swell and redden as he detected insubordination. "I have given you an order you will carry it out."

"I am not questioning the order sir but we have no supplies prepared and half the ala is still on patrol. It seems to me that if we are to spend time isolated from the support we need to be as well prepared as possible. We all want this to succeed don't we sir?"

Realising that, much as he wanted to be rid of the embarrassment he did not want to be accused at some future date of deliberately risking failure. "How long will you need to fully prepare, decurion?"

"Seven days."

"Good, seven days then."

"There is one more thing, sir."

"Another demand?"

"No sir, a request. When can I meet with the centurion in charge of the vexillation so that we may make plans?"

"Decius Brutus arrived last night. You can meet whenever you wish."

The Sword of Cartimandua

Ulpius had been silent since he reported to Flavinius and Bolanus. He had been silent because he was not only mourning the death of his love but imagining life without her. For the past thirty years, he had known only war and fighting interspersed with boring garrison duty. He had only known the comradeship of men. He had been thrust into a world for which he was unprepared. A woman had come into his life and, he had just realised, taken it over. All the things which had seemed important, duty comradeship, Rome had all fallen into insignificance. He was about to spend the rest of his life with a woman who had captivated his heart, he was about to become a father and it had all been snatched away. He was under no illusions; he would not have the opportunity again to feel the comfort of a loving relationship or the intimacy he had known with Cartimandua. It was a bleak future he faced. The only glimmer of a lining to this black cloud was the fact that he could revenge himself on the Queen's killers and then die a warrior's death. That it was more than one killer was obvious to him. Whilst Venutius might want the Queen dead, others were also involved. He might have given the orders but someone had to get the poison and someone had to administer it. He was certain that the poisoner was Gaius Cresens. He needed no further proof than the fact that the man had disappeared following the death. Venutius was known; who had provided the poison? For in his mind they were as guilty as the fat quartermaster. Her death had not been glorious it had been painful and ignoble. The mighty Cartimandua deserved a better death. He would not rest until he had had his revenge and the revenge of his dead love.

There were other thoughts racing through his mind. He was a warrior and he was going to war. He could not help but think of the expedition he was about to command. Despite what he had said to the governor he was not confident. He would be more than a week away from help, even in high summer, and in winter it could take two or three weeks. He would be in a land of enemies, a land unknown to every Roman. He was relying on a man he did not trust. The main driving force in his decision to obey an order which bordered on the suicidal was that it brought him closer to Venutius. All he wanted was the chance to be within a sword's length of that murderer and the

The Sword of Cartimandua

death of Cartimandua would be avenged. Almost without thinking he gripped the scabbard of her sword even tighter.

"Does this not seem a little hasty to you?" Marcus spoke quietly to the decurion princeps as they sat astride their horses waiting for the last of the pack horses to join them.

"The queen must be buried and, cold as it is, she needs putting below the ground." Inside Ulpius was mourning and was as grief-stricken as he had been about anything, never having witnessed a loved one die before but he was trained to be strong. Much as he thought highly of Marcus he would not let him inside his tough outer shell. Perhaps that was hope for the future for Marcus and Macha might have the hope that he and the queen had had. He swore that he would protect the two of them with his life.

"Some of the men say it is suicidal."

"Some of the men may be right and I am sorry that many of our comrades will die and it will be my fault for both the Governor and tribune want us to disappear, to die. Indeed I think they secretly wish I had eaten the poisoned food. It is of no matter. We will survive if only because I promised the queen I would care for her family. I cannot do so in Eboracum but if I can build a fort then I believe I have the chance to protect the sisters, my men and keep this old body alive just a little bit longer." He gripped the pommel of the sword tighter. "I am not ready to meet the Allfather and Queen Cartimandua yet. Once Venutius dies…"

Marcus looked anew at his leader. He knew just how strong his feelings were for the queen. Perhaps he didn't know that there were as strong for his unborn child. If he had known then perhaps he would have seen the still, hard glint in the decurion princeps' eye. "I know that but what of this plan to build a fort on the other side of the country? That seems to me the job for a legion not a vexillation with a handful of legionaries and a few cavalrymen. In my years in the cavalry, I have never known of such an undertaking."

"Nor have I but if I tell you that before she died the queen had that idea too. She spoke to me in great detail of a site on which to build a stronghold." He grinned at Marcus for the first time in a long time, "for sometimes young Marcus we did talk. Her sisters too know of the place. To me, it sounds like a perfect site to defend for it has water to protect it and many natural resources. It also has the advantage that it will not occur to the enemy that we could be so bold as to do this."

"But to travel before the spring has melted the land and made the journey easier?"

"Who said the Roman army ever has anything easy? At least this journey now will show us some of the land we are to travel. We will have longer days when we journey and I think that the enemy will be still wrapped around his women in his stronghold. Do not fear Marcus. I for one am glad to be away from this pestilential hole. It will be good to be away from potential murderers and intrigue. We will be with men we know and trust. I do not know what goes through the mind of the governor. Perhaps it is not good to know. I am a soldier, I have been given orders. I give the orders to you. Life is simple. It may be a short one but it is simple." He looked up towards the hills. "Soon we will arrive at the sacred site and then, she will be at rest." Lowering his eye he tightened his grip on the hilt of her sword.

Marcus turned to check on the progress of the wagon and pack horses. "It is rumoured the quartermaster has disappeared."

Ulpius' face hardened. "I will find him when the time is right fear not. He caused many deaths and I will make him suffer slowly for each one. The fat little weasel cannot run far enough to escape me. But remember Marcus he was but the knife. That poison was directed by another hand and we know who that was."

"Venutius," Marcus shuddered at the tone in his friend's voice. He would not like to be in the sandals of either man when the decurion princeps caught up with them. Changing the subject to a more neutral one he asked. "What do you know of legionary centurion Decius Brutus who is to accompany us?"

"I have not served with him but Flavinius chose him because he is the most reliable centurion in Eboracum. He has served Rome for many years and risen in the ranks. His first action was against Boudicca and it is said that those who survived that war are the best of Rome. He was in command at Derventio. Fear not, Marcus, we can trust and rely on him and his men."

Marcus nodded. Derventio was to the northeast of Eboracum and whoever commanded there had a hard task. It was close to the sea and

The Sword of Cartimandua

they had to contend not only with local brigands but pirates and robbers who came across the cold sea to raid.

Brigante royal tomb south of Stanwyck

The Brigante place of death was a large barrow in a gentle valley to the northwest of Eboracum. It was cunningly hidden on a low crest of land jutting out from the valley sides. Unless you knew where to look it would appear natural. The entrance looked like a small rockfall. They arrived there towards sunset. All the omens looked propitious for the burial; the sun was slowly setting and the evening was as calm as it had been for many days. Overhead the ravens and crows circled and called to each other, it seemed to be an omen from the gods. Macha and Lenta were in charge of this part of the ceremony. In the Brigante, it was the women who buried the dead and said the holy words. Ulpius had left the legionaries and his auxiliaries at the camp and he stood with Marcus and the last of the queen's bodyguards as Lenta and Macha prepared her body for its final journey. The jewels and ornaments brought by Marcus from her capital were placed on her body. Her torc was fixed around her neck.

Marcus wondered how they would get the body into the barrow for they had no tools and there appeared to be no entrance. At last, the women were finished and the bodyguards took up the body lifting it above their heads. Lenta and Macha led the way around the outside of the grass-covered barrow. When they were at the western side they bent down and began to remove loose stones which appeared, to Marcus, to be a rockfall. The auxiliary looked in amazement as he saw the entrance to the barrow. The few stones had hidden an opening large enough for the funeral procession to walk down. The guards had to bend slightly but it was still a dignified group who walked in torchlight into the bowels of the earth. Inside it was not earthen walls but stone which was dressed and, from its look, ancient. This had been here since the time of the ancients and Marcus gripped his charm even tighter. The musty, damp smell was no surprise but it was the lack of a smell of rotting flesh that surprised him. It was not a straight path and when it turned he was plunged into darkness. When it straightened and lit by the torch he caught glimpses of bones in its flickering light as they went further into the grave. Lenta and Macha stopped and Marcus

The Sword of Cartimandua
could see recognisable bodies. Each had jewels and weapons with them but none as fine and rich as those worn by the dead Queen. Now Marcus knew what had been in the box carried from the fortress of Stanwyck. In the tomb there were both men and women; the queen was joining her ancestors. The bodyguards laid the body gently onto the empty bier. Marcus could see others prepared deeper in the darkness. The Brigante all bowed their heads and Marcus sensed, rather than heard the low moaning which emanated from their lips. He did not recognise any of the words but knew that they were all saying the same thing. Suddenly there was silence and the torches were extinguished leaving them in darkness with only the faint light of the sunset coming through the entrance. It was Lenta who spoke the last words. "Allfather receive our queen and sister Cartimandua we honour her in death as we did in life."

No one spoke again even after they had replaced the stones and covered them with soil. Even after they had walked in solemn silence to the camp still no one spoke. Marcus glanced at Ulpius but he could have been the stone they had just used to cover the grave for all the emotion he showed. He was beginning to realise that he did not know the decurion princeps as well as he had thought for he knew the man was mourning but he could not see a single sign.

Later Ulpius asked the question which had been burning in his mind since they had laid the Queen's body into the barrow. "When you spoke over the Queen you said, sister. I thought you were her handmaidens?"

"We were handmaidens but we had the same father. He lay with our mother, one of his slaves and we were half-sisters."

"Doesn't that make the elder the Queen?"

"No Roman. It is for the council to choose and Venutius is still King. He has been crowned. The Queen is dead and so he is the king. He now leads the Brigante."

"But," added Lenta, "many of our people will not follow him as he tried to kill our Queen, our sister."

"Which doesn't help us for that means any Brigante could be a friend or a foe?" He gestured at the Brigante warriors sharpening their weapons.

The Sword of Cartimandua

"These men are oathsworn to protect the Queen. As her family, they are oathsworn to protect us. But you are right we will have to be careful as there are as many untrustworthy Brigante as there are Romans. For was not Gaius Cresens a Roman?" There was mischief in her voice that reminded Ulpius of her half-sister.

"Then it is fortunate for you that I am Pannonian by birth and we are the most trustworthy of warriors."

Laughing the two sisters left the decurion princeps to ponder his next dilemma, how to survive in a land where an enemy could be hiding behind every tree, in every gully and in every hut. He would need all his wits about him. As soon as it was convenient he needed to sit down with the Brigante warriors and Decius Brutus for they needed a plan which, at the moment was beyond his ability.

The party returned to Eboracum in silence each one wrapped in their own thoughts. For Ulpius he was reflecting on the changes the queen had wrought in him. He was gentler with women, he was less mercenary, he thought more of the future at least he had thought on the future until it was robbed from him. She had brought hope into a hopeless, loveless life. He did not know if it was love he had had with the Queen but to his unsophisticated mind, if it was not love, it was the nearest he would experience.

The two half-sisters were also musing on their parlous future. Now that Venutius was king, although in truth he had been king for some time, they were in constant danger. He could pay many murderers to kill them and they were not safe at the fort, as their sister had discovered. The only people they could rely on were not Brigante but Roman and they were the warriors who now rode at their side. Macha determined that, when they left for their new fort, they would be with them. Despite any hardships on the road, they would be as nothing compared with the dangers of Eboracum where every hand could wield a killer's blade.

The day they left Eboracum was both cold and frosty. Rising early Ulpius looked around the fort. It was now taking shape and life would be more comfortable now but even so, he was glad that Marcus Bolanus was sending them away. He knew that the man had his own reasons and those reasons were not thoughtful in any way shape or form. He was an embarrassment and he wanted him away to,

The Sword of Cartimandua

preferably, die on a forlorn hillside away to the west. He saw the governor emerge from the Praetorium a thin hard smile upon his face. For him, the world would become safer with each step the vexillation took away from Eboracum. The days were now longer but the wind was still bitingly cold. It was as though winter had lulled them into a sense of false security and descended a savage, second time.

Ulpius called over Marcus to join the Brigante warriors and Lenta and Macha. He looked at each of the warriors. "You have served the queen to the end and now you are released from the vows you took. We are taking her sisters west to build a fort in her honour. You are welcome to join us there but some of you may wish to rejoin your own people. If that is so then go with honour for you have all served the queen loyally and well."

It was the senior warrior, Orrick who spoke. He was a powerful warrior and his skill was shown by the bracelets and amulets he wore. The scars on his face and chest ably demonstrated that he faced and fought his enemies fearlessly and never turned his back. When he spoke the emotion rang through his words. "Our oath to the queen means that we cannot rest until her murderer is found and killed. We would have died to protect her and we failed. We will find the man who ordered her death. We believe it to be Venutius who did not have the courage to face the Queen and end her life by his own hand. He paid someone and that is base and dishonourable. For that alone, he should die." The men murmured their agreement and Ulpius nodded.

"Are you going after him then? For if so it would be a glorious death, futile but glorious."

"We hold our lives cheaply and would gladly pay with our lives to avenge the queen but you are right. We were known as the protectors of the queen and Venutius would have us slaughtered as soon as we appeared. We would not get close enough to him and we will not kill in the night. When he dies at our hands he will see who it is and know why we do it. No, we will continue to travel with you and we will protect the Princesses." He smiled. "We believe that Venutius will pay a visit to this new fort of yours and so he will come to us."

Ulpius nodded. "That is well but if you travel with us then you obey my orders. You will be as Romans with the same discipline. Is that clear?"

The Sword of Cartimandua

One or two of the warriors looked a little unhappy at the implications of that but Orrick silenced them with a wave of his arm. "You are a warrior; you are the warrior chosen by our queen. You ride with the sword of Cartimandua. We will follow you."

"Good then let us get over these hills before the snows come a second time. This land appears to be in the group of some monster who makes the weather as a weapon to punish strangers such as us. I hope that the place we seek is less unpredictable. Your queen promised much. I long to see this Elysium in Britannia which holds so much hope." He turned to the two Brigante princesses. "I still cannot persuade you to stay?"

Lenta smiled at the word 'persuade' for, in the week they had been back in Eboracum Ulpius had ranted, raved, bullied, pleaded and at times almost screamed to make them stay behind the safety of Eboracum wooden walls. Persuade had not been a word she would have chosen. They had both been resolute in their arguments and, in the end, Ulpius had seen that perhaps they were right and they would be safer away from intrigue. "No decurion princeps, we will not be persuaded besides we know the land as well as the warriors and we know the place you seek. We will not be baggage for we are Brigante and we will do our share we will help to build this shrine to the memory of our queen."

Nodding Ulpius turned to Marcus. "We leave as soon as the pack horses and wagon are ready. Remember it is only a handful of us who know where we are going. Let us keep it so."

The Sword of Cartimandua
Chapter 12

Brocavum

Venutius was drunk and his warriors were drunk. His official coronation had been some weeks before but the celebrations seemed to go on endlessly. He was now King Venutius even though he had been king before he had not been crowned and acclaimed by his people. This made it easier for him to summon the war host for to refuse would be refusing the king. True, there were still those who were unhappy with the death of Cartimandua but, apart from the handful still with the Romans the bulk to the Brigante supported him. He had had the acknowledgement of all the neighbouring tribes and their kings. As the king with the largest tribal area in Britannia, this made Venutius the king who exerted the most influence. Secretly he was pleased that Cartimandua had betrayed Caractacus for had she not, that young man would have grown to be a warrior king with a legitimate claim to be king of Britannia.

He looked out of the gates towards the rising sun in the east, the steam from his piss rising like early morning fog. This was the time of the long nights and short days. It was a time to drink and tell tales of great deeds. His men were drunk because they believed they had freed themselves from the shackles of Rome and were following a leader who had rid himself of a tiresome, meddling woman. Venutius was drunk because he had failed. He had failed to capture and kill his queen; the poison which had killed her was on his orders but not by his hand and he had wanted to see her suffer and die. He had failed, despite what his men believed because the Romans had not been weakened by him; they had absorbed the Brigante and now controlled much of their territory. It galled him to think that he was depending upon the Silures and Deceangli to defeat the Romans and draw off their strength. His pleasure at becoming the official king was soured by the knowledge that he had failed in his first attempt to rid his land of the Romans. He had hoped that the disarray in Rome when they had four Emperors in one year would have distracted them enough to defeat demoralised Romans. The Roman troops appeared to care more about the way they fought than who was Emperor. It was a salutatory lesson.

He angrily turned back, threw his goblet to smash on the wall of the fire lit hut and his men cheered believing it to be a sign that their leader was showing his anger to his enemies when in reality it was a frustration that he had failed. He was angry with himself and with his spies. The information given to him by Fainch had proved false. He had gathered his forces near to the place the Romans called Morbium for it was not far from Stanwyck. He had prepared a trap and his men had waited through the long, dark winter nights but the Roman incursion had not taken place. He was angry with himself for, despite the fact that the information was wrong, he did not know if the Romans had tricked him just to make his men wait needlessly in the cold or if it was a ruse to draw his men away from his capital. He now knew it was not the latter for he had brought all his forces into his stronghold in case the Roman invasion came in the winter, it was unlikely but these Romans did not fight in the way of the tribes. He allowed himself a smile perhaps the information had been true and the Romans had perished in this cold northern land far away from their warm homeland.

He staggered to his feet and, climbing over the recumbent bodies of his warriors, went to relieve himself outside his hall. The frost was hard and the air icy cold. The steam from his urine rose like smoke from a fire. The image made him picture Eboracum burning and Romans fleeing from his merciless warriors. They would be like sheep before his wolves. The thought excited him and he began to sober up almost immediately. In truth he rarely drank as much as his warriors for he knew that a drunk was senseless and therefore defenceless; he had murdered many a man whilst they were lying in an alcoholic haze. Venutius trusted no one. It would be months before the sun began to warm the land again but he was determined not to wait rotting in an alcoholic haze.

He would begin to send out patrols; it would harden his men and tell the Romans that he ruled this land and not them. He needed a base nearer to the Romans in the East. There was no danger in the west as long as the Deceangli and Silures held up the Roman behemoth and it was here where he would defeat them but he needed to create a thorn

The Sword of Cartimandua

in their side, an itch which they could not scratch. Cartimandua's capital had been ideal but now not only was it in Roman hands, but his men had also weakened it. The Roman base at Eboracum was less than half a day's ride away; it would need much work to fortify it and they would have to fight Romans to do so. He needed somewhere new but defensible. He remembered a river and a high cliff a little further south than Stanwyck; if he built a fort there even the Roman war machine would struggle to assault it. It would not be as big as the huge fortifications at Stanwyck but it had the advantage that even the Roman siege engines would struggle to assault its high cliffs. When he had thrown back his enemies he would use that as his stronghold; there he would laugh to scorn their redoubtable war machines. He decided that, on the morrow, they would begin their war against the Romans, they had drunk enough, and they had rested enough. The Carvetii would war again and they would drive the effete Romans back into the sea taking with them their baths, their perfume and their control. Britannia would be ruled again by men; Britannia would be ruled by one man, Venutius.

West of Stanwyck

Even as Venutius was looking eastwards Ulpius had risen early and was facing west. They had crossed the high treeless hills in the icy cold winds. It had taken many days as the line of pack horses with supplies slowed them down and the foot soldiers kept to their own pace but they had had to take routes that avoided the natives. The wagon with the princesses on board was even slower and Ulpius wondered if it might have to be discarded in favour of a faster, though less dignified packhorse. Slow and sure was not always the axiom of the cavalry but in this case, it was his watchword. They had lost a few mounts and they were as cold as any could remember but they were now within sight of their goal. As the sun had set the previous evening Orrick had ridden with Ulpius and Marcus to show them the land spoken of by Cartimandua.

In the distance, they could see the round-topped hills and steep-sided valleys which Orrick told them contained vast lakes as big as seas and forests so dense a horse could not get through them. The tops of the hills were high and treeless rolling away to the west to the mighty seas spoken of by Cartimandua, the western seas leading to the ends of the earth. Ulpius was gratified to see that there were few dwellings or huts in view which meant they might just make their journey's end unseen by the enemy. There were a few sheep and goats which appeared to perch on hillsides that threatened to tumble to the rock-filled valleys below. He looked up at the grey, menacing sky which was beginning to threaten snow although that would be a discomfort it would not stop them as they were within a maximum of two marches to their destination. Orrick had said that, if they pushed hard, they would do it on one march. They were so close that Ulpius felt like gambling. Although the horses were tired they could rest them when they arrived and they would also have the security of wooden walls. His worry was that the snow would show their enemies where they had been; in itself another reason to make haste. He might exhaust men and horses but that could not be helped, as long as he had a marching camp he would be able to defend himself.

Marcus could not help looking over his shoulder as they passed through the tight lake lined valleys. The valley twisted and turned like some mighty serpent. This was not the way Romans like to travel. They were used to straight roads with no places for ambushes. This was even worse for the high crags and rocky outcrops provided cover for ambushes all the way.

"You will get a stiff neck if you continue to look backwards."

Marcus wondered how the one-eyed decurion princeps could see that Marcus was so nervous. "But if there were an ambush we would be helpless. There is nowhere to run."

"True but we have Brigante scouts out and if you look east you will see that the only danger is not from warriors but stones dislodged by the snow and as for west, well unless our enemies can walk on water we are safe." The lake to the west was wide and, according to Orrick deep. The hillsides on the other side looked as steep as the one to their east which reared up, towering over them like the battlements of an enormous fortress. "I tell you, Marcus, I am more content now than for many days. We are almost at journey's end and we have seen no signs of life. Go speak with your woman and stop making the troop nervous." The troopers within earshot grinned; much as they liked

The Sword of Cartimandua

Marcus it was always good to see an officer put in his place by a superior.

Marcus had to agree that it was devoid of humans. In truth, there was little sign of any life. They had travelled over passes from one lake-filled valley to another. The valley suddenly dropped off to nothing. The forest was so thick you could have hidden a thousand warriors but a spear's throw from the Romans and they would not have been seen. This part of the journey had the narrowest pass and the troopers, four abreast, filled it. He turned his horse and trotted back to the middle of the column to where Macha and Lenta huddled in a wagon. Even though she was miserable Macha visibly brightened when she saw the young auxiliary approaching.

"Are we warm enough ladies?"

Lenta laughed a bright tinkling laugh which was infectious. "As we have blankets and furs and we are in a warm wagon I think that we are much warmer than you."

"The officer is being polite, sister. I suspect our leader has passed the request on. We are comfortable and we do not have far to go."

"How far is it?"

"No more than the time it takes Romans to put up a camp."

"That quick, but I can see nought that is as was described."

"The track twists next to a little stream and then you will see the mightiest lake you have ever seen. Then we will be there." She leaned over to whisper to Marcus who went closer. "When you have fulfilled your duties tonight I would speak with you."

Marcus' face lit with joy. They had had little opportunity to talk as the sisters and the children had been together in the wagon. Marcus rode back to Ulpius with a lighter heart.

"We are not far away."

"I know the scouts have returned." Ulpius gestured to their left where there was a large natural mound. We will put a small fort there. It will give us a warning of an enemy. Orrick has ridden ahead with the Brigante to guard the site. We are very close." Marcus looked over and saw what Ulpius meant. A thousand paces away the hillside climbed steeply away with thick woods covering its lower slopes. The land before it was a sloping bare plain with a huge column of rock reaching up halfway as high as the hillside. It had a steep northern

The Sword of Cartimandua

slope and a gentler southern slope. He could imagine that a tower would enable a sentry to see almost the whole of the lower lake. A good place for an outpost and a further sign that the omens were auspicious.

Years later Marcus could still remember with vivid clarity the first time he saw the site of the fort they would call Glanibanta. He was totally unprepared for the place. They rode through rocky ground and suddenly found themselves in the open at a promontory surrounded on three sides by water. It was as though an engineer had measured a fort and made the promontory to fit the fort and not the other way around. The ground was perfect and was a horse's height above the water. Two rocky streams tumbled a fort's width apart making a frontal assault the only option for an attacking force. Marcus looked at Ulpius who, for the first time in a long time, smiled and nodded. "This will do Marcus, this will do. This is a stronghold; a cohort of legionaries could hold off the whole of the Carvetii."

The senior centurion of the legionaries set to work as soon as they arrived. The marching camp would be the size of the fort and work could begin to build the fort straight away. There was little snow at the site and the ground was not as frozen as they might have expected. Decius Brutus and his legionaries had much experience in building marching camps but this was the first time they had built a fort. The Roman army trained its men well and every centurion had the plans in his head and with his legionaries the men to build. Already the flags and stakes were in place as the engineers detailed to lay it outpaced the area which would become the vexillation fort.

While the legionaries began to dig the ditches Ulpius detailed Marcus to send out two turmae around the lake, east and west to scout for potential enemies and other places to build fortifications. He conferred with the legionaries to ensure that there would be stables for his horses.

Gaius rode next to Marcus and the irrepressible youth could not help but ask questions. "What if enemies were to attack from the south? We would be helpless."

Marcus smiled a rueful smile; he began to understand what Ulpius had felt when pestered by the turma mascot. "There are few people to the south. You would have to travel for weeks before you came to any kind of numbers. Had you studied the maps you would have known that."

"Then why are we patrolling? Should we not be helping to build the fort?"

"I personally would rather ride than have to bend my back and dig ditches. Besides which our task is important. While there are no peoples to the south it might be a route through which we can be attacked. We need to know how the land lies and prepare. Remember young Gaius we are isolated here. We are a vexillation, not an army and we have many enemies arraigned against us. Remember that."

At the camp, Drusus took a turma on foot to cut down the trees. They did not have to go far for there were hundreds of trees. They also needed to clear a killing zone close to the fort. Ulpius nodded his approval as he saw that his men soon had to take off their armour as it was hot, hard work despite the cold air temperature. The work would harden their sword arms even more. As he swung the axe Drusus was less appreciative than his leader of the workout he was getting. Trees took more blows to fell than warriors and he soon found his arms aching and burning from the repetition. Around him, the other auxiliaries were also gleaming with sweat but their efforts soon began to show as the pile of trees grew. When they had cleared twenty paces of trees they began to drag them back to the ditches which now clearly defined the fort. Already stakes were being thrust into the mounds and would give some protection when the Romans finally rested for the day.

It was almost sunset when the patrol returned. Marcus was not surprised by the speed with which they had erected their camp but he was impressed by the progress towards a permanent fort. There was a double ditch in front of what would become the porta praetorian. They would be defended from a frontal attack if one were forthcoming. He was pleased to see a rudimental tower and sentries already peering into the gloom of twilight. It was not a sight that brought a smile to his face it was the unmistakable smell of, fires producing unleavened bread for the first time since leaving Eboracum. The wagon was in the centre of the camp where the Praetorium would be built and which, at the moment was a tent. He could see the Brigante sisters already making their temporary home as comfortable as they could. At least they

The Sword of Cartimandua

would be sleeping above the ground whilst the common soldiers, the caligae, would once again have the hard cold ground. He was eager to speak to Macha but knew his duty. He reported to Ulpius as soon as he recognised the decurion princeps' broad and muscular back.

"I have to report that the lake is long and narrow. There are woods along both sides and a river at the southern end. We found some huts of woodcutters but they were empty. We could see smoke in the distance to the south but it was faint. "

"What about defensible sites?"

"This is the best one. The ground is low lying all around the lake but it is overlooked by hillsides. This area has fewer trees to cut down and we are protected by water on three sides." He pointed back to the pass they had crossed some distance away. "You see it better from this direction. The ground slopes steadily up to the pass and now that some of the trees have been cleared you can see what a good site it is."

"Is there another site where we could build a dock or jetty?" When Marcus looked perplexed he added impatiently, "think boy we need an escape route. We could build a boat and use it to escape but only if there is somewhere else to land otherwise we would sail around the lake until we disappeared up our own arses!"

"Sorry sir, I wasn't thinking you are, as usual correct and we will need to have some stables as well. They would enable us to spread out the horses. There are a couple of places halfway down the lake where there are clearings. There are many trees around the lake materials will not be a problem. "

Ulpius nodded. "Good. As soon as we have this place up and running I want you to take a couple of turmae, build stables and a jetty. This is a good spot but I don't want to get caught like rats in a trap. Good work Marcus." He looked towards the wagon and smiled an almost paternal smile, "and I think there is a lady who would like some of your time. Get your men to look after the horses and then give her some of your time. I think they miss their sister." The 'as I do' was unspoken but Marcus saw the sadness in his face.

Brocavum

"My lord he has just brought the message."

Venutius was about to strike the messenger who had reported a large force of Romans crossing their land. He seethed with rage. All

The Sword of Cartimandua

the time he had been looking east his enemies had been heading west; when he thought they were tucked away in their new fort they were taking the initiative and sneaking through his lands in the dead of winter. The scouts had found tracks in the snow and the remains of a marching camp just west of the high hills but no one knew where they had gone. Could they be, even now, heading north to this his base? Only the barbaric Romans could war in winter.

"Summon the tribe and send messengers to my allies; we must prepare for war."

"But my lord it is still winter and our people have not begun to seed. We are not ready."

"Fool! The Romans do not wait for warm weather. If we do not stop them now there may be no one left to eat the crops you wish to plant. They may be approaching here! Do you not understand? Would you have us fight the legions with this handful of men? We know not how many men there are within our lands. Are they to the north? Perhaps the south or even, Allfather forbid, the west. For if it is the west then they will have come by ship and we will be assaulted on two sides. Now, do you realise why we must act and act swiftly?"

It was then that his chiefs and chieftains realised their plight. They had barely a thousand warriors at Brocavum; their army was at a hundred different hamlets and settlements wintering. It would take many days to summon them. Taking their leave each leader left to gather their forces.

Venutius summoned his guards. "We ride today. I want to see where they were last observed." His men looked at each other. It was unheard of to ride the high hills when the snow was on the ground. Sensing their doubt Venutius turned and snarled. "If the soft Romans can travel through our land I believe that the Carvetii can. We ride."

Eboracum

Marcus Bolanus was enjoying the newly built baths in the fortress of Eboracum blissfully unaware that the letter from Saenius Augustinius had had an effect. The scraping and oiling relaxed him and made him think of his villa near Capua. He had insisted that the baths be built first when he had arrived. He was just stepping into the hot baths when he heard the news of an Imperial bireme approaching. He was more annoyed than worried. One bireme meant it was

The Sword of Cartimandua

someone of inferior rank and certainly no one to worry about. Emperor Vespasian was more concerned with the east. It had been Claudius who had staked everything on Britannia and its riches. He decided not to greet these visitors he would let them wait. In Britannia, he was the ruler. He was therefore surprised when he heard a commotion outside and the door was flung open. He managed to utter, "What is the meaning..." before he saw the Imperial seal on the letter in the hands of Quintus Cerialis.

"I am sorry that you have been disturbed but Marcus Caesius Alasica and I are keen to fulfil the Emperor's wishes and bring this little island under Roman rule. And you will be keen; I am sure, to return to the warmer climes of Rome!"

Bolanus stared silently at the letter. He was to be recalled and the manner of his recall meant that he knew he was in disgrace. As he emerged from the bath into the toga held by his servant he could not help but think that he could have made more money than he had so far if he had been more corrupt. He realised, a little late, that he had been lazy and he had neither served Rome nor himself.

"You are most welcome. As you can see we are in the business of building the fortress."

Galba spoke for the first time, barely concealing the disdain in his voice. "I would have thought stone gates would have taken precedence over baths." Bolanus was stumped for words. Alasica continued, almost dismissing the ex-governor. "Where is the twentieth, I am to command."

"They are still in Lindum."

"And the second, and the Pannonians?"

"The second are here but a vexillation went with the Pannonians to build a fort in the west."

"In winter? What fool ordered that? I will have the commander scourged." Quintus was as angry as Alasica.

Realising the truth would come out Bolanus had to admit to the order. "But we needed to pin down the enemy and with the Queen dead."

"The Queen of the Brigante is dead? How?"

"She...err, after eating, she died." Bolanus realised he had yet to inform Rome of this disaster.

The Sword of Cartimandua

"After eating?" asked the new governor, suspicion in every syllable. "Was she poisoned?"

"We questioned the cooks and they denied responsibility."

"And I take it they died during questioning." Cerialis turned to the young commander of the twentieth. "This is quite a disaster. It means we cannot count on the Brigante."

"Oh, most of the Brigante still support us. The Queen's half-sisters."

"The Queen's half-sisters. Where are they?"

The silence and the horrified expression on Marcus Bolanus' face made the two visitors fear the worst. "They are with the vexillation in the west. They wanted to go." He added feebly.

"Oh, that makes all the difference. So let me understand clearly the situation. You have sent the majority of our cavalry with a sizeable part of a legion and the only leaders of the one tribe in the area we can rely on to build a fort on the other side of the island, in winter?"

There was no need for an answer. Bolanus could merely nod. His future was bleak. When the Emperor found out he would have his lands confiscated and his life would be terminated. Knowing his presence was unnecessary he left. "If you need any further intelligence my aides will supply it. I have to prepare for the journey."

As he left the younger man could not keep the disgust from his voice. "Intelligence is the last thing we will get."

The new governor turned to his military commander. "I realise it is too soon but you have a keen military brain which is why the Emperor sent you. What is your assessment of the situation?"

"Unless the commander of the vexillation is a brilliant commander he will have lost men and animals travelling during winter. He will also be at the mercy of the tribes in that area. They are the Carvetii and led by the Queen's ex-husband, Venutius. He is a cunning leader and it is rumoured that he has the support of the tribes north of him. I estimate that in the spring they could put over twenty thousand men against us."

"And we have?"

"If we bring up the twentieth, and the Samians then, after garrisoning Lindum and Eboracum we could field, perhaps twelve thousand. The thousand horse and four hundred legionaries in the west

The Sword of Cartimandua

would have swung the odds in our favour. As it is we will need to create somewhere further north and west to warn us of an attack. I will speak with the commanders."

"And I will enlist the help of some of these natives to expedite the building of the fortress."

Fainch noticed the change around Eboracum within days. She had watched the old governor slipping secretly away on the bireme with the despatches which would end his career if not his life. She also saw that work on the fortress went on at a much greater pace. There were many stone towers with strongly built wooden walls and two ditches that surrounded the whole settlement. The ground for a thousand paces had been cleared. Her master had planned on an attack in the spring before the defences were finished. He needed to know that the fortress would not be an easy target by the time he had mustered his warriors and launched his assault. In fact, the fortress would be unassailable without siege engines and as everyone knew the only army with siege engines was the Roman army. Rather than trust her message to a minion, she decided to visit his refuge high in the hills. She knew that Venutius' temper might result in the message being ignored by anyone but herself. She needed Venutius to be safe, she needed him to lead the rebellion. As she packed her few belongings she knew she and her sisters would need to dream a powerful dream to halt this unstoppable beast that was the Roman army.

Galba and Cerialis met on the third day after their arrival. "How goes the military preparations?"

"The rest of the twentieth will be here by the end of the week. The auxiliary commander of the remaining ala has told me of a place near to the northern river, not far from the Brigante town of Cataractorium a settlement called Morbium. It is at a bluff near a bend in the river. If we build a fort and a bridge there then Venutius will not be as secure. He could be outflanked for at the moment he knows where our line of march must be, south of the great river."

"Have you tried to contact the vexillation?"

"I think there is too much danger attached to that. First of all, we would have to send a turma and we can ill afford to lose more auxiliaries and if the message were intercepted then the enemy would know of the vexillation. I am not sure that the enemy knows of our

The Sword of Cartimandua

incursion. From what I have been told it is a vast empty high land and few people travel even in summer. Besides, I believe there is too much danger in bringing them back. If they have managed to build a fort then they should be able to survive until spring if not," he shrugged his shoulders, "then they are dead and we would have thrown good men after bad. I am more concerned with the Brigante with them. I hope the vexillation commander treats them well."

The commander was indeed treating them well. Had the Romans in Eboracum known the situation they would have realised that they had no need to fear the isolation of the Brigante princesses. Bolanus had failed to mention the liaison between Ulpius and the queen. The problem the vexillation had was that the snows had come with a vengeance. They went to bed at night with the weather cold and threatening and awoke the next day to a blanket of snow that rose in places as high as a horse's haunches. All movement and work stopped. Fortunately, they had built one stone gate and the towers and as Orrick said, the snows would at least stop the Carvetii from venturing out. It was a blessing in disguise.

Ulpius set the men to training; there would be a fight when Venutius came and it was important that the legionaries, auxiliaries and Brigante behaved as a single unit. He spent many hours with the leaders who then passed on the ideas to the men. When they were not training they were making sure that all their equipment was fully functional. One of the first buildings which went up was the blacksmiths and they were busy making horseshoes and arrowheads as well as sharpening swords and javelins. The younger Brigante spent the shortened days hunting to augment their meagre rations. Daily they brought in rabbits and small red deer. They were surviving.

The Sword of Cartimandua
Chapter 13

Glanibanta
Ulpius had bridled at the lack of work but even he had to admit that the rest allowed men and beasts to recover after a gruelling journey fraught with both danger and hardship. The mid-winter travail had cost them both horses and men. The horses would continually weaken for their fodder would run out and there was no grass to eat. It was a problem he would have to deal with. As he tramped through the snow he inspected the partly constructed fort. The ditches had been completed early on and the legionaries were pleased that the lake provided one whole impenetrable ditch. The walls and towers had been built. The northern gate, the porta praetoria had been built of stone. He smiled to himself the Queen had been right about the abundance of materials. There was a huge quantity of stone and none of it had needed to be quarried; it was just lying on the ground. There was also a plentiful supply of slate so that the roofs of the buildings would be watertight. They had brought some pazzolana with them and had been able to use concrete for the foundations and between the stones. Once the snow melted it would not take long to build the other three gates. He wandered over to the towers, acknowledging the salutes of the guards. They were high enough and, with their elevation, gave them an excellent view of approaching enemies. If the bastards did come, and Ulpius had to admit that was unlikely for a while, they would neither be surprised nor overwhelmed. Ulpius was more concerned that he had not been able to build the three outposts yet, the two on the lake and the one on the mound. Even the tireless Marcus had been unable to complete that miracle. He wondered what had happened to his subordinate since they arrived for he was perpetually smiling and seemed full of life. The cynic in the one-eyed warrior wondered if regular lovemaking had anything to do with it. He determined to ask the question directly the next time he spoke to him. He was disturbed by a shout from the northeast tower.

"Gate. Rider approaching."

Ulpius was pleased that his men were not indolent. The legionaries sprang into action and his auxiliaries stood with bows

The Sword of Cartimandua

notched. Ulpius felt his fingers on the hilt of the Brigante sword and it gave him comfort. Cartimandua had told him it had mystical qualities and he had noticed that whenever Orrick or one of the Brigante warriors saw it they had reverence and awe written all over their faces.

"It is one of my people," shouted Orrick and the guards relaxed slightly although the gate remained closed. Orrick climbed to the rampart over the gate and spoke to his kinsman in their own tongue. The warrior was a young fierce-eyed warrior who looked like a younger version of Orrick. The sword he carried was as long as that wielded by Ulpius and the young man had many combat amulets on his arms. He was, Ulpius decided, a warrior. Although Marcus and Ulpius understood many of the words the two spoke so quickly that all meaning was lost. Orrick turned to the Roman who had joined him at the gate. "It is Esca, my cousin. He wishes to join us."

His one eye staring into Orrick's soul he asked, "Do you trust him?"

"He is not just my cousin he is blood kin."

Ulpius nodded. A Roman might not understand the ties of a blood oath but a semi-barbarian like Ulpius would. "Let him enter."

Ulpius allowed the two warriors to speak with each other before he imposed himself upon them. Marcus stood at his side as did Quintus Brutus the senior centurion. They were all eager to learn any news of the outside world. "The Carvetii know we have crossed the high hills and he searches for us. He does not yet have his forces gathered and my cousin tells me that we have more men in this fort than Venutius has."

"How does he know that?" questioned Brutus.

Orrick smiled wryly, not all the Romans were as trusting as the cavalrymen. "He counted us. Venutius does not know where we are building the fort and he is looking further east. I think we moved too fast for him."

"Where did your blood kin come by this intelligence?" There was just the hint of suspicion in the Roman's voice.

"He was sent a summons by Venutius for a gathering of the host."

"That is sooner than I would have hoped. When do you think he will be ready?"

The Sword of Cartimandua

"Once the snows melt and his other men arrive then he will have enough scouts to fill the land and he will find us."

"How long?"

"For the snow? I know not. For his men? At least ten days and then only for them to arrive at his stronghold. It would take another seven nights for them to set off."

"That gives us fifteen days. Enough time for the fort but, unless the snows melt even quicker than they are we cannot build the outposts. Are there others like your kin who wish to join us?"

Orrick nodded. "When the snows melt there will be many for he has dishonoured us by killing our queen."

Ulpius was already working out how to house and feed the extra men whilst he was also thinking about using them as a battle force. The fort could house eight hundred men and the plan was to put almost twice that number in. It was one of the reasons the cavalryman wanted to use the outposts to spread the load; they could all defend the fort but not, perhaps, live in it. He voiced his ideas to Orrick, Brutus and Marcus. "We need barracks outside of the fort. The lake means we cannot make it any larger we need a similar fort, "he gestured to the southwest. "There is another piece of land which juts out into the lake. It will protect us from the west. We could house the majority of the cavalry and any of the Brigante who wish to join us. That will leave the legionaries to garrison and defend this, the main fort. It need not be a fort more of a barracks. I want as much space between all of us as possible. Close company can lead to disagreements."

They all nodded their agreement for there had already been numerous fistfights and one stabbing from conflict between auxiliaries and legionaries for normally they had their own forts and areas. Brutus was beginning to see why the one-eyed barbarian had been put in command of this vexillation. His initial distrust had evaporated during the march and since they arrived. "I will have my men being clearing the ground ready to start once the snow goes."

Marcus nodded, "And I will take my turma on foot to the outpost mound. As it is a hill we should be able to clear the snow easier." Ulpius looked doubtfully at his decurion knowing, as he did that cavalrymen preferred to ride everywhere. "It is not far and the exercise will do them good. Our mounts are too lean and there is little feed to spare."

Ulpius nodded his agreement. "Good. You all know what you are to do. I leave it to you Orrick to recruit and organise your people. Make sure you can trust them. Remember what happened to the queen."

"We remember and do not worry any traitors and spies will not return to give Venutius any help."

As he expected the men of his turma grumbled when they realised that they would have to walk. They grumbled, even more, when they had to carry axes and hammers as well as their weapons.

"This is foot soldier's work," murmured Decius the grumbler.

"If we took our horses then soon you would be a foot soldier so look upon it as training for your future."

The rest of the turma laughed aloud at the put down. Decius was a moaner, a good soldier, but his comrades knew he could moan even on a fine sunny day. It was his nature and, if truth be told, they were glad to be away from the mundane and boring work within the fort. It was exciting to be doing something different.

The path Marcus took them along followed the bubbling mountain stream. The biggest danger was not the snow which was beginning to turn to slush close to the water but the slippery rocks that could turn and break an ankle quickly. Once clear of the stream it became heavier going and Marcus soon began to alternate the leading trooper to help the breaking of the snow. The bright, cold day had formed a crust on the top of the knee-deep snow and the path breaker soon found his feet chilled to the bone. He could see that their work would be a little easier as the snow was quite thin in part. It would soon be completely gone; easier for his men to work but increasing the danger of a visit from their enemies.

As they approached the mound Marcus admired the skill his leader had shown in spotting the potential as an outpost. The mound had a gentle slope from the south whilst it was sheer from the north. The stand of trees on the summit and at the southern side meant that there would be both protection and disguise for the outpost and men.

While his troopers rested and ate their rations at the foot Marcus climbed to the summit. Once at the summit the view was spectacular.

The Sword of Cartimandua

Northwards he could see the steep-sided valley they had followed to get to the fort. To the west was another steep-sided valley and to the east, there was an escarpment, a fast-flowing river and a plain heading towards the fort. They would need to be investigated. Marcus looked at the sun in the sky. They had most of the day ahead of them and the path to the fort was clear. He would send patrols out quickly while he and the rest began their work. He glanced around the summit and saw that it would not take as much work as he had thought to prepare a defensible, hidden outpost.

He descended and gathered his men around him. "Decius, take Gaius and explore that eastward facing valley. As soon as you know the lie of the land return we have much work here." The last comment was a ploy by the decurion as it would ensure that the moaner did a thorough job and would avoid returning too hastily for manual labour. Grumbling Decius led off his companion. "Julius, take Marcus and follow the stream to the west. I think it must return to the lake. Return here once you know that. As for the rest of us, we have to make an outpost and the sooner it is finished the sooner we can return to a warm fire."

He divided the men into two groups. One of them was detailed to make a stable in the copse at the foot of the mound. He made quite clear to his men that they were to disguise it as much as possible so that, from a distance, it would appear natural. Taking the majority of men to the top he gave them similar instructions. "Cut down saplings and thin trees from lower down. Join up the trees here to make a tower. We will leave the entrance at the south for a swift getaway in case we are disturbed."

The men set too and within no time they had a rudimentary tower. The second phase was harder as they had to build a rampart and a ladder but to the Romans, it took a little longer than the time it had taken to walk from the fort.

"Men approaching!" As soon as the sentry shouted the men took up their defensive positions. "It is the scouts Decius and Gaius."

Marcus noticed that Decius looked pleased that all the hard work had been completed. His report pleased Marcus. "The valley is steep-sided all the way to the head. There is a stream but you could not get a large force down." He pointed northeast, "There is a path which

The Sword of Cartimandua descends through a forest from the northern spur but it would only take a single file of men. Their ponies might be able to cross it but I fear our cavalry mounts would struggle over the rocks which litter the path." Marcus nodded pleased. It meant that even if a large force used that route it would take some time to deploy and the outpost would have time to warn the fort.

"Good work. Well done. We are finished here."

"Men approaching!" Once again they came quickly to arms. "It is the other patrol."

Their report was of a similar nature. The stream did indeed flow to the lake and the escarpment was steep. There was a ford which his men had used and Marcus made a note of it on the rough map he had drawn. That would be a danger to the fort.

"Well done men, now back to a warm fire."

Tired as they were by their exertions the walk back was quicker than the one out and they arrived at the almost completed fort well before dark. Ulpius was satisfied with the report. Brutus also noted the comment about the ford. "I will have my men prepare an observation post at the ford. If we are attacked we may be able to slow them down. If this snow remains I feel we are safe."

"Aye the gods are smiling on us and long may the snow continue. The more work we can complete the safer we will be." Ulpius would have felt even better had he known that Venutius was looking in the wrong place for them and Caesius Alasica was mobilising his forces for an invasion of the north. As it was he had to believe that they were the isolated bait on a trap.

After he had seen to his men and enjoyed his evening meal Marcus wandered over to the wagon which still housed the two Brigante princesses. As the wagon had been emptied the sisters had taken it and divided it into two both for privacy and to avoid squabbles which inevitably arise when two women are in close domestic proximity. He coughed when he reached the dimly lit wagon. "Come in. I saw you from across the fort."

Once inside they embraced and kissed. Marcus felt like a young boy stealing from an orchard. He was happy beyond his wildest dreams. His life could not get any better. Macha lay in his arms. There was a comfortable silence and Marcus nuzzled her hair. She looked

The Sword of Cartimandua

up. "I have news." He wondered what she was about to say. He had heard things from his lover about the Brigante in these private moments. Was it to be news of the enemy? "I am with child; your child."

The shocked silence surprised Macha until she saw the enormous grin spread across his face. "Are you sure? Of course, you are! When will…Are you…"

She put her hands across his lips. "In the summer you will see your child and yes I am well and will remain so. Brigante women are strong." They kissed again and Marcus held her tightly to his body. "It is strange the way the gods work. My sister was with child and was murdered and a new child comes into the world at the same time."

"The gods are wise. Perhaps your sister will be watching over us now."

"Oh, she is Marcus. Lenta and I have felt her presence since we laid her in the tomb. She is here. She is the snow; she is the light, she is the warmth we feel now."

They lay down beneath the bear robes and slept. Marcus would awake before dawn and return to his troopers but all the fort knew of the liaison. It was the biggest open secret and yet no one felt the need to criticise or comment.

The high hills east of Brocavum

Venutius and his bodyguards were cold and despondent. Despite a week's trudging through the high hills to the east and south of Brocavum they had seen no signs of the Romans. They had come to the conclusion that if the Romans had ventured this far they had perished in the cold. There was still a nagging doubt and fear in the mind of the Carvetii king that they would have seen signs of their bodies had that been the case. They scanned the skyline for a sighting but saw a sea of white.

Fainch had watched them approach. After meeting her sisters they had dreamed a powerful dream. The potion they had used was a powerful one leaving them exhausted but they had dreamed a dream and Venutius would be pleased when she told him She had been as still as stone, waiting as though part of the landscape. . She used all her guile and wiles to impress men with her power and she did so

The Sword of Cartimandua

again. She knew they would pass by her, she would be almost invisible and as they did so she stood up. To the warriors, it was as though she had appeared from the ground. With her haggard lime painted face and hair, her ragged grey cloak she looked like a wraith. Even Venutius was startled until he realised it was his spy. The men's hands grasped their amulets and muttered incantations against the evil eye. Fainch just smiled. "Hail mighty king. I bring news."

Venutius ordered his men to rest while he took the witch by the elbow so that they would not be overheard. "It must be powerful news to bring you out onto the hills in such weather and to make you forget my orders." There was a threat in his voice as he spoke.

"It is. I am not one of your mindless minions who cannot think for himself. I would not have made the journey were it not urgent. The Romans have a new leader and, even as we speak, he is bringing an army to attack you. He is building a fort and bridge at the great river and he brings not only horsemen but legionaries."

"Do we know him?"

She nodded. "It is Marcus Caesius Alasica and whilst he is young he is no fool."

"You did well to bring the news to me. I have begun the muster but this weather is slowing it down. Is there nothing you could do about the weather?"

She shook her head. "It would take many of my sisters to make the change. "She looked up into the sky. "I can tell you that within seven nights the snows will be gone."

"That is enough. How many men will he bring?"

"He has a whole legion and some cavalry. Have you found the Romans I warned you of?"

"Not yet. I thought they were in this region but it seems they must have passed us by. They must be in the west. How many were there?"

She shrugged unsure of the actual numbers, "A warband size; some cavalry and some infantry."

"No matter. I will destroy them when I have taught these Romans a lesson about fighting in my lands." He drew her closer to him. "I have been thinking of late. These Romans fight well because they are well supplied, they have solid bases. If we were to make their bases a

The Sword of Cartimandua

little less secure it might slow them down." Fainch remained silent; she was not sure where the king's thoughts were leading. "Fires at the docks in Eboracum. Damage to their ships. Poisoned wells and food. All of these would plant doubt in the minds of the people and make the Romans look over their shoulders. Do you think you have enough people to do this?"

Fainch thought for a few moments calculating the number of men and women she could trust and working out how many she could buy. "I think I could but it is dangerous work. The more people I use the more risk I am discovered."

"Your work at Eboracum will mean nothing if we are defeated. We must risk all if we are to beat these Romans."

She nodded. "Perhaps some of your warriors could raid the settlements of the Roman families. It worked for Boudicca."

"That is why I love you Fainch you have a chieftain's mind in a princess's body."

"There is something else oh mighty king. My sisters joined with me for the dreaming. We dreamed a powerful dream."

"And?" Venutius felt a range of emotions; a good dream would give his men the heart and desire to rid the land of the Romans.

"We dreamed an eagle which took a lamb. Before it could eat it a wolf came and devoured the eagle and the lamb."

"And I am the wolf?" She nodded. Excellent I will tell my chieftains at the muster. With that dream, we cannot lose." He turned to his men. "Mount we return home."

His men cast furtive, curious glances as they left wondering, not for the first time, what powers the witch possessed. Some of them had heard her tell the king of the dream and it both pleased and frightened them. None of them would dream of crossing her even though she appeared to be a slight, pretty female; to them, she was a monster transformed by the gods and they were glad she was on their side. Fainch, for her part, smiled the secret smile of a woman who was superior to all she knew. Venutius was merely a pawn in her grander, greater plan. The Romans were an obstacle that could be removed by Venutius, if not Venutius then another leader; as long as they believed in her supernatural power they would not oppose her. The return to

The Sword of Cartimandua
Eboracum would give her time to plan her campaign of treachery and death. They would pay for the destruction of Mona and her love.

The Sword of Cartimandua
Chapter 14

Morbium

"This looks a good place for a fort." Alasica sat astride his horse on a steeply sided bluff overlooking the river. His engineers had already begun to build a wooden bridge that would enable him to harass the rear of the Carvetii forces.

Quintus Aurelius, one of his young tribunes ventured a suggestion. The area to the north of the river looks flatter and bigger. It would make a better fort."

"You have a good eye Quintus and it may be that we will build a permanent fort there once we have subdued the barbarians but right now this site will protect the bridge and can be held by a small force. Archers could wreak havoc on a barbarian force trying to cross the bridge. Get the men started and keep the cavalry patrols out. I do not want to be surprised whilst we are so few in numbers." Almost without thinking the young general looked over his shoulder to the south almost as though he expected the twentieth to be marching towards him. At the moment his forces were too few in numbers to be anything more than an annoyance for Venutius; the legion would give him real striking power.

"Sir the scouts are back."

Galba dismounted as the three Tungrian scouts returned. Their mission had been to follow the river as far as they could.

They saluted and the leading man spoke. "There is nowhere closer to the sea to cross the river. There are other places to build bridges not far from here but this is the narrowest. The river goes North West to the point where it is a waterfall. From there on men could walk across the river. It would be half a day's travel for the barbarians."

Galba dismissed the men with a wave. His intuitive military mind had chosen the best site for a bridge; the east did not worry him. The Brigantes who lived there were allies. It was in the west where he would face his stiffest opposition. His eyes drifted to the thin line of hills to the west and he wondered how his isolated forces were managing. The white edge to the hills told him that it would still be some time until he could get a messenger to them. He could only hope that they would still be alive and still be able to be an asset by the time the main force arrived.

Venutius' scouts leaned forward over their ponies to keep a lower profile as they watched the Romans like busy bees scurrying around the river.

"I could take the leader out with an arrow from where we are."

"Aye, and if you missed our heads would be hanging from the saddles of those Roman scouts. Our job is to report back to the king and I think we have seen enough."

Brocavum

By the time they reached the King, they were exhausted; a mixture of thick snow and an icy wind as they crossed the summits took its toll. Even so, they were careful to report immediately to the king whose fiery temper was legendary. "They are building a fort and a bridge north of Cataractonium. They are few in number; some legionaries building the bridge, archers and horsemen. "We should attack now lord while they are weak." The speaker was a grizzled old warrior with so many scars it looked as though he had been carved from an ancient oak.

"Eneit you are a brave warrior and if the snows were gone I would do as you advise but not all the warriors we summoned have arrived and we would be weak after travelling through the snow. No, be patient. They believe their fort will help them but it will not. When we have all our men mustered we can strike at their weak points. We are protected by these steep hills while they have their people in wide-open plains where we can make our numbers tell. By the next moon, the snows will be melting and then we will strike."

His men knew of the witch Fainch and felt that she could see into the future. All would be well and they would drive the Romans back into the sea and claim the Brigante land for themselves.

Eboracum

At Eboracum, in the wide-open plains, Venutius' plan was already working. Fainch had set her web of women to cause as much trouble as possible. The plan to fire the ships would have to wait as there were none in port and so the warehouses were empty. There were, however,

The Sword of Cartimandua

many Roman soldiers in the town and although Fainch's spies could not enter they could cause problems when the legionaries left the safety of the fort and ventured into the huts and hovels which were springing up. Food could be poisoned; wine and ale could be tainted. Occasionally an optio could be murdered. Fainch was careful to avoid causing so much fear that the Romans reacted by tightening security.

For the Roman's part, they put the large number of men down with stomach disorders down to the poor local food and climate. The deaths were small in number but the sick list was becoming a problem.

Fainch realised that she had begun to affect the Romans when Alasica and his bodyguard returned to Eboracum. He immediately went to the commandant's house and spoke to Quintus Valerius Corvus. "You have suffered some losses which were not sustained in battle. How did they occur?"

"The men became ill and some died. I do not know where the disease came from."

"Were the men who became ill from the same barracks?"

"No, they were from a number of barracks."

"And the men who were killed where did their deaths occur?"

"They were killed in the town."

"They were all officers?"

Quintus looked up surprised. He had not made the connection but now he had had the suggestion made it became obvious. "All of them. Do you think there is a connection?"

"I think that we need to stop the men frequenting the town first of all. I know the merchants will squeal and the men will moan but I care not. Then I want you to have the preparation of the food supervised. I am worried that, as the Queen was poisoned the men may be suffering the same fate. Let us see if this cures the problem. Increase the patrols and admit no one to the fort. It may be a coincidence but in light of the death of the Queen I am not willing to take any chances."

Fainch realised that her original plan was not working and she began to put in place her secondary plan, not as dramatic but designed to disrupt insidiously, slowly, painfully. She knew that the soldiers might obey orders but they would also obey their lustful needs. They would find a way to seek out women, or boys, who would satisfy their desires. They might not be the officers but it would be a drip-feed. She knew where the objects of the soldier's desires housed and it was simple enough to sell beer at low prices to the prostitutes around the camp. The tainted beer would not kill but would cause such wracks of pain and sicknesses that they would not be able to work or fight for days. The fact that some of them might die would be a bonus. The ships which now made their way up to the new jetties were also a means of subversion; the drinks she sold, again at much-reduced prices, would cause death or illness when the ships were on their way back to Gaul. The effect would not be apparent for a while but it would eat into both the ships and the morale of the sailors. Her final plan was to find some way to rid her land of Alasica who was far too effective to be allowed to live.

Glanibanta

Ulpius and Marcus took a stroll in the first morning light to survey the work at Glanibanta. Even at this early hour, they could see the men picking river and lake mussels to supplement their diet. Once they had built a boat they would be able to fish. "It is going well, sir. The walls are finished and the gates and towers are now ready to be defended."

"It is. We were lucky that there was so much stone around here. Although I think," he looked up and touched the amulet he had taken from the Queen's body, "that the Queen had all of this planned. I think she intended this to be our home. Are the outposts complete?"

"They are and manned. It means that we are two turmae short but they can both be back here in a short time. The docks and jetties are finished but until we have ships they are not needed."

Ulpius nodded and looked towards the barrack fort that Orrick and his men were building. The houses had been the first thing to be built, unlike the Roman way which built walls first but the winter weather had made that decision for them. The plentiful timber and slates had made the job easier; had the enemy harassed them it would have been a different situation for then the men would not have been able to devote so much energy to the building. "I will be happier when their walls are finished. The gods have favoured us so far but with this snow melting so rapidly we must be vigilant for I cannot believe that the Carvetii will not pay us a visit soon." The snows had indeed begun

The Sword of Cartimandua

to melt and there had been no serious snowfall for many days. The paths around the settlement and to the northern outpost were just a slushy mass and the first spring bulbs were beginning to erupt. Soon they would come and as he surveyed his command he realised that his men both Roman and allies would be ready. The Via Praetoria and the Via Principalis both made life moving around the camp easier and gave the men a sense of order. The Praetorium was built and, as in all forts, the hub of activity.

He glanced over at his young subordinate who was looking towards the strongly made home just inside what would be the Brigante fort. He was thinking of his princess and their child. The hurt inside of him did not diminish but it softened his pain to think that someone else would have the family that had been so cruelly wrenched from him.

"How is the princess?"

"She is well. Her condition seems to make her even more beautiful."

Ulpius smiled at the young man's love. "Ay, motherhood will do that. We should thank the Allfather that she has prospered in such a dark and dank climate."

"I have already made a sacrifice."

"Good. It does not do to anger the gods. Who takes out the patrol today?" He asked the question already knowing the answer. It was Marcus' duty but he wondered if his devotion to Macha would have made him delegate that duty. He was pleased with the reply.

"It is my duty. I thought I would take the trail to the northeast. We have seen little sign of life to the south and west."

"Be careful. Now is the time when they will have their patrols out and I would prefer us to see them first. Take no chances." Even though it was still dark Marcus would leave to give him, and the patrol the daylight they needed. This time of year saw the days become a little longer but not by much.

Decius Flavius had not stopped being the moaner of the turma but over the winter he had become a harder working member of the troop and Marcus could see that he had potential as he was both clever and a good soldier. He was someone on whom he could rely. It was for that reason he sent Decius with young Gaius as the lead riders, scouting

The Sword of Cartimandua

just over the horizon. The fact that they were the smallest men in the troop also helped as it meant they were harder to spot on the skyline.

They had already worked out that the eastern valley was a dead end and too steep to allow many men to use it; they had come down the north to south valley and so Marcus head north and west. The first part of the patrol was relatively easy and there were trees and bluffs to hide them. He could see in the distance great craggy mountains which would be impassable to his horse. There was a curving twisting trail through the woods which severely tested both riders and horses but it meant they were shielded from enemy scouts. He could only hope that he could find a pass once he reached the ridgeline.

They were resting their horses at a small lake when Gaius rode in hard and at speed. "Sir, Carvetii."

Instantly his men mounted their horses and took a defensive position around the leader and his scout. "Where?"

"To the north. There is a large lake and the land around it is flatter than here. Decius is hiding and watching them."

"How many are there?"

"It looks to be about three turmae of men, about a hundred. There were others with them, boys and old men but the warriors were armed and some were mounted. Decius thought they were heading for Brocavum."

Marcus nodded. That made sense. Realising that he could be walking into a trap he summoned one of his younger troopers. "Ride back to the fort and report to the decurion princeps. Tell him we are heading North West to investigate a hundred warriors who look as though they are joining Venutius. We will stay with them until we know where they are heading. " The trooper saluted, vaulted his horse and set off at a gallop. Marcus shook his head; at least the message would arrive quickly. "Mount. Gaius, you lead."

His men were now fully alert. They had overheard enough to realise there were three times as many enemies awaiting them as they had; who knew how many others were in their path. They all knew that musters of warbands could number in the thousands and this small patrol was already far from friends. Marcus looked up at the steep mountains which stood like giants to the west and the north. Luckily for the troop, the path taken by Gaius was neither steep nor difficult.

The Sword of Cartimandua

Gaius stopped suddenly and rode next to Marcus. "Just over this rise is a stand of trees and bushes. You can see their camp and still be hidden."

Marcus turned to Julius. Keep the men mounted. I will go and talk to Decius." Dismounting he handed the reins to one of his men. The two auxiliaries dropped to all fours, an undignified manner of moving but one which meant it was unlikely they would be seen. Decius heard them and could not resist a grin as he saw them scurry like drunken men trying to get home.

The spot chosen by his scouts was a good one. The lake and valley stretched northwards and then took a slight North West curve. It was very wide at its southern end. He could have brought his men up mounted as the tree and bush line was quite thick. The barbarian force was moving eastwards. It was an untidy straggle of warriors but Marcus was not fooled they could be on him in moments if he was seen. "Sir!" Decius saluted. "They broke camp just after I sent Gaius to you. I counted a hundred and ten warriors and forty old men and boys. You can see the leaders by the horses and the armour. All the warriors have swords or spears. The old men and boys have bows and slings."

"Good report. Now are they looking for us or are they heading for the muster?" Decius coughed. "Well spit it out, man. If you have an idea then tell me."

"Well there were no scouts out and they looked to be heading east." He pointed down the hillside. "You can see the trail they would have taken if they were heading for the fort and they have passed it."

"Good. You two stay here while I bring the men forward." As he ran back to his men he wondered what Ulpius would do and, not for the first time, he began to realise the weight of responsibility on his young shoulders. If the enemy knew about the fort they could easily assault it, the trick would be to follow them without the Carvetii discovering their presence. Not an easy task. If he followed them closely he risked being spotted, if he trailed them at a distance he risked losing them or worse risked them ambushing him. He peered around the skyline. Soon they would lose the trees and with them their cover; if the enemy continued east they would soon come to a hill too steep for their mounts. He made his decision they would wait until

The Sword of Cartimandua
they had passed and then follow. He could only hope that there were no places for an ambush. He turned to his troopers. "Dismount and finish your meal. We will wait until they have passed."

To the younger men of the turma, it seemed an age that they waited but Marcus wanted to make sure there was not a rearguard watching for just such a move. If he had been with the chieftain and his bodyguard he would have realised that the enemy was blissfully unaware of their presence and believed that the Romans were still east of the mountain range.

Maeve had a small settlement at the northern end of the lake. Although there were only ten warriors in his village Maeve was as proud of them as any king. As he pulled up his breeks he spat. He would have been with the rest of the tribe if it were not for Earl Woolgar his half-brother. Although Maeve owed allegiance to him they had fallen out over some cattle and Maeve had determined that, whilst he would fight for Venutius and drive the Romans from his homeland he would do so as the leader of his own band however small it was. He was annoyed with himself almost as much as he was annoyed with the king for the early muster meant his people would go hungry and he wished he had sown his small fields first.

He turned to look at his men. He was pleased that they had brought not only their spears but also their bows. He mounted his pony and drew his sword, Ban. Pointing the sword at the path skirting the lake to the south they set off, a determined band of warriors who would be the first to strike a blow at the Romans.

Although they were on foot these hardy warriors were able to move at the pace of a pony. The hills were steep around the lake and the men had the stamina of mountain goats. Maeve had no need for scouts; this was his land and he knew every piece of grass on it and his keen eyes scanned the land for anything which was out of place. It was he who noticed the hoof prints. He instantly knew that they were not his people for they were in a line and the size was bigger than their ponies. He held up his hand. "Romans! And they are ahead of us." He gestured to Garve a powerfully built warrior who could run for days. "Head up towards Tor hill you will be able to see into the next valley." The man set off at a loping pace and the rest of the tribe trotted

The Sword of Cartimandua
purposefully forward. Even Maeve was surprised sometime later when Garve appeared, almost from nowhere, like a spirit from the ground.

"You are right. There are Romans on horses. They are following Earl Woolgar and the rest of the tribe."

"How many?"

"There are three for each one of us."

Maeve nodded. An attack was out of the question. He would have to be cunning and use the tactics he had used against the Novontae when stealing their cattle. He would use the dark and see how many of the enemy he could kill.

The first that Marcus or any of the auxiliaries knew about the attack was when the third guard gurgled a scream as the arrow caught him in the neck. The other two had died instantly one to an arrow the other to a sharp knife. It was to their credit that the Romans reacted automatically, hands going to weapons. The Carvetii had the advantage for their eyes were accustomed to the dark and so it was that two more of Marcus' men died before they could respond.

Marcus raced towards the sound of blade on blade and he was gratified to see Decius guarding his left side and behind them both young Gaius, spatha in hand. The first warrior he saw had his back to him and he thrust his spear at the unguarded leg of Aquinius. Marcus' sword severed one arm and then slashed across the neck of the warrior. As the three of them went forwards Marcus began to wonder how many men they faced. It was an ambush but he could see little. It was fortunate that he had ordered his men to sleep in their corselets. Gaius suddenly darted to the side and caught one of the enemy with a glancing blow to his spear. Before he could join him, Marcus found himself facing a huge warrior with a mighty sword. Even as he advanced he sensed a movement to his left and, from the corner of his eye he saw Decius deflect the axe which would have sliced through his leg. As it was the minor distraction had allowed Maeve, for it was the Carvetii chieftain who faced him, to hack down at Marcus' arm. His training took over and he turned the thicker blade easily. He took an easy wide stance, this would not be easy; his opponent had flecks of grey in his beard and his torc told the story, he was a chief. Behind him, the Romans began to gain the upper hand as their numbers told.

The Sword of Cartimandua

Maeve and Marcus were oblivious to it all; thrust was met by counter thrust but gradually Marcus' youth and his training took over. The long reach of the spatha and his superior height meant that the end was inevitable. A trip over a clump of grass-covered rocks made the Carvetii warrior slip and the Roman sank his blade into the unprotected left arm. Maeve did not make a sound but he realised that he would die soon; he could see his dead and dying companions lying around. He needed to get away and warn the king. Recklessly racing forward he hacked at Marcus who retreated slightly giving the Briton the chance to discard his battered shield, run to his pony, mount and gallop away.

Later on, Marcus realised he should have given chase immediately but he did not know how many enemies remained and how many of his own men still lived. By the time they had discovered that their entire enemies were dead or dying it was too late to pursue. Realising that they were safe Marcus set sentries and told Gaius to look after the wounded. "Decius, are there any still living?"

A moment or two later Decius shouted over. "Here."

It was a young warrior and the lifeblood was seeping from his arm. He would not last an hour. "Where were you going?"

The young warrior shook his head. Inside he wondered why the normally brave Maeve had fled leaving them there to die. He felt betrayed and the pain was hurting; he could not believe how much a blade could hurt.

Marcus looked at Decius who nodded. He removed the young warrior's breeks and held his knife under his testicles. "Now I know you are brave but would you go to the Allfather half a man or a whole man?"

"Kill me, you Roman bastard! Kill me!"

"Oh we will but first my friend here will slice off your manhood. Then remove your eyes. You will wander sightless and dickless for all eternity." He paused to allow the thoughts to sink in. "Or you can tell me where you were going and who your leader was and I will put your sword in your hand and we will give you a warrior's death." The sadistic look in Decius' eyes convinced him to tell what in truth was not secret information but it galled the young man to do something so traitorous.

The Sword of Cartimandua

"We were summoned to the muster by the king."

"And who is this we?"

"Earl Woolgar and his warriors."

"He was your leader?"

"No that was Maeve his brother," Marcus nodded; that must have been the warrior he had faced. He would remember the names, both of them for it could help to understand the command structure of the enemy. "And you were headed for?"

"Brocavum."

Marcus smiled. "There, that was not so hard was it?" As he put the sword in his hand he nodded to Decius who thrust his sword into the warrior's throat. "He was brave."

"He was fucking stupid. He could have had you when you gave him the sword and he would still have had a soldier's death."

Marcus smiled wryly. Decius was a fierce warrior in battle. "Then thank the Allfather he was more like me and less like you. What is the butcher's bill?"

"Eight dead and two wounded."

"Can they ride Gaius?"

"Yes sir, they can ride."

"Then let us take our dead and return to the fort we have discovered what we need to." By the time they had tied their companion's bodies to their horses, dawn was breaking. Marcus saw that the older troopers had taken the heads of the enemy. While Marcus did not do it himself he knew that the enemy hated this. It would have an effect.

Glanibanta

"Where is he? He should have returned yesterday?"

Lenta put her arms around her sobbing sister. "Do not upset yourself so you have a child within you. Ulpius said that they might be out all night. He will return. Remember the father of your unborn child is a warrior and warriors sometimes die."

Slumping to the floor the pregnant princess began to dab at her eyes. "I know but I would have some time with him as a husband before that happens."

The Sword of Cartimandua

It was a contentious issue and Marcus and Macha had argued about this. As an auxiliary Marcus needed permission to marry. Lenta wondered why he had not asked Ulpius whom she knew would have given permission. When he returned he would suffer the sharp edge of Lenta's tongue. Her sister had been looking healthy and well but, since he had been on patrol, she was beginning to look a little drawn. Cartimandua's death had been so sudden and so unexpected that both sisters felt vulnerable. When they had hidden from Venutius and fled his forces they had known the risks; it was galling to lose a sister in the safety of a fort. Lenta did not blame the Romans but wondered if her sister's death could have been avoided. Orrick and his warriors had warned Lenta and Macha that the tribes were gathering. They were all in a difficult position; if the Carvetii won then all the Brigante who had supported them would be slaughtered. If the Romans prevailed then Lenta, Macha and Orrick would lose all their power and would be subsumed by the Roman imperial machine. Cartimandua had had a plan but neither Macha nor Lenta was privy to it.

Not for the first time since the patrol had headed north did Ulpius stand in the northwestern tower almost willing his men to return. He had felt disquiet when the messenger told him of Marcus' plans. If the fort was in a parlous position then the patrol was even more so. They were isolated with no friends within a week's march. Every bush and rock could conceal an enemy. It was two days since the messenger had arrived and the decurion princeps had hoped that a second would have brought a progress report. He could not bring himself to chide or castigate his young protégé, after all, Ulpius had trained him and he could find no fault with the young warrior's actions. Even so, the waiting was something to which the man of action could not become accustomed.

"Stand to!"

The gates were slammed shut and the fort called to arms at the sentries warning. The snows had gone from all but the higher hills which made it harder to make out the line of figures. As soon as the horses could be made out it was obvious that it was the returning patrol. The sentry looked at Ulpius to see if he ordered the watch to stand down. Ulpius shook his head. "We'll stay alert. This may be a

The Sword of Cartimandua

trick. They are Roman horses, they are dressed in our uniform but until they speak we will be wary."

He felt rather than saw the two princesses clamber up the ladder. It would have been churlish of him to chastise them for this breach of rules not to mention the potential health hazard of a pregnant princess falling from the ladder and he understood their anxiety.

"It is Marcus! He is alive." Macha's face lit up as she was the first to recognise her man.

Ulpius frowned when he saw the bodies draped over the backs of the horses. He shouted down. "Get the surgeon!"

Even though every part of Marcus yearned to be with his love his duty dictated that he reported to Ulpius and, in truth, his report was vital. Ulpius took him into the now complete fort Headquarters. The brazier in the corner gave off immediate heat which to the half-frozen Marcus was a lifesaver. Ulpius waved his hand for his protégé to sit and handed him a goblet of honeyed warm wine. His desire and need for the valuable information in Marcus' head was counterbalanced by the understanding that he had been through an ordeal; the dead bodies draped over the horses was testimony to that.

Eventually, Marcus told him of the patrol culminating in the ambush. "So Venutius is ready to strike but towards us or towards Eboracum?" Although he was talking to himself Ulpius was also trying to establish if Marcus had any further information.

"I do not think they were aware of our fort here. We saw no signs of armed men either on our way out or back. But I fear that the fact that the Carvetii escaped means they will track us."

"Aye, we will have to assume that is the case. I will waste no more messengers asking for help either our forces will be moving towards us as we were told or we will be on our own. We will improve the defences. But not you. Go see your woman and rest you and your men have done well." He paused and his one eye lit up. "As I knew you would."

The Sword of Cartimandua
Chapter 15

Brocavum

As the battered and wounded Maeve urged his mount towards the muster he wondered how Venutius would take the news. He was not an easy lord to follow as many of his men had discovered. His obvious courage, strength and martial skills were countered by a cruel nature and a violent temper. He gripped his sword and looked to the skies; it was in the Allfather's hands now.

As he crested the brow of the valley before Brocavum he was amazed by the host he could see in the distance. It looked as though every warrior had already arrived. Surely with a host this size, even the mighty Roman army could be destroyed. Riding down the steep slopes he pondered on the Romans he had fought. It was the first time he had been bested and he realised that he could have died at the hands of the young Roman warrior. Hitherto they had respected the Roman ability to fight in tight lines, shoulder to shoulder but every Carvetii warrior believed that in single combat they would win. His dead comrades gave that statement the lie.

The fact that he arrived alone meant that Venutius demanded he attend him immediately. In the huge hall with all the chieftains gathered the High king sat on a raised platform on a mighty throne. He was deliberately intimidating. He had to keep his vassals in awe of him.

"You come alone Lord Maeve where are your warriors or are they with your brother?"

Every eye stared at the warrior whose wounds were still apparent. "We found some Romans and ambushed them but they were alert and they defeated us."

Venutius' eyes narrowed. "They defeated you? Did you outnumber them?" Maeve lowered and shook his head. "You attacked at night?"

"Yes my King, but their guards gave warning and they had armour."

"Where did they come from these Romans?"

The Sword of Cartimandua

"They were horsemen and we found their tracks coming from the land of the lakes."

For the first time, Venutius looked confused. He had expected Romans from the west but he had believed that the south was safe as the Deceangli were still fighting the Romans in Mona. Suppose he had two huge armies to face? He had a mighty host but he could not fight two conflicts against two armies. On the other hand, it could have been a patrol from the army to the west.

He rose, towering over his warriors. "You have disappointed me. You have been defeated by a handful of Romans and you have failed to do as I asked which was to discover where the Romans were. What have you to say?"

"I know that I have let you down but I believed that my information was vital. I would else have died with my sword in my hand." The proud warrior stared defiantly at his king.

"And that is the only reason why you still have a head on your shoulders. Summon Earl Woolgar."

The Earl must have been outside for he appeared within a heartbeat. He glared at Maeve when he entered. It was obvious in an instant that they were half brothers for both had inherited their father's looks. They could have been twins but for their dress. Earl Woolgar had more jewellery and finer clothes than his poorer brother. "Your warrior here has dishonoured your tribe. To redeem you and your people I want you to take your warband to the land of the lakes. Find these Romans without them seeing you. When you find them send a message to me. If it is a patrol you can destroy it, if it is an army then I will come to defeat it. Do you think you can do this?"

The sarcasm in his voice made the older warrior colour. "I will my lord and if it is a patrol I will return with their heads on my lance."

When he was outside he looked with disgust at his half brother. There was no love lost between them with Maeve blaming the Earl for taking his birthright. He had felt humbled and angry when he had heard his people disparaged all because of his half brother. Much as he wanted to kill him there out of hand he knew that family loyalty meant he could not. "Take your miserable self back to your farm. When we have defeated these Romans, I will decide on your punishment."

The Sword of Cartimandua

Morbium

Caesius Alasica stared intently at the almost complete bridge. His legionaries had done well in appalling condition. This northern land was cold and inhospitable; for the Iberian soldiers, it must have seemed to be Hades. The last few touches were being applied and he knew that the following day would see the invasion of the land of the Carvetii. His auxiliaries had kept the lands north and south of the river clear of enemy scouts. The Roman leader's nose wrinkled in distaste as he saw the heads of the dead scouts displayed on poles. No doubt it was an effective deterrent but it showed the Roman that his auxiliaries were but a step away from being barbarians themselves. He looked at the native bridge which had enabled them to secure the two banks. Although it had served his needs the Roman could see that the spring floods would sweep it away. He could see the remains of an earlier bridge. His bridge was of stone and would easily withstand flood damage. He looked back at the watchtower his men were building at the top of the ridge. When completed it would give his soldiers early warning of an enemy advancing on the bridge or fort.

He turned to his aid. "Gaius Agrippa, ensure that the centurion in charge of the cohorts building the forts is an experienced man. The last thing we need is for all our work to be undone because the commander here is inexperienced." Gaius nodded but before he could continue Alasica continued with his instructions. "And you, young Gaius, must ensure that the road between here and Eboracum is defended well. Keep it well patrolled. I want our supplies to be with us as soon as we require them. I wish we were closer to the coast for we could use the fleet." He suddenly stopped as though struck by a weapon. "By Mithras of course! Instruct the fleet commander to sail here."

"But we have not secured the coast yet sir."

"From what I have seen they do not possess any ships, let alone fighting ships. As long as the river is deep enough and wide enough then we can save ourselves the effort of building forts and fortlets all the way from Eboracum. I want to know as soon as the first ship arrives. Once the fleet has achieved this they can escort the supplies. It will save a lot of time. We will not need to unload as many at

The Sword of Cartimandua

Eboracum. Excellent! Excellent idea." He slapped his young subordinate on the shoulder as though it had been his idea. Gaius smiled to himself. This was one of the reasons his men would follow him to the ends of the earth for he shared all his success with his men as well as putting himself in harm's way.

"It will be done, commander."

The simple decision meant that Alasica received his supplies quicker than he would had he been at Eboracum. The river journey was less than that at the fortress. It also meant he was in control of his own destiny. He was aware that some of the officials at Eboracum lined their pockets a little too much and it also diminished the effect of the sabotage taking place.

Glanibanta

It was some days later when Macha brought up the subject of marriage. In truth, she would not have done so were it not for the persistence of her sister who took every opportunity to make direct statements to Macha and oblique ones to Marcus. Marcus, being a warrior just thought that Lenta was being a woman and nagging. He said so to Macha. "Your sister seems a little testy of late is there a problem?"

"No she is just, well she is just Lenta you know," she trailed off lamely.

"Perhaps she needs a man?"

Macha resisted the urge to snap at him. He was so naïve when it came to women but she saw an opportunity to bring up the subject of marriage. "No, she has no need of a man. She had a man, a husband, he is dead. She does not need a man. If she had never had a husband then she would need one for her children. All children need a father."

"Good then, our son will be happy for he will have a father."

"He will until Rome decides to send you somewhere else in the Empire and then where will he be? Will I have to find another soldier to look after us?"

Marcus looked shocked as though the idea had never occurred to him which, of course, it had not. He was happy knowing that he was loved and had a son. He had not thought it through. Now that Macha had suggested it to him it was as though Pandora's Box had been

The Sword of Cartimandua
opened. It was true he could be sent anywhere. He still had fifteen years to serve what would happen if they sent him to Egypt or Parthia. "Well, I er that is."

"That is you have not thought about it have you?"

"No, but I am thinking now." He pulled her over to his lap and nuzzled her ear. "I will see Ulpius. I will ask permission to marry."

Macha threw her arms around him but before either could speak Lenta burst in. "At last! Well done brother."

Marcus looked ruefully at her. "Well, at least it means that we will have our own quarters and there will be no eavesdroppers."

Lenta and Macha both laughed. "It matters not husband for we share everything. There are no secrets."

Lenta looked playfully at Marcus' crotch. "No brother, no secrets."

North of Glanibanta

The scouts of Woolgar's warband picked up the trail of Marcus soon after they cross the ridge near the long lake. The Romans had not bothered to hide their tracks and, although the snow had largely disappeared the weary auxiliaries had left an easy trail. Woolgar was still fuming about his treatment at the hands of his king and was reluctant to send back a premature message. With five hundred warriors under his command, he was confident he could deal with any force short of a legion. He seethed at his half brother. Had he joined the muster the problem would not have arisen; no one would know about the Romans and his honour would be intact. He would have to show the king that he was capable of leading larger warbands than his own. He glanced around at the hills; this was a broken, uneven country and Roman legionaries would struggle to keep their famous ordered formations. His lightly armoured warriors would be able to hide and strike from the safety of steep cliffs. Still, he would call on Venutius if it were a legion rather than risking the wrath of his unstable leader for if he suffered the indignity of defeat again he would not put it past the King of the Brigante to have him murdered by one of his witches.

Spring was definitely in the air when they camped in the valley of the two lakes. Woolgar was being cautious. Soon the valley would narrow to a point where it could be held by a line of twenty men. He

The Sword of Cartimandua

wanted his men fresh when they reached there. He looked up from his mutton joint and wiped his mouth with the back of his hand as he scanned the steep skyline. It was many years since he had been here but he was certain that he remembered a twisting path that skirted the escarpment. He turned to Aetre one of his more trusted lieutenants, the son of his sister. Although he had only seen seventeen summers he was a fine warrior and a leader. More important he was a thinker. "Take ten men and see if you can find the path along that ridge." Aetre nodded and quickly left with a file of men.

Although he had only seen seventeen summers he had proved himself to be a clever warrior and the older man, drawn from Woolgar's personal warband trusted him and his judgement. They left their mounts at the foot of the slope close to a small stream and they set off at an easy lope. The land steadily rose, climbing through rowan, elder and pine. They paused briefly at a pond to drink and to enable Aetre to climb a small knoll that overlooked the valley. He could see that there was clearly a path weaving through the forest and he quickly rejoined his men. The path became more uneven with rises and falls; there were sheer drops and it was barely wide enough for two men but it was a path. Behind him, his men smiled at the young warrior's wisdom in leaving their horses. It was drawing on towards dark when the path began to descend. He wondered whether to turn back when he heard a roaring noise in the distance. They trotted on until they came to a waterfall. They descended the steep sides and found a shallow ford through which they could easily wade. The trail on the other side appeared to head up into the valley to the east and he was about to turn back when one of his scouts suddenly drew his attention to a thin tendril of smoke spiralling from the other side of the trees.

Alert to the danger they began to ford the stream, its icy waters chilling them to the bone. Once they were back on the path the forest masked the roaring of the waters but they began to smell not only the smoke but the smell of horses. Aetre held his hand up. He turned to one of his men. "Go back to Earl Woolgar. Tell him of the path, the stream and the waterfall. Tell him we believe there are Romans ahead. We will find out their numbers. Tell him I will send another messenger when I know more." Once more his men wondered at the

The Sword of Cartimandua

wisdom of the youth. He was not blundering into a situation and he was keeping their leader informed. All of the warriors knew of Earl Woolgar's meeting with Venutius and all knew how angry he had been.

They moved steadily on until Aetre stopped them again. The forest ended and he could see, in the darkening evening a man-made structure; it was the Roman tower sitting atop the steep knoll. There was a glow from the foot of the mound and a glimmer of light gleaning from the top. They had found the Romans. Rather than send another man back with half a message Aetre selected his smallest warrior. "Find out how many are there but do not be seen."

He slipped away crawling through the clumps of dead summer weed and grasses. The wind was coming down the valley from the lakes and he crawled in the opposite direction to mask his smell from the horses. He could see they were Romans by their mail and their horses. He was surprised to see a tower; he had travelled this valley before and never seen a tower here. How long had they been here? He could just make out the sentry in the top of the dimly lit building. The others appeared to be reclining and eating at the foot of the tower close to the tethered horses. He was as silent and motionless as a stone as he counted them. It was completely dark by the time the warrior returned. "There are more than ten men there. I counted at least twelve horses. There are men in the tower and they are Romans."

"Good. Go back and tell the lord what you have seen. We will await his instructions here." As his man trotted off Aetre divided his men into watches. Whilst it was dark the light from the Roman fire allowed his men to see movements in the tower leaving the sentries blind to the Carvetii hiding in the forest. Aetre spread his men in a half-circle and impressed on them not only the need for silence but also for vigilance.

Woolgar started his men off long before the dawn. Following the advice of the scout, they went on foot and they were led by the earl himself. The scout warned him of the dangers of the path but Earl Woolgar was desperate to get to grips with the Romans. He pushed them on at a fierce pace losing two men who fell down the scree on the dark hillside; their broken limbs would rule them out of any further fight but the war chief cared not. Speed was of the essence and from the message he deduced it was not a large party; his fifty warriors would be more than enough. Aetre heard them long before they arrived and he went towards them to ensure they could not be heard by the tower. Lying in the dark he had become acutely aware of how far noise could travel and he wanted to warn his kin of the presence of the Romans. He appeared by the side of Earl Woolgar making his bodyguards grip their weapons in alarm.

"Greetings uncle. They have not moved yet. There are only twelve Romans in the tower. The sentries appear to be looking towards the two lakes rather than over here. They changed sentries in the middle of the night."

"You have done well cousin. Can we approach without being seen?"

"We would have to be as the snake and crawl on our bellies but we could. But lord the sun comes soon we must be swift."

"Aye." He turned to his men. "We will follow Aetre. When he crawls so shall you. Spread out and surround the Romans. On my signal we attack. Any man who attacks before the signal will die by my hand." His last statement was for the younger hotheads who were likely to risk death for the glory of first blood.

The ground was cold and damp as they slithered across the open ground close to the tower. They were helped by the fact that their dull and dark clothes blended into the dark ground. There were tufts and clumps of grass and weeds which helped camouflage the lightly armed and unencumbered warriors. In the tower, the guards were stamping their feet to get warm and peering into the lightening sky to the north and east. Lugotrix was eager to close with these Romans and prove his valour. He had yet to earn combat amulets, this would be his opportunity. His arrow was already notched on his bow. He glanced over at Earl Woolgar who raised his sword; coming to a half-crouch he aimed his arrow at the two men in the tower.

The young optio, Julius Brutus, was enjoying himself as this was the first time his half turma had been given this duty. He was relishing the independence of command. His men were the least experienced which was why they had not been given the duty hitherto; they were, as he was young and the turma had only joined the command a few weeks before they left Eboracum. They had not been involved in any

The Sword of Cartimandua

of the battles nor the long patrol but they were keen to prove themselves to the infamous one-eyed commander. Ulpius was forced to use them as he now had another half turma on the lake guarding the south; he recognised the rashness of youth and wanted to protect the affable young optio from himself. The casualties from Marcus' patrol were beginning to cause problems. He knew that in a short time there would be a lightening of the sky to the east that was when he would awaken the rest of his men. It was essential to be prepared for any Carvetii who ventured down the valley; he was determined not to let down the rest of the ala.

The first that Julius Brutus knew of an attack was when he heard the whistle and felt the air move as the sentry next to him fell with an arrow protruding from his neck. He barely had time to duck below the parapet before a second arrow thudded into the roof of the tower.

"To arms!" Even as he shouted he gripped his shield and drew his sword. His men reacted quickly but they were hopelessly outnumbered. Their reaction was to look to the north but their attackers were all around them. Men who had been soundly asleep woke to find a warrior with charcoal covered face slashing down at them with short-bladed seaxes.

Lugotrix discarded his bow and gripped his razor-sharp, short-bladed knife. He saw a sleepy Roman lurch towards him a spear in his hand. The young warrior waited until his opponent thrust at him and then spun around his blade glancing off the man's spine and plunging into his kidney, a mortal wound. He was a warrior at last! Eagerly looking around he pounced upon a Roman who was trying to mount his horse. The young Lugotrix grabbed his trailing leg and they fell in a heap on the ground. They were so close they could smell the sweat on each other's body but the Carvetii could smell something else, fear. "This morning Roman you die," he ripped the knife across the throat of the auxiliary and felt the warm salty blood splash on his face. Feeling exulted he continued to saw through the cartilage until he felt his blade grate against bone. With a sudden rip, he tore the head from the body and stood shouting his triumph. Now all his brothers could see that he was a warrior and he had kills, not just one, for he had three.

The Sword of Cartimandua

Although they gave a good account of themselves their defence was over in minutes. The last Roman to die was the optio who used the tower from which to hurl javelins at the warriors who were busy slaughtering his men. He was brave and knowing he would die he determined to take as many barbarians as possible with him. He took great satisfaction in watching his javelin take a warrior full in the chest. He released a second and saw it hit another in the leg. When he had hurled the last of them he waited in the tower for the death he knew would come. The Carvetii kept up a steady shower of arrows whilst two men made their way up the ladder armed with long spears. Although the young auxiliary managed to hurl a sword and kill one of his attackers the second one managed to wound him as he came through the door at the top of the tower. Julius Brutus, who was now weakened through the loss of blood, fought bravely on, managing to slice through the cheek of the barbarian. The blood from his wound caused him to slip and his assailant killed him with a thrust of his spear into the unarmoured area between his legs; a turn of the lance eviscerating him.

Woolgar's men were excited by their first, easy victory over the Romans and it took all of his power to stop them from firing the tower. "Fools! We have surprise. This tower is here to warn the Romans of an attack from the valley of the two lakes. We can use this." He gestured to one of his men. Take a Roman horse and bring the rest of the warband."

The man vaulted easily on the horse and set off at a fast gallop.

Quintus Carrus and his companion Gaius Sempricus were looking forward to returning to the tower their duty completed. Ulpius had insisted upon two troopers being on duty at the narrow neck of land between the lower lake and the steep hillside. It would provide early warning of an attack and the narrowness of the area meant that two men could easily spot anyone advancing towards the tower. It was not a popular duty as the only shelter was a rock overhang. They knew that their relief would be coming soon and they prepared their horses.

"I hope they have kept the fire going my feet are so cold that I can't feel them."

"Aye and some hot food would not go amiss. Not long to wait now. I just hope our young optio hasn't decided to redesign the tower

The Sword of Cartimandua

or have us performing complicated military manoeuvres I am shattered. I just want my bedroll." They both laughed. They might make gentle fun of their optio but in truth all of the turma liked him. He was a caring commander if a little keen. Quintus and Gaius were the two longest-serving auxiliaries and Marcus had put them in the turma to stiffen its experience.

Suddenly they heard the thud of a galloping horse from the direction of the tower. They were both experienced enough to know what it meant, danger. They both turned to face the noise and drew their javelins. The Carvetii warrior turned around the huge rock in the trail to be faced by two armoured Roman warriors. The two troopers immediately recognised their foe and their training took over; they only needed one javelin thrust to kill him instantly.

As they removed the javelin from the body Quintus realised that their enemy was riding a Roman horse. "There is trouble at the tower. We must return to the fort and warn the commander. Let us be careful." Leading the Roman horse they trotted back towards the tower. The path to the tower twisted through scrub and brush but then it emerged into the killing ground cleared by the auxiliaries. There was another way; the small river ran in a shallow gully off to the side and afforded some cover.

In the tower, Woolgar and his men had long since finished mutilating the corpses and stripping them of weapons and armour. They had found the food and were enjoying the fire as dawn broke. So it was that the two Romans saw the Carvetii moving around the tower long before they were seen. They used the stream as a path that kept them hidden from the watchers. They were just unfortunate that Lugotrix climbed into the tower, the scene of his first victory, to survey the area as one of the Roman horses neighed as it lost its footing. "Romans!" He pointed to the west where the cavalrymen had realised they were seen and reacted quickly. The advantage that the Romans had was that they knew the path and they knew where the fort was. Realising that they could not hide the troopers whipped their horses into a gallop, leaving the water to the relative safety of the path now well worn by the Roman patrols.

Woolgar shouted to the men nearest to the remaining Roman horses. "Get those Romans now!"

The Sword of Cartimandua

By the time they had bridled them and mounted the horses, the two troopers were in the distance. With daylight now upon them, the Carvetii would soon be upon them.

The sentries at the fort had just been changed and so were as alert as they could be. They could hear the horses before they saw them and the speed told them it meant danger. The standing orders were quite clear and the senior sentry shouted, "To arms to arms!" By the time the troopers arrived at the gate, every wall and palisade was manned. The gates were opened and closed again before the nine Carvetii had arrived. When they did arrive a shower of arrows plucked two men from their saddles and the rest retreated to a safe distance from the fort. To say they were surprised was an understatement. They could see two forts bristling with Romans and Brigante heavily armed and secure. The leader who took them back to the tower did not look forward to passing the message along to Woolgar.

Ulpius knew that they could not escape notice for long but, as Quintus made his report he was disappointed that the tower had failed to give them a warning. It had been fortunate that his standing orders had had the mounted patrol out or they would have been surprised. He turned to the decurion next to him. "Senior officers in my headquarters now." He turned to the two troopers. "You have done well. Rejoin your turma."

As soon as he saw the empty horses being led by the handful of scouts Earl Woolgar knew that he was facing a larger force and it was not far away. He had sent for his men as soon as he realised his first messenger had perished. The first elements were making their way into this new camp. The Carvetii chieftain had decided that this flat area with the Roman tower and water close by would be a good base either to defend against roman attacks or use as a springboard to assault the invaders.

From his scouts, he discovered that there were two forts, one Roman and one Brigante, less than a legion but more than a cohort or century. As he quenched his thirst with some warm beer he considered his options. The Romans could not attack Venutius without passing him. They had chosen the site of the tower well for it was a natural bottleneck. If they chose to head west he would soon know and it would play into his hands as it was still Carvetii land patrolled by

Carvetii warriors. Was this a Roman invasion or a diversion? He would need prisoners. He decided not to send a message to Venutius until he knew more. He was still smarting over his treatment at the hands of the king. He would send to the king when he knew everything. He shouted to Aetre whose success had made him the favoured one. "Gather my blood brothers we will go and see these Romans for ourselves."

Glanibanta

Inside the headquarters building, Ulpius was having similar problems of intelligence. From Marcus' report, he knew that the tribes were gathering. From Quintus' report, he knew that there were enough tribesmen to overwhelm his outpost. Was this a patrol like that of Marcus or was it the main force? He looked around at the faces of his senior leaders; Orrick who spoke for the Brigante; Quintus Brutus who led the legionaries and Marcus now promoted to senior decurion. "Well we are blind are we not?" He was pleased that they smiled at his self-deprecating comment. "Or at least half-blind. We need to know what we face."

Orrick was the first to speak. "I can take my scouts out to discover who they are. We will be less easy to spot than your troopers."

"True but I fear they will be watching the fort. Hidden but watching. It matters not whether it is Brigante or Roman they will be watched."

"If we leave at night?"

"Then there may be a chance. Marcus when you led your patrol you headed west did you not? Could we go that way and outflank them?"

"The problem is the hills and the water." He was pleased that Orrick nodded in agreement. "The water and the mountains force you to travel north for half a day before you can even think about turning east and we still have the problem of the narrow valley of two lakes."

"East"

Orrick spoke. "Your young commander is right and the mountains to the east are even higher. There is also a valley, the

The Sword of Cartimandua

valley of the long lake and it comes out close to where Venutius will have his muster."

Ulpius turned to speak to the legionary centurion who had not spoken. "Any thoughts centurion?"

"It seems to me that my legionaries were chosen because they can defend walls." They all nodded their agreement. "But they are the very troops who could force a narrow pass for that is work for men fighting shield to shield. The barbarians cannot stand against such tactics. They fight as individuals. We are not enough to face a huge army but as long as they are equal numbers, my men could easily force them back."

"How narrow is the pass to the north Marcus? You travelled down it last."

"It is ten men wide until you come to the land where the two lakes join where it is quite flat although boggy and marshy, about three hours march and then it narrows again to forty men wide just north of the northern lake."

A plan was forming in his mind. "So if our legionaries can force them back to the wider part then our cavalry would be able to fall upon them?"

Marcus nodded and Orrick spoke up. "The centurion is right the hills to the west are steep, for horses. My men are hillmen. I could take a warband on foot and attack them in the rear at the neck of land between the two lakes."

Their discussion was interrupted by the shout of "Stand to! Riders approaching."

The men quickly raced to the ramparts. The bolt throwers were already cocked although the enemy warriors were too far away to hurt. "That's him."

"Who?" questioned Ulpius.

"The leader of the men I fought. I recognise his hair and beard." Marcus had mistaken the warrior brother of his defeated opponent but it raised his standing amongst the Brigante.

"You did well young Marcus for that is Earl Woolgar. In his youth, he was a mighty warrior and he is one of Venutius' wisest and fiercest leaders."

The Sword of Cartimandua

"So," continued Ulpius, "we can assume it is a large force but not the whole army." His three lieutenants nodded their agreement. "They will, of course, base themselves at our outpost as it controls the pass. How many men would he have with him do you think?"

Orrick pondered for a moment and then said, "He would have at least a thousand. They would be his warband."

Ulpius looked at Decius Brutus. "You can force the pass against a thousand warriors?" It was more of a statement than a question.

"Against undisciplined warriors with little armour? Yes."

"Good, let us retire and I will tell you my plan. If we all approve then we will proceed."

An hour later the plan was finalised. As soon as it was dark Orrick would take a hundred and fifty of his best warriors west to provide the ambush. Ulpius and Marcus would take ten turma as a screen towards the tower. Decius Brutus would follow with his legionaries and two bolt throwers and attack the Carvetii at the pass. The remaining soldiers both Brigante and Roman would defend the Roman fort. As Ulpius said it was a gamble but if they did not strike quickly then perhaps the Carvetii would bring their whole army and destroy them.

Earl Woolgar turned to his nephew. "What do you think?"

"I think that we would lose many men attacking from here. They have the fort defended by the water. We could starve them out. Stop their men getting supplies or we could inform the king."

Woolgar nodded. He had come to the same conclusion. If they had boats then the assault would be easy but as long as they had the lake behind them and the walls defended by the bolt throwers, archers and javelins then they would be wasting lives. "I agree." He turned to his blood brothers. "You have the honour of the first duty. Watch the fort and let no one leave. I will return with more men."

Both forts were filled with the sounds of blades being sharpened and equipment being checked. For the Roman legionaries, who had been largely guards until this moment, it was a chance to show the barbarian horse soldiers what real Romans could do. For the auxiliaries, it was a chance to hit back at the hated Carvetii. When Woolgar had returned he had also brought the heads of the dead

The Sword of Cartimandua

cavalrymen and they had been placed atop long poles for all to see. The Brigante were warriors first and foremost. The fact that they would be partially avenging the death of their Queen was a bonus and they would take few prisoners. The act angered the legionaries more than Ulpius' men who also understood the gesture of removing an enemy head.

As darkness fell Ulpius called his key leaders together. He spoke first to Orrick. "There will be no signal for you to attack for I know not how long it will take us. You will have to judge the time for yourself. I do not think they will be expecting an attack as it is an almost impossible thing I ask of you."

"We will not fail and we will need no signal for as soon as we see them we shall attack."

Ulpius nodded. He knew himself that warriors lost confidence when attacked from a direction they felt was secure. "Marcus you will take six turmae along the right flank, Lucius Emprenius you will take six to the left and I will command the remaining three in the centre."

"But sir that is the most dangerous part. You will be facing the main body of Earl Woolgar."

"Aye Marcus and that is why it is my duty. The men must see me leading. And besides," he smiled at Decius Brutus, "I will be backed by a cohort of the finest legionaries in Britain. Are you sure your bolt throwers can still be effective firing over the heads of my men?"

"It is true they are more effective firing through ranks of men but believe me they will cause chaos falling amongst the ranks who feel secure."

"Good. If there are no further questions may your gods help you tomorrow."

Marcus waited until they had left. "Commander. I have a request."

"I know you wish to be married."

"But how…"

Ulpius smiled. His craggy face made it seem a little lopsided. "I may only have one eye but it sees well enough and besides Lenta spoke to me or should I say took me to task and berated me."

"And?"

"Of course, you may marry. I would have married her sister if time had allowed. Do it now. It will make the women happier."

The Sword of Cartimandua

"Thank you. And will they be safe?"

"A good question. The men we leave are the weakest we have and if we are defeated they will not hold out long. Had we managed to build a boat then they could have escaped on that so I will not lie to you. If we lose then they will be lost. If we win then they will be safe. Now go and marry her before I feel the rough edge of her sister's tongue again."

In the middle of the night, Orrick silently led his men out. They avoided the Carvetii guards by following the mountain stream which fed the lake. They were in the foothills within an hour of leaving the fort. As a precaution, Esca took fifty Brigante and they watched the Carvetii. They would kill them at dawn before the attack.

In the fort, the cavalrymen were mounted and watching the faint light of dawn begin to creep over the steep-sided mountains to the east. Marcus looked at his men. They were now hardened into a battle-ready team. At his right, guarding his sword side was Decius almost the shadow of the decurion. He looked unconcerned as he chewed on a piece of dried horsemeat. Marcus knew that inside he was as wound up as he was. Perhaps Marcus was in a greater turmoil having married the now heavily pregnant Macha and just as suddenly left her. He had everything to fight for.

Just behind the gate, Ulpius fingered the hilt of Cartimandua's sword. It gave him comfort to know it would be with her weapon that he would wreak havoc upon her murderers. Certainly, the Brigante were in awe of the weapon. As Esca had left he had asked Ulpius if he could touch the scabbard. As the thought entered Ulpius' mind he wondered if the young man had achieved his objective; were the sentries dead? He was answered by the sentry who quietly called down. "The signal, sir, from the tree line."

He turned to his men. "Our allies have done their work now it is up to us. Remember we are fighting for Rome but we also fight for our lives. Fight as you have been taught and we will win."

With that, he led his turma forward. The cavalry quickly exited and formed a skirmish line. Ahead of them, the Brigante trotted forward as scouts. Finally, the hobnailed boots of the cohort of legionaries tramped through the gate. As Ulpius watched them he

The Sword of Cartimandua

thought it was a pitifully small force with which to begin a war but it was his army and they would win.

Woolgar was also awake. Sat in the Roman tower, he had spent the night preparing the report he would send to Venutius. It would be a spoken report and he was using one of his wiser lieutenants who would not deviate from his words. Once the report was sent he would begin to prepare his defences. He called his messenger over to him. "Listen carefully and report my words exactly to the king. Tell him that we have found some Romans and Brigante and they have fortified a site at the big lake. They are the size of a large warband, our numbers. We await his orders. Repeat it."

The messenger repeated the report word for word. Woolgar had been careful to avoid any word which might imply cowardice or doubt. Venutius was too unstable to give him an idea that Woolgar was trying to oust him. He heard the horse galloping north and he called for his food. He would eat and then prepare his camp. Above him at the top of the tower, the guard who had been fitfully dozing suddenly became alert. Before he could shout a warning a Brigante arrow entered his neck and his dead body tumbled down the ladder. Woolgar shouted the warning. "To arms to arms!"

The sleepy warriors grabbed the arms they had slept with as Ulpius' cavalry charged across the flat open field before the tower. On the right, Marcus rode his turma close to the stream as did the turma on the left. In the centre, Ulpius headed straight for the tower. That would be where the enemy commander was. Strike the head from the snake and the body would be easily destroyed. The Carvetii outnumbered the Romans but this was the perfect situation for auxiliary cavalry. The tribesmen had no formation and the javelins and spathas wreaked havoc as the solid line of Romans galloped forward. Marcus had the easier task as the ground sloped from east to west and the men there fell back even faster. To his right rode the ever-present Gaius guarding his weaker side. A small group of Carvetii had hidden in a small fold of land behind a rocky outcrop. As the turma wheeled left to drive the fleeing tribesmen towards the legionaries they leapt out and went straight for Marcus. Gaius urged his horse forward and the trooper next to him followed. Leaning forward in his saddle the

The Sword of Cartimandua

auxiliary slashed down severing the warrior's arm. The trooper next to him tried the same manoeuvre but overbalanced and immediately three warriors began hacking at the body. Gaius was now isolated and Marcus had moved forward with the rest of the turma. One of the warriors thrust a spear into the belly of Gaius' horse and he tumbled to the ground. The breath was knocked out of him and the other two rushed towards him teeth bared in anticipation of an easy kill. He still had his shield and as the first of them smashed down with his sword he deflected the blow but in doing so bared his body for a thrust from his companion. Expecting to meet the Allfather Gaius began to mutter his death prayer. As the spear approached Gaius felt a movement out of the corner of his eye and a spatha smashed through the wooden shaft.

"Not so fast you fucking bastard!" Decius then backslashed to take the warrior in the throat. Just as he did so the first warrior tried to stab the unprotected back of the grizzled veteran. Gaius had his wits about him and his sword sliced through his assailant's ankle. Turning Decius despatched him through the throat. "Thanks, young Gaius now let's get back into this war." He charged off on foot to continue killing Carvetii.

In the centre, the initial charge of Ulpius slowed as the warriors closer to the tower began to form up. Ulpius saw their leader, now armed and armoured organising them. Soon his men would begin to weaken as the ground near the tower rose and their momentum slowed. He looked over his shoulder and saw that Decius Brutus' legionaries were less than a hundred paces behind. He turned to his standard-bearer. "Now!"

At this, he began waving the horsetail standard signalling the two flanks to slow. He shouted, "Halt!" The disciplined ranks of the two turmae stopped. The Carvetii were confused for they could only see a thin line of Roman horse that had suddenly stopped. Ulpius raised his sword and the two turmae all drew the javelins they had reserved. The Carvetii charged forward to hit the stationary Romans. "Release!" His men threw their javelins as one into the charging warriors. He looked again at his aquifer. "Now!" He waved the standard again and as Ulpius shouted, "Fall back!" The two flanking lines of cavalry charged.

The Sword of Cartimandua

The tribesmen saw none of this, they saw the Romans retreating and they charged forward over the bodies of the warriors killed by the javelins. The whole host of tribesmen were now racing forward, a warband enraged and angry, desperate to get to grips with the Romans who had decimated their ranks. Earl Woolgar could do little to control them and, looking out from the tower he saw the trap laid by the Romans. He could see what his men could not, a line of legionaries and as the first bolt took one of his bodyguards in the chest, bolt throwers. His military mind could not help but be impressed as the front line of cavalry fell back and his men charged into a solid line of legionaries. It was like throwing snow on fire for they were slaughtered by the heavily armoured Romans. Scanning the battlefield Woolgar could see that the cavalrymen on the flanks were forcing his men into the centre where they were cut down by the relentless Romans who were fighting almost like a machine with the mechanical slash and thrust of razor-sharp gladii. It was time to retreat. He shouted for his blood kin. "We will retreat but with order. You," he pointed to Aetre, "Ride forward and tell the men to fall back. We do not want to run but we can move faster than those Romans." Aetre galloped off. "The rest of you mount. We will see if we can defeat those Romans." He pointed at the turma who were at the western edge of the battle. They were downhill and had a stream at their rear. If Woolgar could attack them whilst their attention was on those to their front then it could allow his men to escape north.

Ulpius rested his mount as he watched the progress of the legionaries. They were an impressive sight. Their short stabbing swords made light work of the unarmoured Carvetii. He could see the decurion princeps calmly surveying his men as they moved inexorably forward. Few of the tribesmen had helmets and even fewer had armour whilst their blows were taken on stout shields and iron helms. Suddenly Ulpius was aware that a mounted man was ordering them back and they began to fall quickly back. The warrior had organised some archers whose arrows although not causing casualties slowed down the legionaries. This was as he had expected but then disaster struck. Ulpius saw the Carvetii leader charge Lucius Emprenius in the flank. The decurion had lost the cohesion of his line and they were

The Sword of Cartimandua

bowled back towards the stream. The warriors closest took advantage and began hacking at the legs of the horses.

Ulpius turned to his two turmae. "To me! Three lines." His men formed behind him ten men wide and three deep. "Charge!" The brief rest had allowed his mounts to regain their wind and they hit the bodyguard of Woolgar in the flank. Ulpius' mighty sword flashed death as he carved a path through warriors eager to destroy Lucius' men. Soon all order was lost and the cavalrymen were enmeshed and embroiled on all sides. Swords and spears flashed as every man fought for survival.

In the centre, Aetre had extracted most of the men and there was now a gap between them and the legionaries. He kept berating those warriors who would have returned to the fray. It was vital that they retreated to the narrows close to the lake and the steep hillside. Gradually they edged their way back and soon there was a noticeable gap between his men and the Romans who were now approaching the more uneven ground which would break up their formation.

On the right, Marcus had halted his horses as they were blown. He looked around to see which of his men had survived. Both Decius and Gaius were with him although he could see a tendril of blood dripping slowly from a wound on Gaius' arm and both men were afoot. The battlefield was littered with the bodies of horses hacked down as the barbarians tried to get to grips with their riders. For a cavalryman, it was one of the saddest sights they could ever witness. The horses of the turmae were snorting heavily and they were looking weary.

Woolgar could see this from his mount and he suddenly shouted to his men. "Withdraw!" Leaving many of his blood kin in a wall around him Woolgar took his bloodied and blood-soaked survivors back towards the bulk of his army. Although they had lost many men they still outnumbered the Romans.

Decius Brutus had taken this lull to bring up his bolt throwers and they began to hurl death at the retreating tribesmen. This was what his men did well. He roared. "Forward!" and the cohort once more began its relentless pursuit of the enemy.

Ulpius Felix sheathed his sword and trotted Raven over to the legionary who was ordering his lines. "You and your men did well centurion."

The Sword of Cartimandua

"Aye we have only lost one or two men but this ground is no good for us; it is too rough."

Before them, the ground was littered with large pieces of rock, scrubby trees and bushes. The enemy warriors were forming up again with their flanks protected by water and the steep hillsides.

"Now is the time to wear them down. The longer we hold them here the more time that Orrick will have to attack them in the rear. Have more bolts brought up let us see if they have the will to take the punishment."

The centurion nodded and began to organise his men. The bolt throwers were placed on either side of the cohort so that the men could retreat behind the cohort in the case of a sudden attack. Ulpius turned to Julius Augustus. "Lucius was wounded in the last attack. Take charge here. Send the wounded back to the fort and watch out for sudden attacks." Dismounting he led his mount over to Marcus and his troopers. He could see that his young deputy had dismounted his men. "Well done men! Be vigilant the day is not yet ours." The men gave a tired cheer and Ulpius drew the centurion to one side. "Send any wounded back to the fort. It will bolster their defences. How many men did you lose?"

Looking around briefly to confirm the numbers he said, "Eight dead and four wounded enough to merit a trip back to the fort. The rest would not thank me for taking them away."

"Good. I had thought that we would have ended the day victorious but they have a wiser head commanding than we are used to. It will be a slog. Our legionaries will batter at the enemy and I will send a patrol along the stream to see if we can flank them."

Marcus shook his head. "The stream leads to the lake and there is no path this side. The path on the hillside is steep and dangerous we would not be able to travel swiftly. I fear that the only way is through this narrow pass."

"Then we will have to rely on our foot soldiers. Rest your men but be alert. I do not think they will attack but you never know with these warriors. They may decide to make a death or glory charge."

Woolgar was also consulting with his lieutenants. They had not emerged with as few casualties as the Romans. Many of his best warriors had perished in the initial attack and the charge of his blood

The Sword of Cartimandua

kin had also resulted in many of his better armed and experienced warriors dying. The warband remained intact but they were not as solid and controlled as their well trained and disciplined opponents.

The leader had been given a variety of opinions. His men shouted out suggestions without even thinking. They just confused their leader.

"Let us attack now for we are being slaughtered by these machines."

"I say we retreat to the head of the lake and ambush them."

"Let me take me warriors up the stream to attack from their rear."

"Silence you are chattering women!"

Even as they spoke they heard the screams as the bolts flew through his ranks slaughtering whole files of them as they stood awaiting the next order to charge for they were so enraged that all they could think of was a charge to destroy these heartless machines which had made the battlefield a sea of blood.

"My lord our men are being killed here, we need to move to somewhere they cannot attack us with those devilish weapons." Aetre was no coward but he hated to watch men dying without being able to strike back. Their voices were pleading with the young leader to be allowed to fight, to attack and avenge their horrendous losses. Already another thirty men had been killed or wounded as they vacillated.

"You are right but the minute we retreat those horsemen will be upon us."

Aetre looked up at the scrubby trees around them. "We have axes aplenty why not cut down a barrier. They would have to move it and that would give us enough time."

Woolgar slapped his nephew on the shoulder. "That is why you will lead this band, one day nephew. You think." He turned to his blood kin. Cut down trees and build a barrier in front of our men."

The bolt throwers continued to take a heavy toll on the lightly armoured tribesmen. As the wood barrier began to form they were less effective and Ulpius walked over to Decius Brutus. "Our native friends are becoming cleverer."

"Yes and no for it means we can assault them without risk of a sudden sortie. We will prepare our attack. Are your horsemen ready commander?"

The Sword of Cartimandua

"Yes, they are rested." The cavalry leader looked around at the reformed turmae. They were now down to seven effective turmae but Ulpius knew there were at least thirty men back in the fort that would soon be able to rejoin. He could see that they had made the barrier the height of a man. It was time to attack. "Centurion, begin your attack." It would take them some minutes to reach the barrier and the bolt throwers were already being dismantled in preparation for the next attack. "Mount. Single column." The narrow pass meant that they would have to follow the legionaries in a much narrower formation than they would have liked but Ulpius was pleased with the way his troopers had grown and developed into this team.

The legionaries at the front of the column moved slowly to keep their formation intact. The last thing they wanted was for a shield to slip and allow the enemy inside. They braced themselves for the onslaught of missiles which they knew would come and this was made worse by the fact that all that they could see was a wall of wood looming ever larger. Suddenly the arrows, stones and javelins began to shower down. There was a scream of pain and the centurion shouted. "Close ranks! Do not stop for wounded men." It was vital that their momentum continued and as long as they marched shoulder to shoulder, shield to shield there was little damage that could be done to them. Decius Brutus hoped that the weight of men would demolish the barrier and he needed the speed he could muster. Men continued to cry in pain as the missiles began to strike home and the legionary leader could see that they were but a few paces from the wall. "Charge!" They hit the wall with the power of a hundred men but the barrier held for the Carvetii had braced it with more logs which were partially embedded in the ground. The missiles now began to take casualties as the tribesmen fired from many paces behind the barrier.

Ulpius recognised the problem and he called out to Marcus. "Take your archers, shoot over the barrier and clear those tribesmen."

By the time that the obstacle had been cleared and the threat of archers removed the tribesmen were long gone. Their task had been to slow up the enemy and they were gone as soon as they had loosed their missiles. They had learned from their Roman enemies and mounted their archers. Ulpius surveyed the battlefield. They were not in a position to successfully pursue the defeated tribesmen but Ulpius

The Sword of Cartimandua

needed them to be looking behind rather than forward in the hope that Orrick would be able to complete his ambush. He called over to Esca. "Bring your best men. Marcus, take charge here and then give me your turma, Decius Brutus remove the barrier and strengthen the tower I will follow the enemy. We do not want them to return."

Esca and Marcus came over to him. It was Marcus who spoke first. "I will follow them, commander. "

"You could follow them Marcus but Esca and Orrick would like to see the sword of Cartimandua wielded would you not?"

The Brigante nodded. "The sword is worth a hundred men."

"Aye well start your men down the pass and I will follow with my men. Be watchful for ambushes. Their leaders are too clever by half." As he loped off Ulpius turned to Marcus. "I mean you no slight, decurion, for you could do the task as well as I but this is more than a skirmish; we need the Brigante to fight for their land not as mercenaries but as brothers in arms. The sword will do that for with the Queen dead it is the symbol of Brigantia. If we can defeat the Carvetii I have hopes that more tribesmen will come to join us and that gives us our only chance of success for if Venutius brings his whole army we will be defeated." Marcus nodded. "One thing still rankles. Find out from the two men who survived the tower how they believe the enemy was able to get past them. I do not want a repeat of that disaster. If it were not for their survival and quick thinking we could have suffered even greater losses."

"Yes sir."

Orrick had reached the neck of land between the lakes as the battle was raging near to the tower. His scouts reported Woolgar's messenger heading north but were unable to stop him. He knew this area well and the thin, spindly copse would hide his men. He sent thirty archers to the opposite hillside as the enemy was not in sight it would give them the chance to climb high enough to be safe from an attack. Orrick turned to his men. "At last we have a chance to strike back at the deceitful Venutius by destroying this warband. I have no doubt that our Roman friends will defeat them and they must return by this path. You will await my signal to attack. I want to trap them between us and Ulpius. Now hide and rest but be vigilant."

The Sword of Cartimandua

They were too far from the battlefield to hear anything and the late winter morning was silent so it was that they heard the first wounded stragglers dragging themselves towards their camp. Orrick wondered, as he signalled for his men to remain hidden, if he could have attacked their camp but he dismissed the thought as soon as it entered his head for the camp would be fortified and he might not have reached it, no the Roman barbarian had been right. Suddenly they heard the tramp of a larger number of men and the whole of the Brigante force tensed as they sensed they would soon be embroiled in a deadly conflict. Orrick was in the middle of the ambush and he waited until he had counted fifty men pass him. Then with a scream of Brigante invective, he launched himself at a warrior with a chieftain's torc. His sword sliced through the shoulder of the grey-haired leader who died almost without knowing they were being attacked. As the ones further away from the assault turned to face their attacker they found arrows raining down on their unprotected backs. Orrick felt immortal as his sword sliced through thin leather and damaged shields his enemies falling away before him. The momentum could not last for the Carvetii outnumbered them three to one and soon his men began to fall. On the other side of the path, Carvetii archers were picking off the hidden Brigante.

A voice boomed out. "Brigante bandit, face a real man" and he found himself facing Earl Woolgar who was dressed in mail with a mighty helm upon his head. Undaunted the younger warrior leapt forward and slashed at his opponent's head. A shield blocked it and Orrick barely had time to raise his shield as the axe hammered down chipping pieces of metal and wood. Before he had time to counter Woolgar backhanded the hammer end of the axe and it jarred against Orrick' arm making it slightly numb. Earl Woolgar then used the boss of his shield to punch Orrick in the face. As he stumbled backwards the last thing he saw before oblivion took him was the axe head slicing down. The blow was so powerful it split not only the warrior's head but the top half of his body.

The day would have been even worse for the Brigante had not Aetre suddenly shouted. "The Romans, they are right behind us!"

Woolgar turned to his blood kin. "Hold the pass! We will meet in the afterlife." His blood kin gave a mighty cheer and turned to make a

The Sword of Cartimandua

shield wall before the oncoming soldiers. Leaving the remaining Brigante who were still engaged in combat Woolgar and Aetre took his personal warband through the narrow part of the pass and into the wider land between the lakes.

Ulpius and Esca emerged like wolves from the hillside and fell upon the Carvetii still fighting. The rearguard locked shields and began to sing the Carvetii song of death. The Roman in Ulpius wanted to use archers to slaughter his enemy but the barbarian and warrior knew that it was important to kill them as warriors. He formed a line of troopers where the pass was at its widest and, as his men threw their javelins they charged.

Raven was a warrior's mount and as they approached the shield wall the jet-black horse raised his front hooves; as they crashed through one man's skull Ulpius sliced down on another. His blade went through metal, leather and bone. A shield wall was only effective when every shield was locked. Ulpius had taken out two in the middle and suddenly its cohesion was gone; its strength had left it and the end was in sight. The Romans had the advantage of height and their spears allowed them to strike beyond the range of the Carvetii weapons. It was only a matter of time before every warrior lay dead in a lake of blood. Not one of them had surrendered and they had bought their Lord the time needed to get to his fortified camp. The warriors died to a man holding their weapons in their hands, fighting until the last gasp of breath was driven from their bodies and they all died knowing that they would meet again in the Allfather's hall and tell the tales of their bravery for all eternity.

The Sword of Cartimandua
Chapter 16

Brocavum
Venutius' muster had gone well and, as he surveyed the mighty army gathered before him, Carvetii, disaffected Brigante even some Novontae and Selgovae from the northlands, he could not help but feel smug, for it was a huge army. There were chariots drawn by small ponies, men armed with javelins, slings and arrows, warriors armed with huge hammers and men who fought with two seax, one in each hand. It was a hotchpotch and it lacked uniformity but it had a purpose. At the last banquet, he had seen the passion each warrior chieftain felt for their cause. This was the last roll of the bones; the Silures, Ordovices and Deceangli were all but defeated. The last druid strongholds on Mona were being put to the sword by ruthless Romans, bent on revenge for the actions of those savage priests. It was only here, in the north, where there was any resistance. Caractacus, Boudicca and the other figures of opposition were dead or imprisoned. Venutius had managed to gather the last army. He could not help a self-satisfied smile, not noble-born but marriage to Cartimandua had given him the chance to be king of two tribes. This was his destiny and this was his moment. After he had defeated the Romans he could unite the whole of the land under one king, King Venutius of the Britons.

He paused to acknowledge the cheers of another contingent, this time blue-painted warriors from the north. His army was huge the trick would be to ensure that they fought together, He remembered the stories of Boudicca's army, five times bigger than the legions she had opposed but they had been slaughtered. They had allowed the Romans to choose the battlefield he would not fall into that trap. He had already organised his armies into four giant warbands. This played to his strength, loyalty to your tribe. It also meant that within the warband there would be smaller groups of warriors who could be used tactically. He had seen the Roman army enough to know that the century, small though it was, could operate independently or as part of the whole. He could not presume to make his army as disciplined as the Romans in such a small time but he could use the ideas. The other strength of his army was mobility; they were lightly armoured but they

The Sword of Cartimandua
could strike at the enemy and then retreat. He frowned for this was the one weakness of his force. They had a tendency to lose their heads and keep attacking, disobeying orders. Earl Woolgar's experience had shown them all the danger of indiscipline. This was why he had decided to keep one war band in reserve. If one warband failed to keep order he would not have lost the battle. As for the place of the battle, he would fight close to his stronghold at Brocavum. The Romans would be coming from the east and the land, although flat sloped up to his walls. There was more than enough room for him to outflank the Romans and not do as Boudicca had done and give the enemy secure flanks.

Thinking of the flanks made him look westwards. Earl Woolgar had still to send a messenger. Were the Romans he had encountered a patrol or had this Alasica decided to attack on two fronts? He still cursed the failure of his plan to disrupt the Romans at Eboracum. Even though Fainch had begun the work well security had increased with the arrival of the new commander and they were being well supplied. The use of the river to carry his supplies had caused problems. He could not disrupt by raiding the ships he had none. In a single stroke, he had been out manoeuvred. He was now reliant on his army defeating the Romans in battle. His allies and subordinates were arriving in huge numbers, in fact, his biggest problem was feeding such a mighty host. He was only awaiting the return of Earl Woolgar who would report whether he had Romans to his rear or not. As soon as he heard from Woolgar he could begin to plan his battle, the battle that would rid his land of Romans.

East of Brocavum

Galba was having his own problems. He had long left the proximity of his new fort and the supplies which could come up by boat. He needed secure supply lines and that meant wagons; wagons meant a road and that was what was slowing him up. He was building the road across the windswept land to the west of Eboracum. His scouts were constantly in touch with the enemy scouts and he knew that they were close. In five days he would be within striking distance of Brocavum.

Brocavum

"King Venutius, it is Earl Woolgar, he returns."

The Sword of Cartimandua

"Send him to me." It was a bloodied and battered Earl Woolgar who prostrated himself before the mighty king. As he had made his way through the huge host assembled he had decided that he would swallow his pride and bite his tongue. This was not the time to upset the unpredictable king. He could paint his action as a victory rather than a defeat. "Well, Earl Woolgar. Have you brought good news?"

"I have, my king. There is no Roman army to the south and west it is merely a small force of cavalry."

"Whom you, of course, destroyed?" The sneer in his voice was apparent to all who listened.

"Most of them are dead, but a small force escaped and joined with some rebel Brigante in their fort at the head of the big lake. They cannot do anything as my warband has fortified the valley of the two lakes."

"And what if I need your warband, Earl Woolgar. What then? Will they still be trapped? Will they still be unable to attack?" Why did you not destroy these forts? Their marching camps are weak little affairs."

"My lord the fort is not a marching fort. The Romans must have been there over winter. It will take siege engines to destroy it."

For the first time, Venutius was at a loss for words. How had the Romans managed to build such a building over winter? If there were one could there not be more? Perhaps this Alasica was bringing more legionaries from the south. It made the battle even more necessary. "I need your warband. If these cavalrymen are defeated then a few men should be able to hold them." As Earl Woolgar left Venutius, wondered if these Romans were the same ones who had spirited away Cartimandua? Part of him wanted to destroy them himself but he knew his destiny lay in defeating the bigger Roman army.

"My Lord! My Lord! The Romans are on the other side of the valley. We have seen their cavalry."

"Excellent! Then we attack the day after tomorrow." He turned to Aetre, the leader of the rebel Brigante. "Send your warband to the valley and prevent their cavalry from crossing. Send reports as more Romans arrive. We have them. To your warbands, it will not be long before the camp is surrounded by the heads of dead Romans."

The Sword of Cartimandua
Glanibanta

At the Roman fort Ulpius was scanning muster lists of dead wounded and fit. Now that the action was over he felt tired and weary. Would the Carvetii attack sooner rather than later? Although he had fortified the tower again he had had to use even more troopers as they had to watch the path they had discovered to the east. Although not big enough for an army it was big enough, as they had discovered to their cost, for a small group of men to cause havoc. His other problem was supplies. They had used almost all that they had brought and were running low on almost everything. He called in Decius Brutus and Marcus. It was time for some decisions to be made and he was sure that Marcus would not like them.

"We may have driven off the enemy but it has been at a cost. Centurion, how many effectives have you?"

"One hundred and ten, counting those who are lightly wounded. Ten others may be fit within the week as for the rest?" The shrug told it all.

"Marcus?"

"We can mount two hundred troopers which will leave two hundred dismounted and able to fight." The winter had been harsh and many fine animals had died. Their bodies had supplemented the meagre diet of the troopers who honestly preferred any food to horsemeat.

"We have supplies for another week if we go on half rations. There are two hundred Brigante left. Have you any suggestions?" The looks on both men's faces told Ulpius all that he needed to know. "I have spoken with Esca. There is a trail that goes south, then east and then north east. It brings us perilously close to Brocavum but if we take it then we will be heading towards our supply lines."

"But sir the princesses. The wounded. We couldn't move them."

Ulpius held up his hand. Perhaps I was not clear. I was not talking about moving all of us. If we all went we would run out of supplies sooner rather than later. At least here we can fish and forage. No, I am talking about taking my Pannonians. If we take the best horses we can make good time and bring the supplies we need back here. Decius Brutus can command the legionaries, Brigante and unhorsed

The Sword of Cartimandua

Pannonians. By my reckoning, he should have ten mounted auxiliaries for scouts. Well, centurion how does that sound?"

"It is a good plan although," the legionary leader laughed, "We would have plenty of supplies if we all ate horse!"

Ulpius laughed. "It may come to that. Now Marcus what is your opinion?" The steely look in his eye told Marcus that he had had the only outburst which would be tolerated.

"If it means the princesses will be safe and results in more supplies then I am happy."

"Good. Well go and say goodbye," he suddenly became serious, "for ours is the more dangerous mission. If we are not ambushed and do not run into the whole Carvetii host then we might be able to return," he paused and added "as long as we haven't fallen from a crag or drowned in a lake or perished in a thousand different ways. Give the men today and tomorrow to rest. Find any who are weak and let them remain here. I want no weak links when we ride, for we will need our best men and all our strength if we are to survive."

Gaius and Decius went with Drusus to the lake. They took lines and bait for it was not often they were told to rest by the decurion princeps. They did not think they would catch anything but it mattered not for they would chat and engage in the kind of ribald banter which bonded warriors such as these.

"Well I for one am glad that I am not remaining in the fort," said Drusus as he cast his weighted line into a deep channel.

"Then you are stupid... sir. I'd rather stay in the fort where you have a bit of wood and soil to protect you. Out there in the hills, you never know where your enemy is or when he is going to pounce. Remember the patrol we went on? Those sneaky fuckers slit two throats of men on guard, good men and they heard bugger all."

"That can still happen here, Decius. The ones who are left are generally the wounded and those not as fit as those chosen."

Decius spat into the water. "Well, in that case, I should still be here because I am not fit and a lazy bastard to boot."

Drusus laughed. "You cannot fool us, Decius, for we have seen you fight. There is no better warrior in the turma. You might have carried off that act once but now we know the truth. Who knows we might even see you promoted."

The Sword of Cartimandua

"Get away. Me an officer? That'll be the day. I just fought to stay alive."

"That's all any of us do isn't it?"

There was a companionable silence as they watch their lines bobbing up and down. When Gaius spoke it was as though his small quiet voice was a shout and the other started in surprise. "I don't want to die. I am afraid of dying." There was a pause as the two older men looked at the youth. "I am not afraid of fighting; I just don't want to die. Does that make me a coward?"

"Does not wanting to die make you a coward? If that was a rule then the whole fucking turma would be cowards for none of us want to die."

"That's right we don't want nor expect to die but Gaius," Drusus added gently, "it helps to be prepared for it for it can come to any of us. You fought bravely, almost too bravely at the tower. You weren't afraid then."

"No, but when I saw how close we all came to death I knew I had too much to live for and I am afraid of going into a hole, a hole like the one we put the queen in."

"That isn't death. That's just the body being respected. You aren't in your body. You are with the Allfather, Metellus, Julius and all the other dead comrades. Don't be afraid of a small dark hole, for that isn't death."

They fell to silence once again each of them pondering their own vision of death. Decius broke the moment. "And the secret is, son, fight as you did at the tower. When you fight like a mad bastard there's no one who can stand up to you." He sniffed, "Except of course me. Whoa there!" He suddenly stood up as his line became taut. "Got one! Look at it! Got one!"

Suddenly the three of them were as children, all thoughts of death forgotten as they held the small river trout as though it was a mighty beast they had taken hours to subdue.

Macha and Marcus were lying in the shelter of the wagon. Marcus was stroking his unborn child. Each was lost in their thoughts.

"Do you have to go Marcus? The baby is due soon, perhaps in the next few days. He has been kicking. I think he wants to see his father."

The Sword of Cartimandua

Marcus laughed and put his head next to her enormous bump. "I can feel him!"

"Then stay. I know if you asked Ulpius…"

"I have no need to ask for he said I could remain if I chose."

She looked at him, hope in her eyes. "Then you can stay."

"No, my love. Listen, don't get upset. Let me explain." She nestled into the crook of his arm and he nuzzled her hair, smelling the woman in her. "If I stay yes I shall see our son born, yes I will be close to you but Ulpius will not have me at his side. I am a good warrior. There is only Ulpius who is a better fighter than I am; there is only Ulpius who is a better leader. I say this only to you for I would never speak in this way before my men."

Smiling she raised her head, "I know my husband for there is only you who does not know that you are the finest man in the whole ala. They all say so."

"Well I don't know about that but if I go with Ulpius we have a better chance of winning and if we win then you and our child will be safe and I will then return to you both. Believe me, I will return. I have so much to live for that for the first time in my life I can see beyond the saddle cloth of the horse before me. I can see a future. I can see my son and I can see his sister and his brother."

Pulling away in mock indignation she said, "Oh is that how it is to be? You keep filling me with children and then off fighting with your comrades."

"Seems a good life to me!"

"Soldier, it is a good thing you are going off then but mark my words when you return we will revisit this idea of me as a mother to a troop of cavalrymen!"

Laughing she rolled on top of him and they kissed. "Oh, my love I am so glad that we met for I love you so. You have brought hope into my life."

"And you, my husband have brought love into mine and shown me what a real man is like."

As the troopers rode along the lakeside Gaius turned to Decius. "What I don't understand is why we are going south if we are supposed to be heading back towards Eboracum."

The Sword of Cartimandua

"You are a dozy little turd do you know that? There's fish over there, "he gestured at the lake on their right, "with more brains than you. Look there what do you see?" He pointed to the east of the lake.

"A mountain?"

"That's right a fucking huge mountain. Now we could go north but if you remember there are a few Carvetii who would like to nail your balls to their spear so we go south until one of them savages," he gestured at the Brigante, "finds the path that will take us home."

"Ah."

"Ah is fucking right mate. I am not worried about the mountains it is the army we might just find."

"You mean the main army?"

"Aye, remember that little lot we ran into were on their way to join up with that king of theirs; the one who was married to Cartimandua? They were part of the army. We were lucky before but we stand no chance against the whole army and our horses are about ready for the cook to make them into a big stew! Keep your eyes peeled my son. We might end up having to high tail it back to Glanibanta."

They were about halfway down the long lake when their Brigante scouts pointed northeast to a wooded defile that ran between two small hills. It was wide enough for two of them abreast. Soon it widened out and they could see that there was a stream that bubbled and rushed over a wide rocky bed. In the distance, they could see two huge hills. The one to the west they were familiar with as it ran the length of the valley of the two pieces of water. The other was new and Ulpius frowned as he saw how narrow the pass was. He turned to Esca. "Make sure your riders scout that pass. It would be a perfect place for an ambush."

"It is but, fear not Roman, the Carvetii do not know of this path yet. Few people use this valley for even in high summer there is little sun; it is hard for a tribe to find enough food. The woods end soon."

Esca had been entirely accurate for as they crested the pass the leading Romans could see a long narrow lake meandering up between low barren and bare hillsides. Even now in early spring, there was little evidence of any life either human or animal. Ulpius could see why this was an unknown route. He could see no signs of life at all.

The Sword of Cartimandua

The hills rose precipitously on either side and it was hard to see if any animals, even the goats, could survive here. There was little land for grazing and none for crops. The sheep and goats which had been dotted about the hillsides in the other valleys were absent. It was as though it was a dead valley. The valley bottom close to the lake was wide enough for four men abreast and Ulpius took the opportunity to reform his men and warn them of the dangers they would face.

It was mid-afternoon when Sigger's scout returned. Esca drew Ulpius to one side, "My scout reports the main rebel army. There are many, many men far more than the deer in the forest. He has never seen so many even at the tribal gathering. There are warriors from all of the northern tribes."

"Can we avoid them? Is there another trail?"

"There is another valley to the south; it is narrow but it is unguarded. If we travel at night then we may be able to pass them. There is something else; my scout believes he heard a buccina perhaps signalling. It may be it was a captured one and the Carvetii are celebrating but it may be your army."

"Good that gives me some hope at least for that means there could be friends nearby." Ulpius began to wonder who it could be. Had the invasion started or was the Brigante correct and it was a captured buccina? If it were the invasion then Bolanus was behaving in a more aggressive way than he had thought possible. Could he have misjudged the Governor? Speculation would get him nowhere.

"Just ahead will be the main Carvetii army. We will rest at the head of this valley and then try to make our way home without letting know we are there. We will become spirits of the forests. I want no noise from any piece of equipment, man or animal. When we rest, find some cloth and muffle their hooves. If we can get past them we will have a clear run to home and the army. That means food and safety!" He decided not to tell them that there might be friends nearby- if there was not an army the disappointment might make them weaker- if he waited until they knew for certain it would lift his men's spirits.

North of Eboracum

Fainch felt as though she was being followed, she had the sense that someone was in the woods watching and following. She had

The Sword of Cartimandua

twisted and turned a number of times, she had doubled back upon herself, she had been as motionless as a statue waiting for what seemed like a thousand moments and yet she could neither shake off her pursuer nor find out who it was. Perhaps it was her imagination for when she dreamed a powerful dream the mushrooms and herbs seemed to make her both weaker and yet more attuned to slight sounds and sensations. She decided that she had kept from her hearth long enough and she quickly made her way to her hut. Once there she felt safe and should anyone try to do her harm she had the means within her grasp to prevent it.

Atticus was now officially a deserter. Always a loner the transfer to the second ala had been the last straw for he had become the butt of pranks and tricks at best and attempts to do him serious damage at best. The decurion princeps had not been happy about the transfer but he owed Ulpius Felix and had to honour a promise. The trooper was lazy, sly and unsociable. He got on with no one. His turma did not feel they owed this outsider anything and they let him know, in no uncertain terms, what would happen to him if he let them down or even if they thought he had let them down. The fight at the river had frightened the small man who, even amongst reluctant soldiers, stood out as someone who loathed the occupation. Although he did not relish the thought of being caught as a deserter nor did he feel he could countenance another battle where he would not have comrades to protect him. Ulpius had, in fact, done him a favour for had he not transferred him he might even now be lying in a field in the west, with his entrails before him. As it was he was in the safety of the east made safer because of the patrols of Ulpius and his ala. The military governor had taken most of the army to fight Venutius and there were few patrols for him to worry about.

He would get out of this land and find his way to a big city perhaps even Rome but to do so he needed money. His best chance of money was the quartermaster Gaius Cresens. He had been looking for him since the death of the queen with no success. He did remember following him once when he visited a hovel by the river and it was there he had seen Fainch. He did not know she was a witch, he thought her a whore but when he deserted he spotted her leaving Morbium after having met with other women whom he assumed were

The Sword of Cartimandua

also whores. She would be the best chance to find Cresens and if not she would have money for whores were always careful with their money. One way or another he would have money. Her evasive tactics had also made him wonder about her for she took far too much care to hide her tracks. The crafty Atticus assumed that she had to have a good reason; it was, indeed, what he had done to avoid being pursued by his ex-comrades. He had always known where she was heading and so had been able to catch her up no matter how many twists, turns and double backs she took.

He was already waiting inside her hovel behind the entrance. Fainch stood near to her door and scanned the path and woods around her home but she could see nought. She quickly grabbed a handful of dry twigs from the undergrowth and spread them around the entrance. If anyone came she would hear the twigs crack. Feeling relief she stepped inside her home; even as she did so she knew she was not alone there was a smell and a presence but before she could retreat a strong, rough hand had taken her around the throat and a sharp knife was pressing into her neck.

"No no my little whore. You are going fucking nowhere."

She remained silent wondering who it was. She did not recognise the voice and, from his words, it seemed he only knew her as a whore. The thought puzzled her for she had never worked as a prostitute merely gave the appearance of being one.

"This can go one of two ways. First I find out what I want and you live or I don't and you die, painfully and slowly. Now that is simple enough isn't it?" When she remained silent he pushed a little harder with the blade drawing blood. "I know you can talk because I heard you talking with the fat man."

She felt some relief; from his voice, she knew he was a Roman; she had been worried that he was an agent and that others knew of her. If he only knew Gaius Cresens then he knew nothing and she knew how to play the game.

"I didn't know Cresens had any friends."

"He doesn't but you can't be a choosy whore if you let him slide his greasy fingers all over you." Now that he was close to her Atticus could see that she was both prettier and younger than he had assumed. Before he took her money he might have fun with her. It had been

The Sword of Cartimandua

some time since he had had a woman and young Brigante slave boys were not as exciting.

"What do you want with him? Rumour has it he has disappeared."

"He has but I thought you might know where he went or," he added meaningfully, "where he left his money."

She had the measure of the Roman now. He was a thief. She dealt with thieves on a daily basis. "I don't know where he went or where he hid his money. Have you tried his domus?"

"You think I am stupid? The tribune has guards around it. Now perhaps if you were to distract them."

"First of all, it is hard to do anything with a knife at my neck and secondly what is in it for me? I have to make a bit of money as well."

"I know you whores, you have money all over the place." The conversation was making Atticus relax a little. She was neither fighting nor shouting, she might be a reasonable woman and the money might just drop into his lap. For her part, Fainch felt the knife begin to slip away and she began to slowly slide her right hand down to the folds of her dress; in it, she had secreted an eagle's claw, each talon sharpened until it was as a razor and each one tipped with poison. Holding it by the ankle she drew it slowly out talking all the time.

"How about if I have half of what he has?"

He laughed an evil laugh, "Half! Don't get above yourself, you might get a tenth if you are good." He realised he could promise her anything for she would die once he had it but he also knew that if he didn't haggle she might be suspicious.

"Thirty."

"Twenty, take it or leave it." Thinking the deal done he relaxed his grip with his left hand and lowered the knife so that it was pointing at her back.

She spun around and saying," Done," she raked the eagle claw from his eye to his chin. She was quite powerful and the talons were sharp; the whole eye came out and the talons raked to the bone. He screamed in pain but still had enough strength to stab out at her. Although she was quick and already twisting away the sharp blade sliced into her side making her gasp with the pain. Before he could

The Sword of Cartimandua

attack again she removed his other eye and the blinded deserter flailed around as she moved easily out of his flailing arms.

"Where are you? You bitch! I'll gut you. I'll fucking cut you into little tiny bits!"

She knew that if she remained silent he would not be able to find her and she needed to save her strength to enable her to stem the bleeding. She knew it was not fatal but she didn't know if he also treated his blades with poison. As she staunched the bleeding with a cloth she watched him sink to the floor the pain of the poison taking over from the evisceration of his eyes.

"Aarrgh. What have you done? You bitch! You…" Atticus, the deserter, had his miserable life ended on a dirt floor in a tiny hovel, dying as he had been born screaming, alone and miserable.

Fainch knew that she had had a lucky break and she kissed her charm thanking the mother that she had protected her daughter. Eboracum was becoming too dangerous for her. She determined that, once she had secured her wound she would head back to Mona. Perhaps others of the religion would travel there too but she hoped that the hidden places with the secret herbs and roots would still be there and help her to regain her strength. Before the next dawn had broken all trace of Fainch disappeared from Eboracum and all that remained to show what had transpired was the emasculated body of Atticus the deserter.

West of Brocavum

Caesius Alasica was pleased with his legionaries. They had made much better time than he could have dreamed possible all those months ago when he began planning this campaign back at Eboracum. Although not up to full compliment he had six thousand legionaries and two thousand cavalry. No matter what the barbarians threw at him he knew he could defeat them. According to his scouts once they crossed the river they would be within a day's march of Brocavum. He had yet to see a barbarian stronghold that could withstand his siege weapons. He thought back to the fortress at Stanwyck he had visited whilst his men were building his new bridge. Although it had been deserted by the barbarians his inspection had convinced him that an onslaught of bolts and stones from his onagers would have made it

The Sword of Cartimandua
simplicity itself for his legionaries to carry the feeble walls. The very size of it meant that it would need a huge army to control the walls. He could only hope that Venutius would hide behind his walls. He wondered, as he did every day, where his lost vexillation was; he had had no word of them. Had they perished at the hands of the enemy or had they succumbed to the climate of this inhospitable land? Not for the first time he cursed the order which had left him shorthanded for the cavalry he had with him were new to Britannia and untried. It was the one area of weakness in his army.

"Sir, sir," The rider who galloped up to Alasica was one of the young auxiliary optios. "The decurion told me to tell you we can't cross the river sir."

"Why not optio?"

"There are hundreds of barbarians stopping us."

Taking only his aide and the young trooper Julius rode to the river to see what the problem was. When he arrived, he could see that the boy had not been exaggerating. There were indeed hundreds of barbarians; they were painted for war waving spears and swords and they had the high ground. He had no doubt he could carry the crossing but he would lose many men in doing so and his legionaries' lives were too valuable to be wasted. He called over the messenger. "Prevent them from crossing if you can but if they do manage to cross your orders are to get to me as quickly as possible." He paused and looked sternly at the auxiliary. "And no heroics, without the Pannonians you are my only cavalry."

"Sir."

As he rode back Julius began to search for a solution to his problem. Heading towards his men he could see the road climbing away to the west. He could not allow the enemy to take the road for if he were to be cut off from his supplies then the barbarians could starve him out. He was reluctant to retreat. He saw the solution as he closed with his aides. The road began to climb up a terrace. His engineers had had to make a deviation from their normally straight lines. They had made it twist and turn. Although it was nowhere near finished it was a solid base upon which to stand his men. They would all have firm footing. He could use the terrace as it would allow his bolt throwers to fire over the heads of his only infantry and would scythe down the

The Sword of Cartimandua
enemy. It went against his nature but here, as when Boudicca was defeated, defence would have to come first. He did not have enough men to guarantee victory and he was in a perilous position so far from a secure fortress and support. He gathered his officers about him and quickly issued his instructions. He had chosen his men well and soon the legionaries were arrayed on the terrace with twenty bolt throwers above them. His few archers were just in front of the bolt throwers but above the legionaries. His weaknesses were his flanks. He had too few cavalry to guard both flanks. His auxiliaries were placed on the right flank as this faced the barbarians at the river crossing. He placed the strongest century, the first century with First Spear on the left flank. They were his best chance to hold the enemy.

There was the sudden sound of a buccina and then he saw the auxiliaries riding for their lives. The commander of the cavalry on the right flank signalled the decurion and the rearguard fell in behind them. The decurion in charge began to dress his lines and prepare to face the advancing Carvetii.

"Hold your fire." Alasica did not want his missile surprise to be wasted on the few hundred barbarians who suddenly stopped their pursuit when they saw the Romans before them. They were a mass of taunting painted barbarians who were waving the heads of the Romans they had just killed. He had fought such men in Batavia and Germania as had his legionaries. They would ignore such taunts but he was less sure about his inexperienced auxiliaries who could see the decapitated heads of their comrades. The longer they taunted the more likely that his auxiliaries would feel honour bound to charge. Alasica did not have to wait long for Venutius, mounted in a richly decorated war chariot suddenly appeared on the facing hillside ahead of his huge warband filling the skyline from east to west as far as the eye could see. He was armed and mailed with a driver next to him. He looked huge next to the diminutive driver and his armour gleamed in the morning light. The warriors around the king were his oath brothers; they were the best-mounted warriors with the finest armoured helms, shields and corselets. They would be fearless in the fighting and the Roman commander could see that whilst the majority of the warband were second rate there was a huge elite force of well-armed and armoured warriors. They would have to be the target for his bolt

The Sword of Cartimandua

throwers. He was taken aback by the numbers. He would have been taken aback, even more, had he known that a mounted warband of a thousand warriors was making its way around the unguarded left flank of the Roman army. All he could see was an unbroken line of enemies gradually edging forward. He looked at the forces arrayed against him spreading across the skyline. Although hard to estimate numbers when the formation was so loose it looked the equivalent of eight or ten legions; almost fifty thousand men. It would be a bloody day and would test the mettle of all his troops.

Ulpius and his men were exhausted. Even though they had rested for a couple of hours their nighttime ride skirting the camps of the Carvetii had sucked all the reserves of energy from the hungry troopers. When Esca had told them that there were at least two warbands to the north and east Ulpius and Marcus had had no choice but to begin a detour south and east to get around them. It was demoralising to move further away from hope and food and friends but with only two hundred men and a few Brigante scouts, Ulpius could not hope to take on two warbands. As the early morning wore on they gradually found themselves climbing a saucer-shaped hill. They had long left what passed for a path and were picking their way through scree and tumbled rocks. Suddenly Esca and his scouts ran back. "There is a warband," before Ulpius could even begin to formulate a new plan Esca continued, "and Romans."

Even though he was well outnumbered by the host of barbarians before him Caesius Alasica was unworried. His archers and bolt throwers would make a thousand paces before him a killing ground. The barbarians wore little armour and had few defensive tactics. Waiting until they were but five hundred paces away he gave the signal and the missiles flew, carving a path of death and destruction through the enemy lines. The bolts took out whole ranks of men whilst the arrows plunged like a deadly rain from the skies. Not only did the front ranks fall and falter but the whole of the warband shuddered to a halt as they met missiles, fallen men and the upslope. The bolts were so powerful that they went through three or four warriors. The arrows began to take an even bigger toll as they plunged down onto unprotected bodies, painted but without any armour. The barbed tips tore through necks, backs and shoulders to kill in huge numbers.

To the west, the two cavalry forces were engaged in mortal combat. Although the Carvetii outnumbered the auxiliaries the superior horses, weapons and training meant it was an even match. Alasica cursed again as he realised that his shortage of cavalry might cost him the day. The cavalrymen were holding their own; with another ala, he might have been able to turn them. He was pleased that they had at least restrained themselves from a headlong attack and their fight was now revenge dedicated to their lost comrades.

Venutius signalled a third warband into action and these began to press towards the weaker left flank. Although the missiles were still causing devastation there were not enough to cover the whole of the front and their fire was slightly slower on the left added to that was the inevitable nature of missile fire the closer to your front ranks the less effective they would be. So it was that they inexorably began to draw closer to the front ranks of the Romans. With a sudden roar, they leapt forward free from the torment of bolts and arrows. The legionaries released their pila and the front ranks fell only to have their places taken by the second rank who hacked and chopped with axes and swords, oblivious to both pain and wounds. It was as though they had regarded the arrows as fleas or insects and were now free from the torment.

The tribune from the left flank suddenly appeared at Alasica's side. "Sir they are forcing us back we need support."

"And I have no reserves. You will hold them, Titus Quintus. You will hold them."

In his mind, the young commander began to work out how to extricate his men from this trap without being routed. A collective shout from the left ended that train of thought. Earl Woolgar's warband had worked around the left flank of the Romans and suddenly launched an attack on the unprotected edge of the defensive line. Even as he watched he saw the westernmost cohort begin to fall in lines as they were assaulted from two sides. The First Spear was a good leader but his men were being attacked on two fronts. "Gaius Aurelius take two cohorts from the right and support the left. Antoninus begin to pull back our forces on the right but slowly use the cavalry to screen

The Sword of Cartimandua
our withdrawal." Was this to be the early end of what had promised to be a glittering career? Alasica knew that defeat would mean the slaughter of his men and the loss of the eagle something which had never happened on these islands before. It could mean the beginning of the end of Roman rule in Britannia for defeat would leave the whole of the north unprotected. It would also mean the death of every Roman north of Lindum for with only a skeleton force at Eboracum this warband could sweep Rome's influence from the north of Britannia. "Today gentlemen we all fight or we will leave our bones to be scattered, whitening on these desolate hills." Drawing his sword, he urged his horse towards the left flank which was in imminent danger of collapse.

Ulpius, Marcus and Esca sat on their horses just below the skyline. They had a perfect view of the battle and they could see the effect of the charge of Woolgar' warband. The unthinkable was going to happen, Romans were going to lose. No matter how disciplined they were, they were outnumbered and outflanked. They would die. A whole Roman army would be destroyed it would be like Crassus in Parthia, the republic at Cannae or the most recent slaughter in the Teutoburger Forest. Their only chance was for the Pannonians to destroy the warband. Ulpius looked at his hungry, tired and battle-weary warriors. The warband outnumbered them five to one even if they saved their comrades they would all die. He looked at Marcus. "There is but one chance the arrow formation, the wedge." Marcus nodded. "Prepare the men" He turned to his troopers. "I know you are tired, I know that we are outnumbered but before us we see friends who will be slaughtered unless we intervene. You know me I don't lie and I don't bullshit." His men laughed a tired laugh. "We are going to die but we are warriors and we will die together. Are you with me?" The roar from his weakened men raised Ulpius heart. His men would not let him down. He turned to the Brigante," Esca we ride to our death take your men back to the fort and protect the princess. You can do no more here."

"No Roman, we can do something here. The enemies before us have killed our Queen and our brothers; we win or die with you here." Clasping hands in a warrior's handshake they roared their defiance.

The Sword of Cartimandua

The troopers were now riding hard towards Ulpius with Marcus and Decius leading three men and then four so that a wedge fanned out. Ulpius drew his sword and kissed it. "For Cartimandua and Rome. Charge!"

The noise of the battle hid the sound of the thundering hooves crashing down the hillside and the first that Earl Woolgar and his band knew of their doom was when the arrows and javelins of the auxiliaries sliced through the rear ranks of the Carvetii. The shock was a palpable ripple that ran through the enemy ranks. The most frightening event for a warrior in a battle is to be attacked from the place you think you are safe. With enemies to their front and enemies to their rear panic spread through the ranks of the warband. The sword of Cartimandua carved a bloody path of death, the blade almost singing as it sliced through the unprotected ranks of Earl Woolgar's men; Decius and Marcus widened that path. The backs of the bodies before them were like the practice targets they had used back in Eboracum. Their only problem was ensuring that the blades did not become entangled or trapped in the dying bodies. As in all battles and wars, the bravest and the most fearless are at the front so the opposite is also true, those at the rear are not as brave and not as fearless. Some of the Carvetii decided that they could avoid the swords and hooves of the Roman horses by breaking back towards their own lines. The pressure on the Roman line dropped and the legionaries were able to get a second wind. First Spear recognised the weakening. "Dress your ranks we are not finished yet!"

The Roman commander had no idea who had launched the attack on the Carvetii but he suspected and hoped that it was his lost vexillation. The battle was at a crucial stage and the pendulum was swinging in the Roman's favour. All along the Carvetii line warriors were slowing, wondering what was happening on their right flank. Alasica's voice sounded above the din of war. "Sound the advance." The buccina sounded loudly in the cacophony of noise that was the battlefield. "Romans forward!"

Venutius could not believe his eyes. A few minutes earlier the battle had been won. He had seen the Roman left crumbling and the right withdrawing. Suddenly the appearance of a handful of cavalry had caused his men to retreat. Some of his allies had decided that

The Sword of Cartimandua

discretion was the better part of valour and were retreating at full tilt north and east. He still had his own warband. If he could attack the Roman left open the field the impetus could swing the battle in his favour again; perhaps his allies would be shamed into returning. He could still win this battle. Even with some of his allies deserting him he still outnumbered the Romans and he had seen them falter, one more push would do it. Shouting to his driver to whip his ponies he cried, "Charge!" and the whole host began to charge forwards. His oathsworn brothers urged their mounts forward pleased to be released from the punishment which had been the bolt throwers. Those warriors on foot formed a solid, unbroken line of iron. They longed to sink their blades into Roman bodies. Their collective scream was a terrifying sound and they all raced forward to present a deadly line of blades. They knew they had longer blades than the Romans who had spent most of their deadly pila. If they could close these combat-hardened veterans would save the honour of their king and defeat once and for all these Romans.

On the right flank, Earl Woolgar recognised the Romans as the ones who had beaten him twice. He saw the leader, a huge one-eyed wild warrior wielding a Brigante sword. He would defeat the Romans by killing their leader and in doing so he would regain the honour he had lost in his last battle; he had seen the weakening of his king's allies. This was his moment of glory. This would give him the revenge for his lost warriors. Either he or the Roman would stay on this field. He urged his horse towards the undefended right side of the decurion princeps. Ulpius was focused on the enemies to the front. He could see the wavering lines begin to stiffen as the legionary centurions and aquifers steadied the ranks and began to start to edge forward. He heard the buccina announce the charge and could see the huge figure of the First Spear begin to lead the legion forward. This was their moment and, unlikely as it had seemed a short while earlier, they might just survive.

Marcus, in the place of honour on the unguarded right of his leader, saw the Carvetii chieftain hurtling towards his friend. He recognised him from their battle in the lakes and saw that he fought with a sword and a short axe; he knew he was a cunning and ferocious warrior who had despatched Orrick himself a mighty warrior. Ulpius

The Sword of Cartimandua

would be dead before he knew he was being attacked. He did not hesitate; his own horse was a powerful Roman mount whilst his adversary's pony was far smaller though nimbler. Marcus' horse crashed into Woolgar and his mount throwing him to the ground. As he passed the Carvetii war chief he back slashed with his sword and felt it grate against bone. By now the wedge had lost cohesion and, seeing no more enemies to threaten Ulpius he wheeled his horse around to face his enemy again. He had, indeed, wounded Earl Woolgar but the grizzled old warrior was like a wounded bear. Behind him, Aetre stood ready to protect his liege lord. Marcus rode hard at Woolgar keeping his sword between him and his enemy; as the decurion passed he felt the axe crash against his shield and he struck at the unprotected head of the war chief. Aetre appeared from nowhere and his sword stopped the blow connecting. In the follow-through, his blade caught the flank of Marcus' mount which reared and threw him. As he hit the ground he was winded and dazed but still held both sword and shield which saved his life for Lord Woolgar saw his chance and sliced down at the recumbent Roman with his mighty sword. Aetre saw his chance as Marcus lifted his blade to defend himself from the war chief's strike. In doing so he left his right side unguarded. The young warrior plunged his sword towards the decurion's armpit.

"No, you don't you sneaky little fucker." Decius' spear took Aetre full in the throat. "Now if you'll finish off this bastard, sir, we can get back in the war and beat these fucking barbarians once and for all." Grinning he wheeled his horse back into the fray. With a shout of anger Marcus leapt up hitting the boss of his shield into the face of the war chief who half fell backwards; as he did so he exposed his right side when his weakened arm dropped his sword to the ground. Marcus did not hesitate but sliced under his arm and through his neck. Withdrawing his sword, he decapitated the head of Earl Woolgar and raised it with a roar of victory. The warband saw it and were dismayed; Woolgar and Aetre were now dead, the blood kin of Woolgar were all slaughtered, killed either in the pass or defending their lord on this lonely, desolate hillside and the rest, warriors summoned for the war ran, eager to be away from the wall of death which had appeared from the mists. They would return to their homes,

The Sword of Cartimandua
plant crops, raise families and forget the disaster to which Earl Woolgar had brought them. If he did but know it Maeve would soon be heralded as Earl Maeve and Woolgar's lands would be his.

If Venutius had been angry before he was, by now, furious with red hot rage. The one-eyed Roman who had stolen the queen from him and defeated his warriors had now turned the battle. His surprise attack had been itself surprised and defeated. He cursed Woolgar as the remnants of his warband fled unhindered eastwards. Realising that the Roman was now alone and isolated, he raced his chariot towards his enemy. Soon the sword of Cartimandua, which he saw the Roman wielded, would be his and with it the allegiance of any wavering Brigante who would see it as a sign from the Allfather that Venutius was the rightful king of the Brigante. The king had one last gamble which could win him all. Ulpius was busy despatching two wounded enemies and did not see the chariot making like an arrow towards him. While he was still some distance away his driver was thrown from the chariot having been struck by two arrows. The king of the Carvetii threw his shield to the floor and grabbed the reins. Venutius was barely thirty paces away when he hurled his spear. Although the spear missed the Roman it took Raven in the neck and Ulpius faithful beast reared on to its hind legs mortally struck. The misfortune turned to disaster when the dying beast fell on Ulpius' leg leaving him helplessly trapped beneath the steed. Realising he would have to dismount to finish off the Roman and retrieve the sword Venutius halted the chariot. Ulpius struggled to extract his trapped leg. The Carvetii blade arced down towards the decurion princeps' head as it did so Raven's death throe released some of the pressure and Ulpius dragged his leg out. The blade missed his head but sliced down his left arm.

"Roman you fight well, let us see if you die well." Venutius was a powerful warrior; he had been a war chief before he had married the Queen and become king. He knew how to fight and Ulpius was a wounded, weary warrior but in his heart, he had a fire and a need for revenge. He resolved to take Venutius with him to the afterlife. They both hacked at each other furiously, swords beating on shields and glancing off helms and armour. After a dozen thrusts at each other, they paused to gather their breath. Ulpius was weak both from the fall

The Sword of Cartimandua
and the wound in his arm which was weakening his defence. In contrast, Venutius was uninjured and filled with passionate anger giving him extra strength. The end would not be long in coming and Venutius could not miss the opportunity to gloat. "It is a shame the witch did not poison you as well as the bitch Cartimandua for then I would have won the battle and I would have the sword." Venutius spat the words at Ulpius hoping to make him lose his temper and forget his Roman training.

The decurion princeps did become angry but his training had been over twenty years and it was as though his body took over from the seething mind of the Roman auxiliary. With a roar Ulpius raced forward, his sudden charge catching his opponent unawares. He felt his blade strike the unprotected thigh of Venutius. The thick blood began to gush from the fatal wound. "You should know Carvetii that whoever carries this sword cannot be defeated." The now dying Venutius tried ineffectively to break down Ulpius' defence but his lifeblood was spilling across the hillside for it was a fatal wound. Realising that he himself was wounded and seeing the weakening of the king's blows Ulpius ended the fight with a mighty stroke which all but severed the king in two. As he raised his sword to scream "Cartimandua" the arrow from Venutius' war chief Brennus struck him in his side. The barbed tip entered below his right arm, tore through his body and emerged near his left hip. It was a death wound and Ulpius sank to his knees on that muddy, bloody battlefield.

As he lay there amidst the carnage and slaughter he did not know that the death of Venutius marked the end of the battle and that the warbands, largely leaderless, were fleeing. He barely heard the cheer from the Roman ranks as they celebrated their victory. The sound of the buccina ordering a pursuit was dim, a faraway echo as though in a tunnel. He began to slip away to the comfortable world of sleep, eternal sleep and peace. His only thoughts were for his men; he hoped that many would have survived and he prayed that Marcus would live. The sky was going dark and he gripped the sword hilt even tighter. "Allfather your son is coming home. I hope that I have gained enough honour to be admitted." He closed his eyes prepared for death and hopeful of being reunited with Cartimandua.

"Ulpius!"

The Sword of Cartimandua

Opening his eye Ulpius realised he was still alive. "Is that you Marcus?"

"It is. Rest I have sent for a surgeon."

"No my friend for I will not recover from these wounds but do not weep for me for I shall be with the Queen and the Allfather." He coughed and Marcus could see the flecks of blood which told him his friend had deep injuries and had suffered a death wound. "I want you to do two things for me."

"Anything but you must live."

"We both know that cannot be so for I am dying. First, take the sword of the Brigante back to her people. The princesses will know what to do and," he coughed more blood and spittle, "you must find and kill Cresens and the witch."

"Witch?"

"It was not just the fat one who caused the death of my Queen, there was a witch; paid for by Venutius. Look to Eboracum that is where you shall find her." He opened his eye. "Marcus you have been as a son to me now be a father to our men." Marcus nodded and gave the Roman salute; the oath was sworn.

Although the eye remained open, Marcus told Decius and Gaius later that he saw the life leave his leader as Ulpius Felix, decurion princeps of the auxiliary smiled and passed over to be with his queen and his warriors.

Alexandria

The newly appointed Emperor Vespasian sat in the cool throne room in the Imperial Palace in Alexandria. Now that the East was subdued he could turn his attention to Britannia, the site of his first action with Aulus Paulinus. He had determined whilst serving there that one day Rome would rule that northern outpost of the known world. He summoned his clerk. He knew just the man to take charge and conquer that barbaric wild land.

"Send an order to Gnaeus Julius Agricola he is on the Rhine. He is to assume command of all the forces in Britannia and take control in the name of Emperor Vespasian and Rome."

The Sword of Cartimandua
Epilogue

It was a cold clear morning as the wagon and small escort made their way across the spring hills sparkling with a sharp frost. Leading the way was Marcus with Gaius and Decius in close attendance. The silence in which they rode was a reflective silence as they carried the body of the warrior who had led them through many close encounters with death. As warriors, they knew that the death of Ulpius Felix was the only death they could expect. So far no Pannonian had reached the goal of retirement and citizenship with all the benefits that brought. He had died on the battlefield, he had died undefeated, he had avenged the death of his love; what more could a warrior desire?

In the wagon Macha and Lenta were also thinking about the man who had brought love late in the life of their half-sister; the man who had saved them and their children from at best death and at worst slavery. As Macha suckled the young warrior to be named Ulpius by his father she dwelt on the thought that her husband, the new commander of the Ala, Marcus would probably end his days much as Ulpius Felix with a sword in his hand. She determined to make the most of every second they had together.

The newly-promoted decurion Decius was perhaps also thinking less about Ulpius and more about Marcus for he now saw that the young warrior had changed him, had made him a better soldier and if he was honest, a better man. He came on this journey not only to honour Ulpius but to protect Marcus. Although the Carvetii and Brigante rebels had been beaten Decius knew that there were still rogue bands wandering the lonely fells. Alasica had not yet begun the long process of mopping up all the dissident tribesmen.

The barrow loomed into sight, the earth still fresh from the burial of the Queen. This time they found the entrance instantly. When it had been opened they reverently took out the shrouded body of Ulpius. His hair was combed, his armour polished, his amulets and torcs shone; he looked resplendent, the complete warrior.

"Are you sure you do not want me to put the sword in the grave with him? The three of them would be united forever."

The Sword of Cartimandua

"No. Ulpius made it clear to you, did he not, that he wished it to be passed back to the Brigante?" Marcus nodded. "We are now the leaders of the Brigante and we want the weapon wielded by a warrior. And when your son is old enough he too is Brigante and he will honour both his people, Brigante and Roman by fighting with the sword of Cartimandua."

So it was that Ulpius Felix warrior of Rome was laid to rest in an unmarked barrow with the last Queen of the Brigante, Cartimandua whose fabled sword continued to be used by Marcus Aurelius Maximunius decurion of Rome. The warrior who had been known as Lupus, The Wolf, when he first joined the Roman army joined his lover, Cartimandua in the Otherworld.

From the cover of the high cliffs, Fainch peered down. Her work was not over, it had hardly begun. When she returned from Mona she would be even more powerful and the little group in front of her would be the first to feel her power and she burned their faces on her mind. They would all die, the Romans, the Brigante traitors and even the suckling child, all would feel the wrath and revenge of Fainch.

In the land of the lakes, Earl Maeve viewed the returning remnants of his half-brother's warband. They were a pitiful sight but they were now his warband and he swore that when he had built them back up into a fierce fighting force he would rid his land, the land of the lakes, of this insidious invader.

The Sword of Cartimandua
Author's comment
This is a piece of fiction! It is based on some historical characters. Cartimandua was the Queen of the Brigante, she did betray Caractacus, met Claudius, married Venutius, took a shield-bearer as a lover and vanished from history in, about, 69 AD. Rome did have four Emperors in 69 AD.

Roman auxiliaries came from newly conquered nations and fought in a turma of about thirty-two; each turma forming part of an ala or wing of cavalry. They fought in much less formal situations than the legions. Stanwyck is a superb Iron Age fortification and it was substantially improved by Venutius. Following its destruction by the Romans the capital of Brigantia moved down the road a mile or so to Alde borough. There is a fort at Ambleside called Galva or Glanibanta. There is no record that it was built by auxiliaries and certainly no suggestion that they built it as suggested by my novel. However, it was not a legionary fort and auxiliaries probably built it. When the unit left a fort, they would normally destroy its defences but would frequently bury such items as they could not carry. Glanibanta has seen numerous reincarnations.

History is written by the winners and the main records we have are from Tacitus and other Roman writers. There are no Brigante records and I have surmised and speculated about what might have happened.

I have used Roman names for places as that is the only record we now have. I suspect that the Brigante would have had their own names for them. The big river is obviously the Tees which formed a natural boundary for the Romans. The archaeological records for the auxiliaries in Britain suggest that they took Roman names and I have used Roman names for the auxiliaries. I have taken liberties with dates to suit the stories. Venutius was still alive a couple of years after my book is set. The idea of a common soldier taking a Queen as a lover was suggested by the fact that the Queen herself left her husband for a warrior.

Griff Hosker September 2014

The Sword of Cartimandua

Other books by Griff Hosker

If you enjoyed reading this book, then why not read another one by the author?

Ancient History

The Sword of Cartimandua Series
(Germania and Britannia 50 A.D. – 128 A.D.)
Ulpius Felix- Roman Warrior (prequel)
The Sword of Cartimandua
The Horse Warriors
Invasion Caledonia
Roman Retreat
Revolt of the Red Witch
Druid's Gold
Trajan's Hunters
The Last Frontier
Hero of Rome
Roman Hawk
Roman Treachery
Roman Wall
Roman Courage

The Wolf Warrior series
(Britain in the late 6th Century)
Saxon Dawn
Saxon Revenge
Saxon England
Saxon Blood
Saxon Slayer
Saxon Slaughter
Saxon Bane
Saxon Fall: Rise of the Warlord

The Sword of Cartimandua
Saxon Throne
Saxon Sword

Medieval History

The Dragon Heart Series
Viking Slave
Viking Warrior
Viking Jarl
Viking Kingdom
Viking Wolf
Viking War
Viking Sword
Viking Wrath
Viking Raid
Viking Legend
Viking Vengeance
Viking Dragon
Viking Treasure
Viking Enemy
Viking Witch
Viking Blood
Viking Weregeld
Viking Storm
Viking Warband
Viking Shadow
Viking Legacy
Viking Clan
Viking Bravery

The Norman Genesis Series
Hrolf the Viking
Horseman
The Battle for a Home
Revenge of the Franks
The Land of the Northmen

The Sword of Cartimandua
Ragnvald Hrolfsson
Brothers in Blood
Lord of Rouen
Drekar in the Seine
Duke of Normandy
The Duke and the King

New World Series
Blood on the Blade
Across the Seas
The Savage Wilderness
The Bear and the Wolf
Erik the Navigator

The Vengeance Trail

The Danelaw Saga
The Dragon Sword

The Reconquista Chronicles
Castilian Knight
El Campeador
The Lord of Valencia

The Aelfraed Series
(Britain and Byzantium 1050 A.D. - 1085 A.D.)
Housecarl
Outlaw
Varangian

**The Anarchy Series England
1120-1180**
English Knight
Knight of the Empress
Northern Knight
Baron of the North
Earl

The Sword of Cartimandua
King Henry's Champion
The King is Dead
Warlord of the North
Enemy at the Gate
The Fallen Crown
Warlord's War
Kingmaker
Henry II
Crusader
The Welsh Marches
Irish War
Poisonous Plots
The Princes' Revolt
Earl Marshal

Border Knight
1182-1300
Sword for Hire
Return of the Knight
Baron's War
Magna Carta
Welsh Wars
Henry III
The Bloody Border
Baron's Crusade
Sentinel of the North
War in the West
Debt of Honour (May 2021)

Sir John Hawkwood Series
France and Italy 1339- 1387
Crécy: The Age of the Archer
Man at Arms
The White Company (July 2021)

Lord Edward's Archer
Lord Edward's Archer

The Sword of Cartimandua
King in Waiting
An Archer's Crusade
Targets of Treachery (Due out August 2021)

Struggle for a Crown
1360- 1485
Blood on the Crown
To Murder A King
The Throne
King Henry IV
The Road to Agincourt
St Crispin's Day
The Battle for France

Tales from the Sword I

Conquistador
England and America in the 16th Century
Conquistador (Coming in 2021)

Modern History

The Napoleonic Horseman Series
Chasseur à Cheval
Napoleon's Guard
British Light Dragoon
Soldier Spy
1808: The Road to Coruña
Talavera
The Lines of Torres Vedras
Bloody Badajoz
The Road to France
Waterloo (June 2021)

The Lucky Jack American Civil War series

The Sword of Cartimandua
Rebel Raiders
Confederate Rangers
The Road to Gettysburg

The British Ace Series
1914
1915 Fokker Scourge
1916 Angels over the Somme
1917 Eagles Fall
1918 We will remember them
From Arctic Snow to Desert Sand
Wings over Persia

Combined Operations series
1940-1945
Commando
Raider
Behind Enemy Lines
Dieppe
Toehold in Europe
Sword Beach
Breakout
The Battle for Antwerp
King Tiger
Beyond the Rhine
Korea
Korean Winter

Tales from the Sword Book 2

Other Books
Great Granny's Ghost (Aimed at 9-14-year-old young people)

For more information on all of the books then please visit the author's website at www.griffhosker.com where there is a link to contact him or visit his Facebook page: GriffHosker at Sword Books

Printed in Great Britain
by Amazon